POSTHUMOUSLY YOURS

By

MAGGIE WHITLEY

This paperback edition published in
The United Kingdom 2020

Copyright © 2019 Maggie Whitley
ISBN - 9798713633295

Cover illustration by Piers Schofield
The image on the front cover is Crown copyright

All characters in the publication are fictitious and any resemblance to real persons, living or dead is purely coincidental.

All rights reserved.

No part of this publication may be reproduced, stored in a retrieval system, or transmitted, in any form or by any means, without the prior permission in writing of the publisher, nor be otherwise circulated in any form of binding or cover other than that in which it is published and without a similar condition including this condition being imposed on the subsequent purchaser.

ALSO BY MAGGIE WHITLEY

For Adults;

Cuddles and Custard

Arctic Moment

Green

For Younger Readers;

The Adventures of the Great Alfonso (and his brother Ronnie)

The Kettles Boil

Bushed!

The Man with the Tattooed Eyebrows

Plug

This book is dedicated to my amazing proof readers,
Glyn, Angela, Lynn and Christine. Any mistakes are theirs!

PROLOGUE

There was nothing in Betty Mortimer's Admission Record to suggest that she was a serial killer. Even under 'Hobbies and Interests', where she had written in her distinctive, but almost illegible, copperplate handwriting, 'Reading, playing Patience and watching TV' (she'll fit in nicely here, Mrs King, the owner of the retirement home had thought at the time), there was no clue to her being anything other than what she appeared to be – a sprightly, well-dressed, mentally acute 75 year old widow in need of a bit of support and company in the later stages of her life. But serial killer? No, not a mention.

CHAPTER ONE

"I can come and live with you, Mark."

"No you can't, mum. We've been through this a dozen times. You need a bit of support in your life now and I can't give you that."

"Please," she whined. "I won't be any bother."

Mark took both his mother's hands in his and shook his head. "You've had two falls recently. The last one you were out cold for hours and both times you ended up in hospital. God knows what might have happened if I hadn't dropped by when I did."

"I just lost my balance, that's all. Tripped over the hall rug. I'm fine. Really. I can manage."

"Mum, I live in a one-bed flat above a launderette. There's no room and you wouldn't be able to manage the stairs. Plus you'd be on your own. I'm off on tour soon, remember? This is my big break. I can't not go." He stroked his mother's face gently. "Honestly. This is for the best. And anyway," he said, "your house is far too big for you. And you never know," he added, pointing at the large, nondescript, cream-coloured two-storey building in front of them, "you might actually like this place. It's the best that money can afford."

Still holding her son's hands tightly, Betty Mortimer took a step backwards to take in the full building. It was what she called a 'nothing' building – it was just there. Purpose-built as a residential care home in the '80s and set in its own grounds, it was located in a growing village, Nether Rising, which was separated from the town of Stratton-on-Ouse by the outer ring road and thousands of bland new infill houses. It was a twenty minute bus ride into the town centre. Mother and son stood in front of a pair of glass doors above which a hand-painted sign read 'Friars Rest Reception'. To the left and right, the two wings of the building stretched away symmetrically for several hundred yards, cream pebble-dashing interspersed at regular intervals with white, plastic-framed windows. At equal distances wooden benches were set along the paths that followed the contours of the building and there were more benches on paths which wandered off into the trees. It looked in good order, she'd give him that, and she liked the way the windows reflected the late afternoon sun. At least they'd been cleaned recently, she thought. Inside and out. You don't get a sparkle like that without doing both sides.

"But Friars Rest? What sort of name is that? It sounds like a place where people who work in fish and chip shops come to die. And anyway, shouldn't there be an apostrophe?"

"What? What are you talking about, mum?"

"Friars Rest. Where's the apostrophe? Is it one friar or two?"

Mark shook his head. Was this a sign she was starting to lose her marbles? "Nice gardens though," he said, trying to distract her.

"I suppose," she said grudgingly. But he was right. What the building lacked in style and grace it made up for by the beautifully manicured lawns and carefully maintained flower beds, even now a riot of late summer colour. There were trees aplenty and Betty liked how quiet it was. You could hardly hear any road noise from here. And she did like a nice tidy garden, especially one she didn't have to look after herself.

"You must be Mrs Mortimer and Mark." A pleasant, friendly voice drew their attention away from the garden and back to the building. Standing in the entrance was a large woman dressed in a tight black suit and a bubble-gum pink blouse which matched her hair perfectly. "Admiring our gardens, I see." She walked forward, holding out her hand. "I'm Mrs King. The owner and manager of Friars Rest Retirement Home."

Mark took her proffered hand. "How do you do. Mark Mortimer. And this is my mother. Betty Mortimer."

"So very pleased to meet you both. Won't you come in?"

Betty didn't know which to stare at first as she followed Mrs King into the building – the outrageously coloured hair which had been back-combed and teased into a bouffant perched high on the woman's head and held in place with industrial amounts of hair spray and garish plastic combs (Betty hadn't seen a style like that since the '60s) or the enormous backside straining against the too-tight skirt, mesmerising, with a rhythm all of its own. Six inch high stilettos completed the spectacle. There was so much to take in just with Mrs King alone that Betty paid little attention to her surroundings.

"I thought we'd have a cup of tea in my office before I give you the Grand Tour," said Mrs King, majestically. "How does that sound?"

"Grand," said Mark. Betty said nothing as the owner turned right and led them down a long corridor, both walls and carpet the same shade of magnolia. Large prints of flowers added vibrant splashes of colour to the otherwise monotone décor. She stopped in front of a closed door marked Private.

"It may say Private but my door is always open," quipped Mrs King. "Well, metaphorically speaking." She opened the door and ushered them in. "We have no locks in this place. Except on the bar!" she snorted. Betty shuddered. "Please, have a seat. Tea? Or would you rather have coffee?"

"Tea's fine, thank you. Mum? Mum?"

"Sorry. Yes. Tea's fine." She was still unable to take her eyes off Mrs King. Why would anybody deliberately choose hair that colour? Must have been on special offer. Or maybe a mid-life crisis of some sort. Whatever, Betty thought it unbecoming in a woman of her age, because she must be what? 55 if she was a day and she wasn't wearing it well. Mrs King ordered tea for all by pressing a buzzer on her desk then came to join them on one of the two cream leather sofas arranged on either side of a glass coffee table.

"Welcome to Friars Rest Retirement Home," she said grandly. "We're very proud of what we do here."

"And what's that?" asked Betty, curtly.

"Oh, it's quite simple," said Mrs King, completely unfazed by the sharp tone. "We provide a home for those of a more mature disposition and we cater to their every need, every whim, with dignity, respect and warmth. We pride ourselves that this is a home from home for those discerning few who have been used to the better things in life and who want a bit of comfort and want to be care-free in their later years."

"Yes," said Mark, "we saw that in the brochure you sent us. It all looks very impressive. You seem to take care of everything."

"Oh, we do!" exclaimed Mrs King. "We care but we are not a Care Home. We are a Retirement Home. There is a difference, you know. But one thing we do guarantee is that our guests don't have to worry about a single thing."

"Except how to pay!" said Betty. "It's hugely expensive."

"Mum!" admonished Mark.

"Well, it is. It's exorbitant."

"It may seem that way, Mrs Mortimer, but it's all down to quality, you know. You get what you pay for. And by charging what we do, we get, how shall I say, a certain type of people, if you understand my meaning." Betty nodded. She understood perfectly. Rich. "And although it may seem expensive," she continued (seem? thought Betty. There's no seem about it. It is eye-wateringly exorbitant. I suppose it has to be to pay for all those hair appointments and specially upholstered suits), "that's because we do cater for any personal requirements. And when you see what our accommodation's like, the food we provide, the service we offer, well, I think you'll agree it's money very well spent."

A light tap on the half-open door revealed a young man dressed in a dark green, open-necked, short-sleeved shirt with trousers the same colour, bearing a tray on which stood the wherewithal for tea for three and a plate of home-made biscuits.

"Thank you, er...Raoul," said Mrs King peering at his name badge. "Just pop it on the table and I'll be mother." He did as he was bidden and left, smiling broadly. "Now, tea."

The Grand Tour was just that. Mrs King left nothing out.

"Now, we have two wings, the Flower Wing, which we're on – you'll have noticed the lovely flower paintings – and the Forest Wing, with Reception just to the right of the main entrance here. There are suites on both floors but more on the first floor, and all of them are named after flowers or trees. Lovely, don't you think?"

"Lovely," muttered Betty unenthusiastically.

"And we can accommodate up to 80 guests at any one time. But we'll start with what our guests probably think is the most important place in the entire home and is certainly mine. The Dining Room."

The room itself seemed larger than it was because it was currently empty of diners. It was light (magnolia again) and because of its location, situated in the apex of the two wings of the building directly opposite the front entrance, and with a glass conservatory with French doors opening onto a small secluded garden, it was bright and cheerful. Ten tables, each with six places, were arranged around a smaller central table on which was displayed a vase full of dried flowers.

"You can sit anywhere you want," said Mrs King, "but most of our guests tend to eat with their friends. Or you can have your food in your room if you don't feel like socialising. We're very flexible. And here," she led them through a wooden swing door, "here is where our chefs create miracles." Spotless stainless steel was everywhere. "One of our chefs, Geraldo, he's even won the famous Golden Globe Artichoke Award. Pinched him from one of the cruise lines, we did. That's how seriously we take our food in Friars Rest." Betty looked round the empty kitchen. "But not at the moment, of course." She looked at her watch. "The kitchen crew are on their rest break just now. We run a tight ship here and we look after our staff as well as we do our guests. One big happy family, that's what we are."

"Very nice I'm sure," snarled Betty.

"I just want you to see behind the scenes as well as front of house," explained Mrs King theatrically. "Just to show you that our highest standards extend to where the eye doesn't necessarily see."

On they went. Past the Beverage Station in the corridor. "Tea, coffee, whatever you like, 24 hours a day," Mrs King explained. "As much as you like whenever you like." On and into the Television Lounge where large, comfortable, multi-coloured armchairs were arranged in a semi-circle around an over-sized TV screen. A few chairs were occupied and Mrs King beamed at those who could bear to tear themselves away from whatever afternoon chat show they were watching, mildly interested to see who was disturbing their viewing. "Of course, there's a TV in each suite too, so you can watch whatever you want, when you want, if you don't want to be with other people. And we do have a Quiet Lounge upstairs for those who like a bit of peace and quiet but don't necessarily want to be on their own."

"You seem to have thought of everything," commented Mark, clearly impressed.

Mrs King nodded. "I do believe we have."

Betty sighed. This wouldn't be much different from her present existence. Lonely meals eaten in front of a TV. Except here she'd be paying a prodigious amount for the privilege.

"And we have a Games Room too. The cupboards are simply full of jigsaws, board games – you name it, we've got it. Books too, if you're a reader. Shelves and shelves of books. The local library comes and changes them for us every three months so there's always a fresh selection. And now we'll take the lift up to the first floor and I'll show you a couple of suites."

"How often does a suite become available?" asked Mark, wondering ahead as to how soon he could reasonably sell his mother's house and make the necessary arrangements for her to move in.

"We usually have a couple empty all the time. People move on, you know."

"Die, you mean?" asked Betty.

"Well, yes. But some go to other homes or even move back in with their families."

Betty snorted in disbelief. Oh yes, she thought. As if!

Doors led off the entire length of the corridor, most of which stood open. "We encourage our guests to keep their doors open so they feel part of what's going on but you can always close it..." Betty finished the sentence for her, "...if you don't feel like socialising."

"Quite!" They walked past an open doorway. Inside, a small group of green uniform-clad staff were sitting, mugs of tea in their hands. Immediately they leapt to attention guiltily. Mrs King beamed at them and carried on. "As you were. Don't mind me. Just showing a prospective guest around." The disturbed staff remained standing. "Our helpers are on duty 24 hours a day so there's always someone there if you need them." Helpers? thought Betty. It sounds like something out of a bad Christmas movie. Mrs King smiled at the helpers and pulled the door closed after her. "They are our lifeblood, bless 'em. Now this," said Mrs King, as she opened a door marked Daffodil Suite, "is one of our standard suites." The room was currently empty, the previous occupant presumably either having died or returned to the bosom of their family. It was bright, airy and spotlessly clean. "As you can see, there's a large comfortable bed," she waved her hand imperially round the room, "and we even have a choice of pillows." Betty bit her tongue. "En-suite, of course." Mark peered into a compact but adequate bathroom. "There's a buzzer by the bed should you need any assistance. Ample storage space," she said, opening the wardrobe door to prove her point, "and a matching chest of drawers." Betty thought Mrs King was sounding increasingly like one of those over made-up women on those dreadful TV shopping channels that she sometimes watched in despair, desperately trying to sell pillows or fake leather handbags. A robust leatherette armchair had been placed in front of the window overlooking the gardens. "And, of course, you can personalise the suite as much as you like," she continued. "Bring in your own pictures or some nice family photographs. Even the odd piece of furniture, if it'll fit. Obviously there's a limit to the number of things you can bring but we want to make your suite as homely as possible for you. After all, we want you to think of Friars as your home."

"Can you change the colour?" asked Betty. "I don't like magnolia."

"Nobody's ever asked that before." Mrs King sounded piqued. After all, she prided herself on her choice of the colour scheme. "But I don't see why not. Especially if you buy your own paint."

"It's a bit on the small side," said Mark. "Have you got any other rooms?"

"Suites," Mrs King reminded him. "We call them suites. We do have one other which is gorgeous but it is currently occupied."

"Could we see it?"

"Of course. It really is the best suite in the entire establishment. I'm sure Lizzie won't mind me showing you. Follow me."

They did as they were told.

The Rose Suite was at the very end of the corridor, on the right hand side, next to the fire exit. Mrs King pointed at the name on the door. "This is the only suite with a THE," Mrs King told them. "I thought it was worthy." Betty looked at her son, her eyebrows raised. "Worthy?" she mouthed. Mark shook his head. Mrs King tapped gently on the closed door.

"She likes to keep herself to herself," whispered Mrs King, conspiratorially. Then in a louder voice, "Lizzie? Mrs Hetherington? Can we come in?"

A faint voice from within could just be heard. It sounded like "Bugger off!"

Ignoring it, Mrs King opened the door and walked in. "Just showing these good people around, if you don't mind."

"I don't think it would matter if she did," Betty whispered to her son.

A frail, very elderly woman sat in an armchair, a blanket over her knees despite the warmth. Badly arthritic hands lay on top of an open book.

"And how are we today?" Mrs King asked.

"I don't know about you, Tabatha," snarled Lizzie, "but I'm very well, thank you for asking."

Tabatha, thought Betty. Didn't see that one coming.

"Lizzie's been with us longer than any of our other guests, haven't you dear?"

Lizzie ignored her and returned to her book.

"As you can see, it's a corner suite with a double aspect. Much more space of course." And there was. As well as the armchair there was a window seat under one of the windows and a small writing table and chair were placed in front of the other. "The en-suite is bigger too and has the added advantage of a walk-in bath. It really is a lovely suite."

Betty could only agree. "It is so much nicer. Presumably it's more expensive."

Mrs King nodded gravely. "Very much more so, I'm afraid. And there's a waiting list, too," she whispered, glancing at Lizzie. "It's so lovely and peaceful here. All you can hear in this suite is the wind in the trees." She

11

sighed deeply. "Well, that's the tour over. Shall we go back to my office and have another chat?"

Back in the owner's office, more tea was produced.

"Now is there anything you'd like to ask me?" Mrs King asked as she delicately nibbled the edge of a biscuit.

"Where's the apostrophe?" demanded Betty.

"What?"

"Mum!"

"Well, it should have an apostrophe."

Apostrophe? What was the woman talking about? Mrs King was puzzled. She'd never been asked for one before. "I'm sure you could bring your own with you, if you wanted. We'd find room for it somewhere." Betty glared at her. Before his mother could open her mouth again, Mark got there first.

"Why is it called Friars Rest anyway? What's the history?"

"I believe it was built on the site of an old friary. Concubine monks or some-such. Anyway," said Mrs King, "why don't you go away and think about it and let me know what you decide. I don't think it will be a difficult choice for you. We're very easy-going here. We've got very few rules and regulations. In fact, the only thing we insist upon here is no incontinence. We don't do bowels, if you know what I mean."

"What have you got against bowels?" asked Betty. "Everybody got 'em."

Mrs King gave her a long, hard look. Was this was the sort of person she wanted in her beautiful retirement home? Perhaps Mrs Mortimer was going to be more trouble than she was worth. She'd dealt with some oddballs over the years. After all, old people had more than their fair share of little peccadilloes, didn't they? But this woman? She seemed to have more than most, not to mention an attitude with knobs on! But money was money. She stood up and proffered her hand.

"I'll wait to hear from you," she said.

CHAPTER TWO

"Well, what do you think?" Mark asked, as he unwrapped a Waitrose ready meal and popped it in the microwave. "At least you'd get fresh food there and lots of it. No more microwave jobs. Did you see that sample menu she gave us? I wouldn't mind some of that."

Betty looked sadly at her son as she watched him set the kitchen table for one. "Aren't you staying?" she asked.

"Can't. Got rehearsals tonight." He poured them both a glass of red wine and sat down opposite her. "Really, what did you think of the place? I thought it was pretty classy. Much better than I thought it would be. I expected it to smell of wee and boiled cabbage."

"I didn't like it."

"But Mum, whyever not?"

"And I certainly don't like her. Tabatha? What sort of name is that? Awful woman." She shook her head vigorously. "Anyway, I want to stay here. In my home."

"It's too much for you, this house, Mum. It would take an army of people to look after it. We've discussed this before."

"You could move in," she suggested tentatively. "I've always said there's plenty of room for the two of us. I wouldn't cramp your style."

"No Mum," replied Mark, standing up as the microwave pinged. "I am 35 years old. I am definitely not moving back in with my mother." He spooned the Cottage Pie with Added Meaty Gravy onto a plate.

"I'd pay you."

"What?"

"I'd pay you to come and live with me."

"No. It's not going to happen. This tour is just about the best thing that's ever happened to me. I'm doing okay and I'm happy but if this series of gigs proves to be a success, I'm set for life. The whole band is. Fame and fortune could be just around the corner."

"No-one ever got to be famous playing the mouth organ, Mark."

"Thanks Mum. Say it as it is, why don't you. And anyway, what about Larry Adler?"

"Mark, you know my taste veers more towards classical and Radio 3 rather than mainstream."

"I don't think you could describe Larry Adler as mainstream, Mum. And anyway, he died over 20 years ago."

"My point exactly."

Mark looked at his mother, puzzled.

"I'm sorry, Mark. I didn't mean to denigrate what you're doing. It's just suddenly everything is changing. I'm going into a home and you're going away. I just feel I'm going to lose you and you're all I have."

13

"I'll be back, you know I will. Korea's not a million miles away. I'll be back at the end of six weeks."

"Couldn't you stay here and play locally with another group? You could come home each night."

"Mum, I've been with the guys in this band for years. We're mates and we like playing together. This is our big chance and I'm not going to blow it. For them or for me." He pushed her plate closer. "Eat up."

"Not hungry."

Mark took a large gulp of wine. "Look, I think Friars Rest will be good for you. You'll have company, make new friends, good food. You'll be looked after. I mean, how many other retirement homes have hairdressers and beauticians when you want one? And a doctor on call. And a chiropodist, for goodness sake." He nudged the Home's glossy brochure towards her. "Look. It's all there. It's got so much to offer. All these activities. Day trips. Trips to the theatre, art galleries. Concerts. Visits to restaurants. What's not to like? You can do as much or as little as you want to. Look!" he said pointing. "Here! It says so."

"But it costs a fortune, Mark."

"So? It's not as if you can't afford it. Even without selling this house you could easily afford to live there. Dad left you a fortune, I know. So spend it. On you. Live a life of total luxury with non-stop pampering. What else are you going to spend your money on?"

"You. You could have all this money. Then you wouldn't have to leave."

"I don't want it, Mum, I never have. You've never been able to understand that, have you? I like being independent. I like making my own way in life. I may not live in the lap of luxury but I'm happy with that. But now this opportunity has come up and all that may be about to change. That's why I'm so excited about this tour. If I'm a success, it's because of me and me alone. Can you try and understand that?"

She couldn't but she could see her son was resolute. "I wouldn't want one of those poky rooms."

"Suites," Mark reminded her.

Finally Betty smiled. "I'd want the Rose Suite."

"Maybe one day you'll get it. But honestly, Mum, I think you could do a lot worse."

"But how can it be any good if it's not got an apostrophe?"

"Mum, I'll get you one for your birthday. I promise. Now eat up. Your dinner's getting cold."

"You'd still come and visit, wouldn't you? You won't forget me?"

"You do talk rot, you know that."

"I suppose I could give it a go. And if I decided I don't like it, well, we'll see. Maybe I could try somewhere else."

"Now you're talking. Another glass of wine? To celebrate? Then I really must go."

Just over two months later, Betty Mortimer checked into Friars Rest, alone, arriving by taxi with two large suitcases and a heavy cardboard box marked "Things". Mark had put his mother's house up for sale two days after they'd had the Grand Tour of Friars Rest and it sold within a week and that was after a bidding war. Houses like hers didn't come on the market very often – large, six-bed Victorian villas with wrap-around gardens on quiet leafy streets were in high demand, even if it was a bit down at heel with a hugely overgrown garden. There were few bills to settle so Betty was left with a prodigious amount of money after the house was sold. She added it to the money she had inherited from her husband, Mark still insisting he would not take a penny of it. He arranged for a local auction house to sell some of her furniture and her antiques – more money – and for a house-clearance firm to get rid of her junk. Then he left.

Betty had clung to him. "I'm going to miss you so much," she sobbed. "You're all I have."

"Mum, I'll be back in six weeks. You'll be fine. The sale has gone through and all the financial stuff is sorted. I've booked you into the Chard and Chattels Hotel for a couple of nights just until your room is ready at Friars. Mrs King is having it redecorated."

"In bloody magnolia, I expect," sniffed Betty.

"She'll call the hotel to let them know when you can move in and they'll arrange a taxi for you. Isn't it exciting? I'm excited for you."

"Couldn't I come with you?" she pleaded.

"I don't think so," laughed Mark. How many other bands took their ageing mothers with them on tour? "You'd hate it. We'll be on the go the whole time, Korea first, then Japan. It's six solid weeks of hotels, late night gigs. Travelling non-stop. A different city every night. I'm going to find it hard to keep up, I can't see how you'd manage. Anyway, Friars Rest is sorted and I know you're going to love it."

"Remind me what your group is called."

"The band is called Cornflour Blues."

Betty nodded. "I suppose it's got to be called something." She looked sadly round the empty dining room. Gone was the oak table which could seat ten comfortably but never did; gone, too, the red velvet padded ladder-back chairs, the mahogany sideboard and matching court cupboard, long since emptied of all its fine crystal and the unused twelve place-setting Noritaki dinner service. She wondered whose home it all would be gracing now. The faded wallpaper remained – darkened patches showing where fine prints of long-gone hunting scenes (her husband's choice) and delicate watercolours of

15

landscapes (her choice), once hung. "I shall miss this old place," she said softly.

"I know. But it's time to move on. For both of us."

"I had some good times here, once. With your father. You never had a chance to know him. You were so young when he died."

"You've never talked about him, have you?" said Mark quietly. "All these years and you've never told me what he was really like."

Betty walked round the echoing room, her heart full. "He was your father," she said simply.

Mark looked at her. Clearly she wasn't going to say anything more. She never had. As far as he was concerned, his father had sired him and that was about it. He came, literally, and then he went. Not much of an epitaph. It had always been a bone of contention between him and his mother – no matter how many times he'd asked over the years she refused to tell him anything about his dad. All she would say was that he died shortly after he, Mark, was born. And that was it. So he'd stopped asking.

Mark sighed. Concentrate on the present, he told himself. "Anyway, I think you'll be very happy at Friars Rest. Think of it as a new adventure. New home, free from worries. All you have to do is take it easy and enjoy yourself."

"I don't think I know how any more. How to enjoy myself."

"Well, maybe now's the time to find out." He gave his mother a lingering hug. "Gotta go, Mum. Early flight tomorrow. I'll phone when I get there."

"Take care won't you?" She bit her bottom lip.

"Don't I always?" And with that he was gone.

"Do you want a help unpackin'?" asked the helper, smiling, as he effortlessly manhandled her suitcases and the box from the taxi, through the front doors and into the lift. He was tall, dark-skinned, with crinkly black hair showing signs of grey, and was dressed in the dark green uniform of the Home. Not from these parts, thought Betty. She looked at his name-badge. Ephraim. Did this place specialise in people with odd names?

"No, I can manage."

"No, lady," he said in his dulcet sing-song voice. "I gotta help. Else de boss have my gusset for me garters!"

"Okay. Thank you," Betty added as an afterthought.

She followed him slowly down the Flower Wing corridor and for one dizzy moment Betty thought they were heading to the Rose Suite. But they stopped at the last door but one on the opposite side from the much-vaunted suite.

"This is you," said Ephraim. He pointed to the name on the door. Violet Suite. "This is you," he repeated. "Mrs King say to tell you she come shortly to see yourself."

Betty re-arranged his words in her head so they made sense.

Ephraim held the door open for her and gingerly she stepped into the room. Yes, it was poky. Just what she didn't want.

"Are you absolutely sure this is my room? I had asked for something bigger."

"Positive, lady," replied Ephraim as he struggled to put her suitcases on the bed and her box on a small wooden table. "You real sure you don't want a help?" he asked again.

Betty shook her head. No, she didn't want a help. She wanted to get out of here.

"You like it here," he promised her. "We look after you. You be happy." And with that, he closed the door and left her.

Betty sat on the edge of the bed and looked round her. It didn't take long. Bed, wardrobe, table, armchair, bathroom. She'd been right about the magnolia, she noted ruefully. This was to be her home now. This was it. There had been a few occasions in her life when she'd felt utterly bereft. This was another to add to the list. She wasn't the crying type but this time she might make an exception. Why had she let Mark talk her into coming here? At least at home she had space to move. Now she was trapped. Where could she go? Before she could provide herself with the inevitable answer there was a knock on the door and in walked Mrs King carrying a small bunch of fresh flowers in a vase. She was dressed in a pale green suit this time, every seam threatening to give way under the unrelenting pressure.

"I thought you might like these," she said, pretending not to notice Betty's stony face. "I'll just put them here on the window sill. There. Don't they look lovely? I'll leave you to unpack and let you settle in. I'll get some dinner sent up on a tray in a little while. A lot of our new guests like to eat alone for the first few nights. Perfectly natural." She stood in the doorway. "You really will like it here, I know. It may not be what you're used to but it will soon feel like a home from home. I promise. Now, how do you like to be called?"

"By my name," replied Betty snidely.

Mrs King ignored her and carried on. "So, is it Mrs Mortimer or can I call you Betty? We do prefer first names here at Friars. More friendly, don't you think?"

Do I have a choice? wondered Betty.

"Welcome to your new home, Betty." Apparently she didn't.

As she closed the door behind her, Mrs King could have sworn she heard a howl.

17

CHAPTER THREE

Friars Rest
Nether Rising
September

Dearest Eva,

I'm so sorry I haven't written for such a very long time – I really can't remember when exactly it was but it feels like it was centuries ago. I think it must have been just after Barry died, which would make it nearly thirty-five years ago. My goodness me! But the reason I've not written, apart from the fact that I'm not good at keeping in touch, obviously, is because there's been nothing to tell you. Life has just plodded on, one day after another. And when I do finally realise that I have some major news for you, it's as if I've suddenly woken up and found that decades have slipped by. A lifetime. Do you remember Dad saying time flies like an arrow, fruit flies like a banana? I never really understood the fruit bit but suddenly I know all about the arrow. Can you believe that? Thirty five years! But honestly, there has been nothing of import to impart, as they say. I have lived, and that's it. But now, at long last, I have some news so I thought it was time to put pen to paper.

It's the worst possible news, I'm afraid, Eva. Well, no. That's not quite true. The last time I wrote, that was the worst news ever. When I told you that my darling Barry had dropped down dead from a massive heart attack. That was the most earth-shattering news I could ever have imagined. And, of course, what followed after. But this is pretty grim too. Well, it is as far as I'm concerned. Mark, my son – do you remember me telling you how he was born shortly before his father died? Well, he decided it was time for me to give up our beautiful family home I once shared with Barry and move into a care home. Sorry, it's called a Retirement Home. There's a distinction, apparently, though I'm blowed if I know what it is. But that's beside the point. Can you believe it, though? Me, in a HOME. Yes, I know I had a couple of tumbles and knocked myself out – I am 75 after all – I think I'm entitled to the odd fall. Anyway, he decided that it was time for me to be 'taken care of' – his words not mine and I did think it sounded a bit ominous – and to move into a retirement home where I could spend the rest of my days forking out huge sums of money for the privilege of having someone cook my meals for me and cut my toenails every once in a while. I tried to argue with Mark but he wouldn't give. Said he had things to do, opportunities had beckoned and he couldn't always be around to look after me. Told me it was in my best interests. So off he's gone, somewhere in the Far East, off to make his fortune. Bit old at the age of thirty-five, if you ask me, but that's Mark for you. Still won't take a penny of my, or his father's money. Headstrong. Now where do you think he gets that from? You keep it, he says. It's yours. I don't want it. Spend it on making sure you have a comfortable retirement. So here I am, Eva, spending it on keeping a certain Tabatha King (more of her later) in badly-dyed hair and expensive, ill-fitting suits, and funding her retirement plan by moving into her care home, Friars Rest. Yes, I know. I can hear you asking. I asked the very same question, but that's how it's spelt. No apostrophe. The woman had no idea what I was talking about when I mentioned it. It's a sign of the times, I'm afraid. Anyway, Care home. Retirement home. Call it what you will, it amounts to the same thing. A very bleak future with only one outcome.

Two weeks ago I finally moved in and I can truthfully say I'm hating every minute of it. Everybody is ever so nice – even Tabatha – but I always get the feeling that they're trying too hard. To be honest, I have never felt so lonely, not even when I was rattling round my huge house, all on my own. I don't think I ever sent you a photo of it but it really was a lovely place but not the same, of course, after Barry died. And now I'm stuck in a tiny room which is about as soulless as they come. True, I've got them to hang two of the small paintings I brought from home and I have a few knick-knacks dotted round the room, my jewellery box and a lovely Lalique vase in the shape of a horse's head that Barry gave me on our first wedding anniversary, but the place has no heart. It was funny though, packing up my entire life into two suitcases and a cardboard box. I was surprised at how easy it was. At the end of the day, they're only possessions. Over-rated, if you ask me.

The staff, or helpers, as they're known, have gone out of their way to make me feel welcome, right from the very first morning when there was a knock on my door and this tiny little Asian woman burst into the room carrying a breakfast tray almost as big as she was. I'm pretty, she said, and she was absolutely right. She was gorgeous. But it was only when I read her name badge, Priti, that I realised that that was her name and she wasn't being boastful. Petite in every respect except for her huge, black, almond-shaped eyes and the thickest hair you've ever seen, which she wears in a plait. It almost reaches her knees, I kid you not. Her startlingly bright smile would have been a tonic for anyone but I am still convinced she doesn't like me. I get the impression all the helpers are laughing at me behind my back. I've no reason to think that, of course, I just seem to be on such a downer at the moment. They come from every corner of the world, the helpers – except Janice, who's from Doncaster, and Mikey, who's from Bradford originally, (but more recently from the Young Offenders' Institute at Marketby, on some sort of day release scheme, he told me. I didn't ask). There may be others I don't know about, locals I mean, but I haven't actually been outside my cell, sorry, suite, since I arrived, so it may be that I just haven't met them. Why haven't you left your room? I hear you ask. And what do you do all day? Both good questions. What do I do all day? Not much, to be honest. I watch television – mostly rubbish, as that's all there is on. I read the paper. I play Patience. Lots of Patience. I eat. I sleep. Not much of an existence, is it? And as to why I haven't left my room. That's a bit more difficult to answer. Lack of confidence, I suppose. Or maybe I'm just scared. One of the first things that Mrs King said to me when I moved in was that they encourage residents to mix and make friends. Social intercourse is so important, she told me. I thought for a moment I'd misheard her! But I lost the few friends I had when Barry died and I don't want any now. I'm not a very sociable person, you know that, and I've never made friends easily. But I certainly don't want to try with this lot of geriatrics with their dribbling and I was going to say incontinence, but that's not allowed here. Before I even moved in, I was told that was a no-no. So I'm just going to have to hope that my bladder and bowels play ball. I'll be on the streets if they don't!

Anyway, after two weeks of not venturing out of my room, I must admit to feeling a bit stir crazy. I've had a bellyful of dreadful television and I've even started cheating at Patience, just to liven things up. But I just can't seem to see the point in making any effort, Eva. Can you understand that? My meals are brought to me, invariably by Priti and Janice. Priti tends to do nights whilst Janice does mainly day shifts, so she can take care of her three children. Not easy, she said, when your husband runs off with a contortionist from Latvia. I made sympathetic noises in all the right places. To be honest, she doesn't look old enough to have so many children. She's a pleasant girl but I do wish she'd do something with her hair – it's all colours of the rainbow and is done in those deadlock things. And she has the most awful tattoo of a spider's web stretching from behind her left ear and down into her frontage, if you get my drift. But she's very kind-hearted, as is Priti, and I'm sure they both mean well. I just seem to have all these doubts at the moment, about everything. The other day Priti saw me writing to you. What lovely hand-writing you have, she commented. It's really fancy. Where did you learn that? I sat back to look at what I'd written. I used to be proud of my lovely copper-plate but not any more. A touch of arthritis in my right hand means even I find it almost impossible to read and I know what it says! I do hope you can manage to read it, Eva. She asked me who I was writing to and I told her I was writing to you, my sister. In Canada. She has a sister in Canada too. And one in India and two in Dubai. And one in the US. But she never writes to them, she tells me. Nobody writes letters any more. Only phones or messages them. Probably thinks I'm dreadfully old-fashioned. I don't care. She offered to post my letters for me, bless her. See what I mean about being kind? They do try and I think they mean well. But I just can't shake off this suspicion that they are all too good to be true. I'm not used to people being so friendly. It makes me feel they've all got an ulterior motive. Paranoid or what?

I had a good long look at myself in the bathroom mirror last night before I went to bed, Eva, and I really didn't like what I saw. It's one of those mirrors that is so well illuminated you can see every nook and cranny in your face, should you want to. It's also got one of those magnifying mirrors on a stalk – brilliant for those annoying little chin hairs that keep popping up unannounced. Irrelevant, sorry. What I was going to say was that I hardly recognised the old woman I have become. I'm only 75 but I look so much older. Everything about me is grey. My hair is grey. I could dye it if I could be bothered but what's the point? My skin looks grey. My outlook is grey. I look gaunt and I've got awful crows' feet and a horrendous mannequin mouth. Gottle of gear! Gottle of gear! I seem to have lost what little twinkle I had, I suppose. All the animation has gone from my face and I look empty. Do you know what I mean? I keep thinking, is this all there is? And, sadly, I think it is.

On a brighter note though, I must say the food here is really very good indeed. They sold it as one of the highlights of the Home and they weren't kidding. I actually think I've put on a pound or two since I've been here but that's not surprising because, truth to tell, I hadn't been eating properly for a while, not since Mark left. But I still sit here alone, in front of the television or listening to my radio, meal on a tray in front of me, so life is not very different in that respect from before. Mrs King does all she can to encourage me to mix with the other residents but I don't feel ready yet. And when I sit here and think that I may have another ten, twenty or, God forbid, even thirty more years of this, my heart sinks. The thought is almost unbearable. I told Mark if I didn't like it here I could go somewhere else but where could I go? Every place is the same for the old and unwanted, it's just that this one has better food and costs more. So here I am. Stuck. With nothing to look forward to. Left here to fade and rot. Not a happy prospect. In fact this morning I woke up with tears pouring down my face — never was one for crying as you know — but I'd obviously been crying in my sleep. No-one was more surprised than me. I didn't think that was physically possible. But something must have set me off and the only thing I can think of is that I'm going to spend the rest of my life in this place. I'm sorry to sound so gloomy and depressed, Eva, but that's the way I feel. What can I say? Things can only get better? Somehow I doubt it. In a way, I feel I've already died. Which is why I sign myself,

Posthumously yours.

Betty. Your loving sister

CHAPTER FOUR

"How are you settling in, Betty?" asked Mrs King, who today was dressed in a dapper, if over-stretched, pale grey woollen suit, with a dark grey roll-neck jumper. The colours complemented her immoveable pink hair perfectly. With great difficulty, she pulled up the armchair next to the bed where Betty was lying, fully clothed, on the duvet, and sat down heavily. There was a whoosh of air as the seat cushion admitted defeat. At least, I presume it was the cushion, thought Betty grimly. After several attempts at crossing her legs, Mrs King gave up and planted her feet squarely on the floor.

"I don't like this room."

Mrs King looked around. "What's the matter with it."

"Well, for one thing, it's small."

"I did tell you before you moved in that most of the suites were this size. We only have one large suite and that's taken. Don't you remember?"

"Of course I do! I'm not senile!" Betty snapped.

"It's got everything you could possibly need," Mrs King told her.

Betty scowled at her. She didn't have to live in it! She tried to imagine the house that Mrs King went home to at the end of every day. Something quite palatial, no doubt. In magnolia. Not a rabbit-hole, like this.

"You said 'for one thing', Betty. There's more?"

"It's noisy. Listen! Can you hear it? Machinery of some sort. It's like an engine noise in the room beneath me."

Mrs King tilted her head and leaned forward, listening hard. "I can hear a slight whirr, if that's what you mean."

"It's more than just a whirr. It keeps me awake at night. Is there something in the room below?"

"It's the plant room for the central heating and water system. But it's not really that loud, is it? Not much louder than the air-conditioning. I'm sure you'll get used to it. We could get you some ear plugs."

Betty looked at her in astonishment. "I don't pay all this money to have to wear bloody ear plugs!"

"Language please, Mrs Mortimer. There's no need for that."

"And anyway, ear plugs won't deal with the smell."

"Smell? What smell?"

"When I open the window, I can smell cigarette smoke."

Well, don't open the damned window, Mrs King was tempted to say. She stood up. The chair groaned quietly.

"Do you often have the window open? It is November you know."

"I know what month it is! I like fresh air. Always have done. And anyway, it's always so stuffy in here."

Mrs King tottered over to the window. How does she walk in those shoes? wondered Betty. "And I can hear voices," she added.

Oh God! The woman's hearing voices now, thought Mrs King. What next? Perhaps it was time to call in Dr Chatterji to have her assessed.

"Voices, you say. What sort of voices?"

"Foreign ones. They're not speaking English, I can tell you that."

Mrs King pushed the window open wide, inhaled deeply and looked down. Three faces looked up at her, the smiles on their faces and the cigarettes in their hands both disappearing with equal alacrity. She stared hard at the men below then slammed the window shut. "I think I've identified both your problems," she told Betty, "and I can assure you that neither the voices or the cigarette smoke will be a problem again."

"I'm not imagining it then?"

"No Betty, you're not. Some of our staff appear to have been enjoying an illicit smoke outside the plant room. It's not a designated area for a staff break and it won't happen again."

"And the whirring?"

"I'll see what I can do. Now, is there anything else?"

"I'd be happier if I was in a bigger room," repeated Betty. "I'd really like to move."

"I know, and I'm sorry, but as I keep telling you, there is only one Rose Suite and as I told you before, there is a waiting list for it. So even when Mrs Hetherington vacates the room..."

"Dies," interjected Betty.

"Well, yes, whatever, when she goes, wherever she goes, Mr Latimer is next on the list. Have you met him? No of course you haven't, because you haven't left your room, have you? It's been well over two weeks now. You can't take advantage of everything we have to offer if you stay cooped up here. It's not good for you, you know. And trust me, we do have so many activities laid on for the residents. Why won't you join in? Why not come down to the Dining Room at least, Betty, and meet some of your fellow guests? They don't bite," she added cheerily.

That's only because they haven't got their own teeth, thought Betty unkindly.

"I can't force you to come down and join the others but I do wish you would. You'll feel so much better. I know you will." She took Betty's hands in hers. "We do really want you to feel part of the family." She sounded earnest enough but Betty found all this concern for her well-being, genuine or not, uncomfortable. For so long, she'd always had to look after herself, pretty much, and now being surrounded by people who were always expressing concern about her welfare, she was finding it overwhelming. Everyone, from Mrs King to the woman who cleaned her room and the helpers who brought her her meals. She hated their incessant questions as to how she was feeling and if they could get anything or do anything for her. It simply didn't feel right. She wanted to believe they were genuine but it all seemed so unnatural. She decided to give Mrs King the benefit of the doubt.

"Thank you," said Betty, "I'm sure you mean well. It's just that I find it all so strange. So very different from what I've been used to. I've lived on my own for a long time now, so to be in a place like this with lots of other people, people I don't know, well, it's going to take some getting used to."

"I can understand that," said Mrs King sympathetically.

"And I'm so used to doing what I want when I want. Having meals at set times and things like that. I like to eat when I want."

Mrs King nodded and sat back down. Betty's son, Mark, had warned her. When he'd called her to tell her that he'd finally persuaded his mother it was a good idea to move in to Friars they'd had a long chat on the phone. "My Mum can be a bit brittle sometimes," he'd told her. "She's been very independent ever since my father died. That's something she prides herself on. And because of that, she's very used to having her own way. She may take a little while to settle in. She's very proud and very single-minded. You're going to have to be patient with her. I think she's lonely but she'd never admit it. Don't try and push her too hard – she'll come round in the end."

"Thank you for telling me about your mother," Mrs King had said. "I'm a mother myself although I doubt that my son knows me as well as you know your mother. She sounds very special to you."

"She is," Mark agreed.

"But please don't worry. Some of our guests do take longer to settle in than others. Everybody's different."

"She can be very strong-willed, I'll warn you," Mark added, "and once she gets an idea in her head, well, dogmatic isn't the word! On the outside she can come across as abrasive and sharp. But once you get to know her, she really is an absolute sweetie. You just have to dig quite deep."

"Does she have any, you know, how can I put it...mental issues?" Mrs King was thinking about all that nonsense to do with, what was it? A postrofy? She'd Googled it but that hadn't helped.

"Oh no! Not at all." Mark was quick to reassure her. "There's nothing wrong with her brain. Bright as a button. Razor-sharp mind. And there's nothing wrong with her bowels, either," he added hastily. "Apart from these couple of falls at home, I've never known her have a day's ill health in her life."

"Well, that's good to know."

"No, it's just her attitude that can be a bit challenging. As I say, she can be quite pig-headed at times. Opinionated's probably a better word."

Mrs King laughed. "Opinionated we can do. Now please don't worry about your mother, Mark. We will take very great care of her."

"I know you will."

Mark had been right. His mother was proving particularity recalcitrant and awkward in almost every respect and now Mrs King was discovering this for herself. Take this business of Betty staying in her room all the time. It wasn't healthy. She couldn't recall another new arrival who'd not ventured out after a couple of days to see what was going on or simply to talk to somebody. Anybody. But Betty clearly didn't want, or need, company. Her door was always shut to the outside world.

"Why don't you leave your door open, Betty? Every time I walk past, it's closed."

"I don't want people putting their heads round the door for a chat. I don't do chat. I like my own company. It's what I'm used to."

"Janice tells me you play a lot of Patience."

"So? I like it. I can do a lot of thinking when I'm playing."

"Can I get you some books from the library? Some magazines perhaps?"

Betty shook her head. "Janice brought me a couple. Not my style at all."

Mrs King was fast becoming exasperated. Everything she suggested was rejected out of hand.

"What about some of our activities? We've got Serviette Folding in the Quiet Lounge later this afternoon. Back by popular demand, I'll have you know." Betty did not even deign to answer her. "I'm just concerned for you, that's all. I want you to be happy here. To make the most of your time with us. It really isn't such a bad place, you know." Betty said nothing. "You will try, won't you?"

Betty nodded. The armchair sighed as Mrs King stood up. It was the first time Betty had ever felt sympathy for a piece of furniture.

"Oh, I nearly forgot. Got some post for you." She pulled a couple of letters from her jacket pocket and placed them on the bedside table. "Now, you will remember what I said, won't you?"

Betty nodded again. She'd agree to anything if the woman would just leave. Letters! It was the most excited she'd felt in a long time. These were the first letters she'd had since she'd moved in and she was desperate to see if there was anything from Mark. Apart from the one promised phone call to her the day before she moved into Friars she hadn't heard a peep out of him. He'd arrived safely, he'd told her, though she'd had to strain to hear him as there was a lot of background noise, wherever he was. He'd had to change planes in Amsterdam. Then a long flight to Seoul but he'd slept most of the way. Suffering from awful jet lag but the hotel was fine, even if the food was a bit strange. She'd smiled and reminded him to eat properly. Their tour started tomorrow, he went on, and he was really excited. You will take care, won't you, she'd told him. He said he would. Before he ended the call, Mark again promised to write. Maybe now he had. But looking at the envelopes it was clear he hadn't. One letter was from her solicitor telling her what a real pleasure it had been doing business with her and if she ever wanted to sell a property again, or if she needed help re-drafting her will, then Rickets, Warble and Jottings (Solicitors) were the team for the job. The other letter was re-directed junk mail offering her a time share in a racehorse. Nothing from Mark. Betty sighed and lay unmoving, staring up at the ceiling. This had all been such a bad idea, moving into this place. She would never fit in. She didn't really want to. And now Mark had abandoned her.

CHAPTER FIVE

Friars Rest
October

My darling Eva,

    I am truly sorry that my last letter ended so very gloomily but I'm sure you of all people can understand how depressed I was feeling. Things have improved marginally, you'll be pleased to hear, in that yesterday I finally summoned up the nerve to leave my room. That dreadful woman, Mrs King, has been chivvying me to get out and about. She really is a strange one, with her over-tight suits (she has them in a huge range of colours) and her stiletto heels. She'll break her neck one day, you mark my words. I could never understand how anybody could walk on those things. But it's her hair that I find amazing. It really is a feat of engineering – mounds of pink candy-floss (you call it cotton candy in Canada, don't you?) piled high. Stiff as a board. I wonder if it's detachable. I can just imagine her taking it off at night and putting it on the bedside table, giving it a saucer of milk (I'm joking!) only to weld it back in place the following morning. That would be the easy way to do it. But maybe she spends hours in front of the mirror every morning beating it into submission. Spraying it with industrial-strength hair spray and ladling buckets of glue on to it. There's nothing the matter with grey, I say. But I digress.

    I have lost track of how many times Mrs King has dropped in to see how I was doing. But all credit to her, she has been as good as her word and the seemingly endless chatter from below my window and the accompanying cigarette smoke have both stopped. The whirring noise seems to have decreased too, or maybe it's as she said, I have become more used to it. Anyway, I decided that the only way to prevent any more of her uninvited visits was to give in. Admit defeat and leave my room. And that's exactly what I did. But rather than join the fossilised relics Mrs King calls her guests, I chose to go and sit on one of the benches in the gardens. It was a beautiful day – brilliant sunshine with a cloudless sky, although a tad nippy, or 'fighting fresh' as Mum used to say. I was content to just sit and admire the flowers – the last of the roses and a magnificent display of fuchsias. And somebody has planted one of the beds with nothing but sunflowers. Some of them are monumental and must be well over 6 feet tall and they provide the most stunning splash of colour this time of year. I sat myself down, minding my own business and who should come and sit next to me but Ephraim. He was the one who helped me with my suitcases the day I arrived. He was dressed in that awful dark green uniform that they all have to wear. Not the colour I would have chosen. But then neither is the awful magnolia which is absolutely everywhere.

    He asked me how I was doing, in that song-like, lilting voice of his. Close your eyes and you're in the Caribbean. Not that I've ever been, of course, but I've seen it on the TV. We never travelled, Barry and me. There never seemed to be the time somehow. Any ting I can get you, lady? Ephraim asked me. Cuppa tea maybe? Or sometin' stronger? He patted his trouser pocket. Hip flask presumably. You would love the way he laughs, Eva. I do. I told him I was fine and just enjoying the peace and quiet, but he didn't take the hint. *Jes look at dem sunflowers,* he said. *Don't dey make your heart sing?* And he was right. They did. *Why you sitting out here in de cold?* he asked me. Cold? This is warm for October, I told him. *Not where I come from.* And where's that? I asked. Ephraim pointed over his shoulder. *Back in dere. Inside, where it's warm.* He laughed again. Such a warm and joyous laugh, I can't describe how it made me feel. *You thought I was going to say sometin' like Jamaica or Barbados or somewhere like dat, now tell me true,* he said. I nodded. He was absolutely right. *Well, you'd be wrong, my dear lady. I'm from Epsom.* And suddenly he was speaking in perfect Queen's English. He laughed again. *Surrey born and bred,* he informed me. I sat open-mouthed, staring at him. Then why the Caribbean accent? I asked him. *Oh, de crumblies in dere,* he nodded toward the building behind us, *dey like it when I talk like dis. It makes dem laugh.* Crumblies? I could not believe he had used such a word. *Yes,* he replied. *That's what most of them are. Some of them because they can't help it. Some of them because they choose to be. You have to make sure YOU choose not to be.*

Honestly, Eva, I could not believe what this man was saying. No respect whatsoever. I'd report him to Mrs King for his insolence. Before I could admonish him for his sheer impertinence, he stood up, pulled me gently to my feet and tucked my arm though his. *Now, lady, how about a little perambulation through the verdure and then I'll take you back to your room — unless you want to go and sit in the lounge? Go and join some of your fellow companions?* He chuckled as he said it. I shook my head. *No? I thought not. But you will have to at some time, you know.* I knew he was right, Eva. At some stage I would have to socialise with my fellow crumblies, as he called us. But I wasn't quite ready for it yet. *Okay then, lady, back to your room it is and I'll bring you a nice cup of tea and a piece of whatever cake the kitchen has managed not to burn this afternoon. But before that, as a real treat, I'll show you where the hedgehogs nest.* And he did.

Thinking back, Eva, I had assumed that Mrs King sent Ephraim out to check up on me - she has this uncanny knack of pretty much knowing where anybody is at any given time. But now I'm not so sure. Maybe he did it out of genuine solicitude. I just don't know. But what a lovely man and he is a veritable mine of information about the wildlife in the garden. Did you know that ladybirds hibernate? Me neither. Or that blackbirds like to sing after the rain? I'm not making it up. I could go on all day with the things I learned. Anyway, that was my first foray into the world outside Violet Suite. One small step, as they say. And I knew that now I'd done it once, it was only a matter of time before I would venture out again. I know you probably think I'm making it all sound terribly melodramatic, like I'm about to take an epic voyage to deepest Antarctica or something, but it took a lot of courage to leave my room, I can tell you. But dread it as I might, if I was going to make anything at all of my life at Friars Rest, the rest of my life I should say, I would eventually have to spend some time with the other residents, repugnant as the thought was.

For the rest of the day I thought about Ephraim's kindness and I was touched. And you know what a cynic I am. But now I had convinced myself that he was being genuinely kind and that he was looking after me. It was a strange feeling. After Barry died, apart from

Mark, nobody, and I mean nobody, Eva, has ever really cared about me and I found Ephraim's actions both moving and unsettling. And for once in my life, I felt uncharacteristically charitable and I thought, if he can be kind, well, maybe I should be too. So, the following day, I walked boldly across the corridor to see Mrs Hetherington in the much-coveted (by me!) Rose Suite. The door was ajar so I knocked lightly and went in. There she was, just like the first time I saw her, sitting in her armchair next to one of the windows, blanket over her knees, reading a newspaper. The scowl on her face was immediately replaced by a beaming smile. Thank God! she said. I thought it was that dreadful woman, Tabatha, again. She can't leave me in peace. I knew exactly what she meant. I was afraid I was disturbing her. Oh no, not at all, she insisted. I enjoy a bit of company. Just not Mrs King's! She beckoned me over. I'll let you into a secret, she whispered. I can't stand the woman. Couldn't explain it if you asked me to. There's just something about her that gets my goat. She's nice enough and I do believe she genuinely cares for all her inmates, but she just irritates me. I couldn't help but smile. Exactly how I felt about her! Come on, plonk yourself down on the window seat and sit next to me, whatever your name is. Betty, I said. Well, Betty, if you stand there any longer, I'll get a crick in my neck. There, that's better. And you can see my lovely view into the gardens. Oh, and I'm Lizzie, by the way. Lizzie Hetherington. She held out a tiny hand, the skin dry and almost transparent. I squeezed it gingerly. I asked her how long she'd been at Friars. More years than I care to remember. She looked so sad when she said it, Eva. I'm 96, you know, and still got all my own teeth! She cackled loudly. There was a wicked glint in her eye and I realised she was being ironic. It's not so bad once you get used to it, she went on. I've got a nice room and they bring me my food up so I don't have to go and sit with all the old farts. I smiled. I could not believe she was 96. She's painfully thin (emancipated is how I'd describe her) and bent with age, no doubt about it, but her skin is almost flawless. Of course, she's got the odd wrinkle but her face is largely unlined with not a single liver spot. So different from mine. Her grey hair is long and thin and she wears it in a single plait neatly coiled loosely at the nape of her neck. And even that belies her age – she has the neck of a swan whereas my turkey crop wobbles every time I speak. So it's not just her room with its fabulous views that make me jealous.

It is a beautiful room, so spacious, easily twice the size of mine, Eva. The views are simply wonderful, I told Lizzie. I nearly said 'to die for' but stopped myself just in time. I gazed begrudgingly at the neat gardens, the meandering paths and the majestic trees, leaves just starting to turn and watched as a gardener slowly raked a few fallen leaves into a pile under an enormous oak. I told her that my views were nothing as good as this. Lizzie nodded. Oh, I know. Nobody's is. There's people here would kill for this room. Some folk are sitting waiting for me to die so they can grab it. That Mr Latimer for one. He's top of the list. Pops his head round the door every Monday morning, right on cue. How are you doing today? he asks me. What he's really saying is 'not dead yet?' But I'll outlive him, sure as eggs is eggs. I asked her if she got many visitors, apart from Mr Latimer checking up on her. She shook her head. No. And I don't mind. I'm more than happy with my own company. Just like me, I thought. Mrs King sometimes puts her head round the door, and good old Ephraim, of course. Do you mind me coming? I asked her. No, of course not.

Delighted. Which room are you in? I told her I was in Violet. It's small and I overlook some outbuildings and sheds. Totally different from the view that you've got. I think there's some sort of workshop or something underneath me. There's a constant thrumming. Sounds like machinery. Get yourself moved, Lizzie advised. If only, I thought. You don't have to put up with that, she went on. I mean, you're paying a small fortune so tell Mrs King you want to be moved. I said Mrs King had it in hand and that at least she'd sorted out the cigarette smoke and the chattering that went on. Lizzie was clearly unimpressed. Sounds like you drew the short straw. It's not good, is it? I mean, this place doesn't come cheap. Can't you move to another suite? I didn't want to tell her that there was only one place I wanted to move to and that she was the current occupant.

I didn't stay much longer after that as it was clear Lizzie was getting tired. Her eyes kept closing and her head would droop and then she'd wake up with a jolt. I got up to go and as I did so, she laughed out loud. Not dead yet! No, not by a long chalk.

I realised now that it was time to go to the Dining Room. It had nothing to do with Ephraim or Mrs King telling me I should meet the other guests — I felt no desire at all to spend any time with my fellow slipper-shufflers. Oh no! There was a much better reason than that. I wanted to see what the impatient Mr Latimer, the Death's Head of the Flower Wing and Mrs Hetherintgon's Angel of Darkness, waiting in the wings to whisk her off to the other side, looked like. Of course, I knew she was joking about anyone wanting to kill her just for her room. Can you imagine anything so bizarre? I think she may be a little crazy to even think that but some old people do have a really vivid imagination. But I still wanted to see what the man looked like.

So whilst I wouldn't exactly say I have a spring in my step, Eva, there is something I need to do.

As ever, your loving sister,

Betty

CHAPTER SIX

The Dining Room.

Betty was doing fine until the lift stopped on the ground floor and then she almost changed her mind. The temptation to press the button to take her back up to the first floor and back to the safety of her own private sanctuary was overwhelming. Was this really such a good idea? Up until now she had not spoken to anybody except Mrs King and a few of her band of helpers, and Lizzie, of course. And now, for the very first time, she was going, willingly, to enter the Dining Room and meet some of her fellow residents. She shuddered at the thought. Standing in the doorway she peered in. The room was full. Every table was fully occupied as far as she could see. Perhaps she'd try tomorrow, she thought with relief.

"Now, if it isn't my favourite Mrs M," came a familiar voice and a hand touched her elbow gently. "You ready to try de lion's den?"

Ephraim. Betty wondered if he could feel her trembling.

"I can see it's full," she said. "I'll come back later."

"No you won't. I'll find you a space or my name's not Ephraim Ezekiel Isaiah Walford Lemington."

Betty looked at him. "Is it?" she asked him.

"Nah! Just kidding you. Who would call their son Walford? I mean! Come on, let's find you a seat."

"No, really. I would rather not. I've changed my mind, Ephraim."

"Now why would you do that? It's a nice menu today – even I'd eat it! Come on." And he steered her into the room. The loud buzz of conversation and the general clatter of eating continued unabated as they walked unnoticed slowly past table after table, looking for a seat. Finally Ephraim spotted one at a table near the conservatory doors. "Here we are, your throne awaits."

Betty looked at the five upturned faces, as they in turn, stared at her, eating temporarily suspended.

"Ladies and gentlemens," sang Ephraim, "let me introduce Mrs Mortimer. Betty. She goin' to be joinin' you for a light repast today."

Betty smiled awkwardly as Ephraim pulled the empty chair out for her and waited until she sat down before he continued. "Mrs M, let me introduce your fellow diners. First we have Miss Agatha Dove. Den Mrs Ruby Piper. Den dere's Mr Ashley Robinson, Mr Reggie Dawson, and las' but no least at all, Mrs Melanie Crowther." No Mr Latimer, then. Betty nodded shyly at each of them in turn as she unfolded her serviette and straightened her cutlery. "Now, y'all, Betty's new here so you be nice to her. They're a bunch of rogues, dis lot," he said loudly so they could all hear. "You take care now, Mrs M. I'll leave you to get 'quainted wid one another." Ephraim gave Betty's shoulder a reassuring squeeze and left her to it.

31

"We're not really a bunch of rogues," said the lady on her left. "He says that every time someone new joins us." She held out her hand. "Melanie Crowther."

Betty shook her hand and glanced round the rest of her fellow diners. Apart from Melanie, they had resumed eating immediately Ephraim had left and now completely ignored her. Not one of them a day under 140, she thought. She stared at the strapping, muscular woman sitting directly opposite whose bilious yellow hair contrasted sharply with the most startling black eyebrows Betty had ever seen; they looked as if they'd been drawn in by hand – badly – by a child wielding an unmanageable wax crayon. Her lipstick, a luminescent orange, had obviously been applied by the same child. The woman scraped up the remainder of her gravy with a spoon and sat back.

"Ee, I've had some voluminous meals here," she said, burping loudly. One of the men sitting next to her, Reggie, was it? patted her gently on the back. Despite being almost skeletal, the man had a florid face and sported a veined, bulbous nose. There's a man likes a tipple, thought Betty.

"Better?" he asked. The woman burped again. The man smiled.

"Ruby Piper," whispered Melanie behind her hand. "Likes her food, that one."

And her make-up, thought Betty. Obviously struggles with both.

"Not just her food," whispered Melanie. "The woman has other gargantuan appetites, if you get my drift."

"Really?" Betty found it hard to believe. "At her age?"

"Three choices for each course lunch and dinner time," said Melanie, handing her a menu. "We're supposed to order what we want at breakfast but they always put a menu on the table because some of these good folk can't remember their own names, let alone what they ordered to eat three hours ago. Mealtimes can be a bit crazy, no doubt about it. Lots of arguments over who ordered what. But the staff are very tolerant. They have to be. They won't mind that you're a bit late."

Betty didn't want to let on that she knew about the menu system and that she had in fact been here a few weeks already, eating all her meals in her room. But she suspected that Melanie guessed as much as she said nothing when Betty's selection – Cream of Cauliflower soup, and Fish Pie followed by sponge pudding and custard – appeared unbidden. She'd chosen her lunch this morning; she just hadn't really expected to be eating it here. As she waited for her soup to arrive she turned to Melanie.

"Do you know everybody here?"

"Pretty much. I've been here over ten years now. There's a lot of comings and goings in a place like this, as you can imagine, but you get to see most people at some stage or another. There's one or two who never leave their rooms for whatever reason, but most of us enjoy having company."

Betty wanted to ask Melanie about herself but felt too shy.

"How are you finding it?" Melanie asked her.

"It's taking a bit of getting used to, to be honest."

Melanie patted her hand. "You will get used to it. Regard it as a 4 star hotel full of the old and bewildered and you'll manage fine. Just don't expect non-stop intelligent conversation. It's in short supply, I can tell you. Don't get me wrong, though. Most people here have got a full set of marbles. They just choose not to play with all of them all the time."

Betty smiled. At least there was one nice person at the table willing to make an effort.

Once pudding was served and eaten people started to drift off.

"Coffee in the lounge," explained Melanie to her new-found friend.

Betty looked round at the rapidly emptying room. "Do you know Mr Latimer?"

"Mr Latimer? Which one? There are two of them."

Two of them? This was unexpected and complicated matters somewhat. Which one was in line for the Rose Suite?

"They're brothers. Johnny and Sinclair. Been here for a long time too. That's them over there. Sitting at the table by the entrance."

Even at this distance Betty could see the similarity. Rotund, fat-faced with thinning grey hair, they were clearly arguing. Fingers were being pointed and voices were raised.

"They're twins. In fact I believe this is the only retirement home in the entire country with resident twins. But they argue and bicker the whole time. Over nothing at all."

"Do they always sit at the same table?" asked Betty. "I know Mrs King said you could sit where you like but that most people tend to eat with their friends."

Melanie nodded. "It's first come first served but there's hell to pay if they can't have their table by the door there. Droit de seigneur they insist on calling it, although I'm not sure that doesn't mean something else altogether. They've always sat there for as long as I can remember. They think they're lords of the manor, kings of all they survey. And we," she opened her arms wide, "we lesser mortals, we don't count."

Betty smiled. "I'm detecting that you don't like them."

"Got it in one!"

"What do they argue about?"

"Anything and everything. Who was born first. Who is the most intelligent. Who made more money. Whose wife was the worst. Which wife got the biggest divorce settlement. But it's always about them. They really only care about themselves."

"What would happen if I went to sit at their table?" Betty asked.

"Why would you want to?"

"No reason."

"Rather you than me. I'd prefer Mrs Piper's mild dyspepsia and her questionable make-up any day to their incessant and futile quarrels. Just don't get caught in the cross-fire, my dear." She stood up to leave. "Coffee?"

"I'll pass, thank you."

"As you like."

Betty was in a dilemma. She didn't relish joining the argumentative Latimer brothers at their table but if she was going to find out who was waiting to grab Lizzie Hetherintgon's still warm bed once it was finally vacated, she didn't have a choice. Somehow she would have to pluck up courage and sit with them for as long as it took to get the answer. Or maybe she could just ask Mrs King. She could tell her, couldn't she? It wasn't a state secret, after all. She'd give it a go.

Contrary to what she had been told by Mrs King herself on the day of the Grand Tour, her office door was still closed. Betty knocked timidly. There was no response so she knocked louder. A helper, Mercy by name, staggered past, a huge pile of freshly laundered towels pressed against her enormous bosom.

"Can I help, darlin'?"

"I was hoping to speak to Mrs King."

"She's away for two weeks, my lovely. Gone somewhere warm and sunny. Does it every year at this time. Somewhere nice, I expect. Can I do sometin' for you?"

"I don't know. I'm trying to find out about waiting lists for rooms."

"Why? You want to change?"

"No. Yes. I mean maybe."

"Well, I'm sorry, dear lady, but Mrs King's in charge of all dat stuff. You'll have to ask her when she gets back."

"When will that be?"

"Truth to tell, I don' know."

"But isn't there anybody else in charge? I mean, what if something happens when she's away?"

"Like what?" Mercy looked alarmed.

"I don't know. Somebody dies or something."

Mercy threw up her hands in horror, dropping the towels on the floor. "Oh Lordie!" She crossed herself furiously. "We never use words like that round here! Nobody dies here! They pass."

"Pass?"

"S'right. We never talk about dyin'." She whispered the last word. "We only pass into the tender lovin' arms of sweet Jesus. He's always there. Waitin' for us."

Betty looked round. "Where?" she asked. "I can't see him." She was feeling deliberately provocative.

"He is everywhere, darlin'. You just got to open your eyes."

Betty made a great show of looking up and down the corridor. "Nope, I still can't see him."

Mercy didn't find it funny. "Dat's cos you ain't tryin' hard enough."

Betty swore under her breath. "Alright, then. So you don't know where Mrs King has gone, when she'll be back, or who is looking after the shop whilst she's away."

"In a nutshell, lady." But Mercy looked confused. "No shop here, though. Dis a care home."

Betty took a deep breath. "What happens if someone passes into the tender loving arms of sweet Jesus whilst Mrs King is away sunning herself?" She could not believe she had just asked that question.

Mercy looked blank. She shook her head slowly. "Now, you got me there." With difficulty she bent down to pick up the towels. "I'll be sure to ask her when she gets back."

"Are you telling me that there is nobody in charge? No deputy manager? No-one? The place can't just run itself."

"Listen darlin', I just do de laundry. Dat's my job an' I do it well. I don' know anytin' about anytin' else. Okay?"

It was going to have to be.

It was now clear to Betty that the only way to get the definitive answer about which Mr Latimer was next in line for the Rose Suite, was to ask the men herself. But that was to prove a lot more of a challenge than she ever could have imagined.

CHAPTER SEVEN

Friars Rest
October

Well, dearest Eva,

Can you imagine it! I finally plucked up courage and went to the Dining Room and I have been going every day now, breakfast, lunch and dinner. You have no idea how proud I am of myself. The reason I went, as I hinted in my last letter, was not because of some great need to socialise with people. I've always been quite content to be left to my own devices, as you know, and if I wanted to chat I could pass the time of day with the helpers who brought meals to me in my suite, Janice and Priti, even Mikey on occasion. I haven't seen much of him. He's a nice young lad but he only works here one day a week. I think I mentioned he was a young criminal. No, what is it they call them? Young offender, that's it. Though you wouldn't know to look at him. He's very presentable in his green uniform, short hair, big smile. Although I did notice the other day he has a tattoo on the inside of his upper arm. Lots of writing. That must have hurt, I thought. All that soft flesh. But why is it these young people have these awful tattoos, Eva? I could never understand it myself. What's that? I asked him, pointing. He rolled his sleeve up as far as it would go to show me the whole thing. I do believe he blushed. It's a recipe. A recipe? Mikey nodded. Another big smile. For what? Scrambled eggs. Eva, I nearly fell off my chair. Why Mikey, do you have a recipe for scrambled eggs tattooed on the inside of your arm? It's my daughter's favourite food. Reminds me how to make it, he said. I don't know what surprised me more. The fact that he had a recipe tattooed on his arm, the fact that he couldn't remember a recipe for something as simple as scrambled eggs, or the fact that he has a daughter. If you'd asked me, I would have said he looked about twelve – clearly he's not but he's far too young to have a daughter, in my opinion. I asked him what she was called. Dimitra, he told me. It's old Greek for lover of the earth. You could have knocked me down with a feather. People are so surprising, aren't they? But I call her Dimbo, for short. Ah well. You give with one hand and take away with the other. Lives with her mother, he said, producing a tatty photograph from his back pocket. She really is the most adorable little girl, all rosy cheeks and curls, and I told him so. One day, she's going to be proud of me, he said. Oh Eva, he quite touched my heart. Something like that does restore one's faith in humanity just a little.

But back to what I was trying to tell you. I do seem to get side-tracked so very easily. The real reason I had to go down to the Dining Room was to find out about Mr Latimer. Both Mrs King and Lizzie had told me he was next on the list for the Rose Suite after Lizzie vacates the room (or goes to be in the arms of sweet Jesus, which according to Mercy, one of the helpers, is what happens when you leave Friars – no dying here, you'll be pleased to know. Jesus' arms are ready and waiting. I sleep easy in that knowledge). Anyway, I simply had to see for myself who this Mr Latimer is. I wanted to see what the competition looked like. I would have asked Mrs King but she's away on her annual holiday and it seems that nobody is left in charge when she's not here. Which I must admit, I find a bit *alarming, so it's good to know that sweet Jesus is keeping an eye on us all. Somebody needs to. But it did mean that I had to find Mr Latimer all on my own.*

Well, as it turns out there are two of them, Mr Latimers I mean, which somewhat complicates matters. I found this out when I first went down to the Dining Room last week for lunch – my, but it's popular. The place was heaving and I was lucky to get the last seat on a table with five others, most of whom completely ignored me the entire time I was there. Can you believe it! One kind lady, Melody Something, pointed the Latimer brothers out to me – twins would you believe – Johnny and Sinclair. From what she says they're an unpleasant pair, constantly bickering and commanding, and I do mean commanding, the best table in the house. So there was only one option – I had to get a seat at their table and find out from them which one was in line for the best suite in Friars. Easier said than done.

It actually took me a whole week, can you imagine, before I finally managed to get a seat at their table. In the meantime I got to sit at a lot of other tables with a variety of souls. Honestly, Eva, there's a real mixed bag here. One or two of the detainees are alright and some of them can even hold a reasonable conversation. And there's one or two who are real characters. But most of them, well, being hit over the head with a shovel and buried next to the hedgehogs would be the best thing for them. Anyway, as I was saying, it's taken me a week before I finally got to meet the Latimers. I don't know why sitting at their table is so sought after. I thought the only waiting list here was for poor Lizzie's room but it would seem that there's a veritable queue to join the brothers, though after sitting with them I can't think why. Perhaps people get some sort of strange, questionable satisfaction or even pleasure possibly, from the free entertainment they provide when they're at loggerheads with each other (which is most of the time). Up until last night their table was always full but finally I hit the jackpot. Yesterday I went down to dinner very early and was at the head of the queue waiting for the Dining Room to open. (Can you believe these people will queue for their meals? They know they're going to be fed. They know the food is going to be good. They know there's plenty to go round. But there they are, every day, every mealtime, lining up just to make sure they don't miss out. Amazing). I stood for a full fifteen minutes, (not an easy thing with my knees) and I got to the table before anyone else, so I was already sitting at what I've called the Latimer Table when the twins arrived and my! You should have seen their faces.

Are you sure you're in the right place? one of them asked me very rudely. He turned out to be Sinclair. I thought I could sit anywhere I replied, somewhat innocently. He harrumphed (is that a word?) and sat down opposite me. His brother, Johnny, sat down next to him and they both stared at me. So I tried to stare back but I lost my nerve. They are twins, no doubt about it. Their features are almost identical – same wispy grey comb-overs, same round, sweaty, fat faces, flushed cheeks, bright red-veined noses (there seems to be a lot of that round here) and they even sound the same too. Also they dress similarly, both favouring tweedy jackets and ties. The big difference is that Sinclair wears black glasses and Johnny, pretentiously in my opinion, sports a monocle. The last time I saw one of those was in one of those black and white films they made centuries ago – Carruthers up the Limpopo, or some such. I got the impression they weren't too impressed with what they saw in me for soon they were consulting the wine list (did I tell you there is a very extensively stocked bar and cellar here?) and arguing over whether to have the Chateau Neuf du Pappy (as Sinclair pronounced it), or a full-blooded Hungarian Viszla (I'm sure that's what he said although I always thought that was a breed of dog. But I could be wrong). Once the wine was chosen (they went for the Pappy), they turned their attention to me again. Clearly they had their priorities sorted.

Sinclair, peering at me over the top of his glasses, asked me in very peremptory tones who I was. I did not like his manner at all. I told him my name, feeling totally intimidated. I'm sure that was what he intended. Johnny asked me if I was new. I nodded. I watched open-mouthed as he held the breast pocket of his Tweed jacket open wide and let his monocle drop into it merely by raising his eyebrows. Must be some sort of party piece. Then I could have sworn he winked at me.

Why do you want to sit here, Betty Mortimer? Sinclair asked me. I'm trying to get to know as many people as I can, I told him. I can lie easily when I want to. Another harrumph. Sinclair again. No bad thing, said Johnny. Getting to know new people. Not much of a turnover here. Did he mean what I think he meant? Could do with some fresh blood here in Friars, he went on. Lively things up a little. And I do like it lively. And I'd like to get to know you. What did you say your name was? I repeated it for him. Well, Betty, he said, licking his lips, I'll save you a space if you like. You can always sit next to me. I could actually feel myself blushing. Can you believe that, Eva? At my age!

There was no opportunity to ask them about the Rose Suite, or anything else for that matter, as the two of them dominated the whole conversation. Melanie, or whatever her name was, was right. All they could talk about was themselves, although it was not so much talking as arguing. What I was able to establish was they they had been partners, owning several factories manufacturing some sort of indispensable gizmos for the aircraft industry and that they had sold their business for a fortune shortly before they retired. At that point both of their wives had left them, depriving each of their husbands of a not inconsequential sum of money with the assistance of the divorce courts (both ladies arguing mental cruelty – they certainly had a strong case). Since none of their respective children wished to have anything further to do with them either, and both brothers being unable and unwilling to cook and clean for themselves, they saw Friars Rest as an ideal solution to avoid a long and lonely retirement. At least here they would have a comfortable existence and a guaranteed audience, both obviously equally important to them. Sinclair insisted that his factory was the larger of the two, at one time employing over 2000 people but Johnny declared that while his brother's factory had been bigger, his had been more important as the thrunge-gromit-separator, or whatever it was called, that he manufactured, was more important than all of the other bits that Sinclair made. So size is not always important, he said, looking straight at me and winking. No doubt about it this time and it put me right off my sherry trifle, I can tell you. And that was the tone of the whole meal. Johnny's three children had all gone to Oxford whilst Sinclair's daughter had only managed Manchester Poly. Sinclair's house in Wilmslow may have had six bedrooms and an indoor swimming pool but Johnny's had had an underground wine cellar. You get my drift.

Honestly, Eva, it was like listening to two children squabbling in the playground. Mine's bigger than yours! I don't like you, give me my toffee back! Nobody else at the table said a word, either because they didn't want to or more likely they couldn't get a word in edgeways. Meal over and Johnny came round and pulled my chair out for me. I stood. You will join us again, won't you, he said, his hand in the small of my back. It wasn't a question. I wriggled uncomfortably and he pressed harder. I smiled through clenched teeth but it only served to encourage him. We so enjoyed your company, he went on. It's not often we get a pretty lady round here and I do like a woman with a good body. Firm and buoyant. And he actually squeezed my bottom.

Eva, I could have happily vomited. The following day I didn't go near the Dining Room at all. This is not going to be easy, I can tell.

Your loving sister,

Betty.

CHAPTER EIGHT

Betty would have been happy if she never had to spend another minute with the Latimers but knew she had little choice if she was to find out who was heir to Lizzie's throne. After breakfast she popped into the Rose Suite for her daily visit to Lizzie. She was concerned to find the old lady lying in bed, propped up by half a dozen pillows and a breakfast tray on her lap.

"Are you alright Lizzie?"

"Betty! Good morning my dear."

"How are you? Aren't you feeling well?"

"Just lazy, that's all." She nodded towards the tray of largely uneaten food. "Didn't fancy getting up this morning so I'm having breakfast in bed. That's the joy of this place. Do what you want when you want. What have you been up to?"

"Nothing much. I had dinner with the Latimers last night, for a change."

"You said the Latimers. Is there more than one?"

"Didn't you know? There's two of them. Twins."

"Well, I never. I had no idea. Fancy!"

"So you don't know which one of them wants this room."

Lizzie shook her head. "No idea at all." She sipped a cup of weak tea. "It's funny. I always feel that there's someone sitting on my shoulder or hovering behind the bed, ready to pounce. I never realised that there are two of them. Are they both waiting to leap into action as soon as I've drawn my last breath?"

This was something Betty hadn't considered. It was bad news if they were both on the list as that bumped her even further down the line.

"You don't know which one of them has been popping his head round the door then, checking to see how you are?"

"No. No idea at all. But if they're twins, do they look alike?"

"Tweedle-Dum and Tweedle-Dee," said Betty laughing, "but Dum wears glasses and Dee wears a monocle."

"Fancy that! Now you mention it, sometimes it was glasses, sometimes a monocle but I never really gave it any thought. I just assumed it was one and the same man."

"So they could both be on the waiting list for your room, not just one of them"

"I don't know. Does it matter?" Lizzie was getting peevish.

Did it matter? It did to Betty. And what if there were more after them? The best suite in the entire Home was rapidly disappearing out of sight.

"Don't tell me you want it too?"

"No, I don't," she lied.

Lizzie looked at her disbelievingly. "You sure? Every other bugger wants it, why not you?"

"I just think there may be people more deserving than the Latimers. They're awful men. I don't think it's right that anyone so obnoxious or unbelievably nasty should have this lovely room, that's all. I think there are much nicer people here who are more worthy."

"It won't bother me who has it when I'm gone," said Lizzie. "But I'm not planning on going anytime soon."

"I'm very glad to hear it." But Betty had decided. Once Mrs Hetherington no longer occupied the suite she would do her damnedest to make sure that neither of the Latimers got it.

Betty missed lunch altogether. Finally, that morning she'd got a letter from Mark and was so distressed by the contents that she took to her bed for the rest of the day. Ephraim brought her a cup of tea shortly after lunch, concerned not to have seen her in the Dining Room.

"Are you okay Mrs M?"

Betty waved the letter at him. "From my son."

"Not bad news I hope."

"Yes and no. But mostly yes. He's not coming home any time soon." She explained to him about Mark's make or break tour of the Far East as a mouth-organ playing musician in a group. The tour was going so well that it had been extended for another six weeks. Their sort of music was fairly new to Far Eastern ears and it was going down well. They'd now been asked to play in Thailand and Hong Kong after their stint in Japan and Korea. He wasn't even sure he'd be home for Christmas. She'd understand, surely, and wouldn't want him not to go? It was all going so much better than expected and there would be at least two record deals out of all this. Plus what with the merchandise sales, he was on track to make a small fortune. They all were. And who knew what next? If they could break into the American market, he was set up for life. He'd enclosed a couple of newspaper clippings showing a sea of swaying fans, arms in the air, illuminated mobile phones held high, at a huge flood-lit arena. Unfortunately it was all in Korean so she had no idea what they said. She passed the clippings to Ephraim.

"Don't suppose you read Korean?"

"Not one of my many skills I'm afraid." He smiled at her. "But you should be so proud. I would be."

It suddenly struck Betty that she knew nothing about Ephraim, nothing about his personal life. Or why such a clearly educated man was working in a retirement home in the north of England. What about his family? Did he have any? Children? She had been so wrapped up in her narrow little life and her perceived misery that she'd never given any thought to this man, or to any of the other helpers in Friars Rest. She knew a little bit about Mikey and Janice. Priti too. But it was all superficial. She had often wondered about Mrs King and what she was really like but all the helpers who looked after her and made her life as pleasant as they could, she barely gave most of them a second thought, forgetting they were ordinary people with lives and loves. How selfish was that? She was ashamed of herself.

"Have you got family, Ephraim? Children?"

"Lord no! Not the marrying kind."

"Why not?"

Ephraim thought for a while. "D'you know, I don' rightly know. Must have never met the right person. Or maybe I just like to be footloose and fancy-free. No ties that bind. I can keep me options open." He winked at her.

Is he flirting with me? Betty wondered, delighted at the thought. When did somebody last do that?

She smiled. "No children even?" she asked mischievously.

"No Mrs M. Not a one."

"But I thought..."

"What?"

"Well, you know."

"What? You was goin' to say dat people like me, my type, always have lots of chil'un here and dere." He'd slipped back into his melodious, Caribbean lilt.

"I would never suggest that of people from Epsom!" Betty sounded appalled.

Ephraim looked at her and burst out laughing. "You one okay lady, Mrs M." He stood up to go. "Now mind you eat tonight. I be checking."

Betty read her son's letter again. There was no address so she couldn't reply. Maybe she should order the Korean Times instead of the Daily Mail, so she could keep track of his progress on the other side of the world. He'd mentioned giving up his flat – no point paying for it if he wasn't going to be there, so he'd asked a friend to clear it out for him and find someone else to take on the lease. It was beginning to sound as if he wasn't coming home at all, let alone for Christmas. She tried not to think about how alone she felt.

Betty forced herself to go down to dinner but her heart wasn't in it. Still, there was no way round it. She had to find out which Mr Latimer was next in line for the Rose Suite, Sinclair, Johnny or even worse, both.

"Where were you?" demanded Johnny Latimer as Betty walked into the Dining Room. "I missed you at lunch time. I kept a seat for you as promised but ended up having to give it up. I had to spend my entire lunch next to that old crab, Mrs Blakeney. Smells like an old tea towel, that one."

"I felt like spending a bit of time on my own," Betty replied. She wasn't going to mention Mark's letter.

"I would have come and seen you in your room if you'd wanted company."

Her stomach heaved at the thought. "I didn't."

"You women. No idea what makes you tick. But at least you're here now. Come and sit next to me." He patted the chair seat next to him. Betty had no option. Sinclair took the seat on the other side. Trapped.

"Now that's much better. It's high time we got to know one another. How about some wine?"

"Oh, no, thank you. I'm not really a big drinker."

"We can work on that. Loosens the inhibitions, that's what I always say." Johnny leaned into her as he spoke and she sat back. "Got any inhibitions need loosening?"

Betty poured herself a glass of water, her hand shaking.

"Cold?" whispered Johnny. "I could warm you up."

It was all Betty could do to stop herself tipping the water into his lap.

He leaned across her to pass the wine bottle to his brother, placing one hand on her thigh to steady himself.

"I've been pining for your company, you know," he whispered in what he believed were irresistibly seductive tones.

Betty grimaced.

"You know how to tease a man, don't you?"

"I don't know what you mean," she replied indignantly.

"Playing hard to get. You shouldn't hide yourself away in your room all day. Not unless you let me come and visit you."

"Absolutely not!"

"Are you sure? Well then, you could come and visit me."

What did she have to say to this man to get it through his thick skull that she did not want him anywhere near her? She was only putting up with his company until she could find out what she needed to know. But how could she casually drop the subject into the conversation? He saved her the bother.

"You'll sing a different tune when I move."

She turned to look at him. "Move? What do you mean? Are you going to another home?" she asked hopefully, trying not to sound too pleased.

"No. I'm going to be moving from my suite on Forest Wing to the best suite in the Home."

"The Rose Suite? But how?"

"You've seen it?"

Betty nodded. "I visit Mrs Hetherington, Lizzie, every day."

"That old crow! She's not long for this world and when she goes..." Johnny rubbed his hands together, "I'll be in there like a shot."

"But she's not going anywhere."

"Don't you believe it. She's on her way out, that one. Can't be soon enough for me. And when she's gone, we can party." He pinched her thigh. It was all Betty could do not to slap him.

"She's not on her way out. She's got years left." She was outraged.

"Pah! I doubt she'll see Christmas."

43

Betty's heart sunk at the thought. It wasn't just at the idea of losing Lizzie that upset her. It had soon become a habit of hers to pop into her room every morning for half an hour or so. Any longer and Lizzie was exhausted. But she always seemed genuinely pleased to see Betty and to enjoy her company, and Betty herself was surprised at just how fond she had grown of the old lady in a short space of time. She enjoyed their chats far more than she could possibly have imagined. And Lizzie was one of the very few people in Friars Rest that Betty would consider a friend and who really meant something to her. But it was more than losing her companionship that upset Betty. To listen to this dreadful man wishing her dead, that was unspeakable. She was now even more resolute. If she did nothing else, she would stop this man getting the Rose Suite at all costs. But how?

Johnny passed her the menu.

"I've already ordered," she said peremptorily.

"If I could have anything on the menu, it would be you," he whispered, moving closer.

"Just as well I'm not on it, isn't it!" she snarled in reply.

"Ooh, you little minx you! I do like a feisty woman."

Betty clenched her fists tightly under the table.

"What have you ordered for tonight, then?" he asked her.

"Ravioli."

"Foreign muck. Not real food, that pasta." Johnny grimaced in disgust.

"Well, I like it."

"Doesn't agree with me. Upsets my stomach."

"Really?" Something stirred in Betty's brain. "That's such a shame."

Johnny shrugged. "I don't like it and it doesn't like me."

"When you say it upsets your stomach..."

"Gives him the squits," Sinclair decided to join in the conversation. Johnny glared at his brother. "Well, it does."

"You don't have to bloody tell everyone, do you?" snapped Johnny.

"You've always had a weak stomach. Slightest thing and whoops! Off it goes. Not like me. Made from cast iron, my guts."

"Oh you poor thing, Johnny." Betty sounded genuinely sympathetic. She laid a hand on his arm.

Johnny looked at her. This was the first time she had ever called him by his name, let alone touched him voluntarily. Perhaps the way to this woman's heart was through his bowels. Maybe he should milk it for all it was worth.

"Lifelong problem," he admitted. "I do have to be very careful what I eat. Especially here."

"You mean the Dining Room?" asked Betty innocently.

"No. The Home. Friars Rest. You know about their policy, don't you?"

"Which one is that?"

"I'm surprised Tabatha didn't tell you." He looked furtively round the room then lowered his voice. Betty had to lean forward to hear him, wincing as she inhaled his stale breath. "Incontinence."

"Incontinence?" repeated Betty loudly. Several heads at neighbouring tables turned briefly then eating was resumed.

"Sshh!" scolded Johnny. "For goodness' sake!"

"What's the matter?" She couldn't remember the last time she'd had so much fun.

"There's a policy here. Slightest whiff, so to speak, of you know what, and you're out."

"Oh, that's right. I vaguely remember Mrs King saying something about that when I first arrived. But surely you don't have a problem. Do you?"

"Oh no. Absolutely not. And I want to keep it that way. So I watch what I eat and keep the beast under control."

Betty smiled at him, a germ of an idea beginning to form in the back of her mind. "You really will have to be careful, won't you? Is it just pasta or are there other foods that set you off?"

"Mainly pasta, thank goodness, so I avoid it like the plague."

"Still, I think we will have to keep an eye on what you eat, just in case."

Johnny was touched. Typical woman though, he thought. Didn't want to know him before, but mention some illness or weakness and all she wanted to do was mother him. Well, he'd let her. No harm in that. And who knows where it might lead. He squeezed her hand and this time she let him. He was on a roll.

CHAPTER NINE

Friars Rest
November

Dearest Eva,

More gloomy news I'm afraid. I had a letter from Mark. His tour with the group is going so well they're going to be out in Japan and wherever for an awful lot longer than planned. Which is wonderful news for him — he certainly sounds happy. But not good news for me. He doesn't think he'll be home for Christmas. What am I going to do? I don't feel I've taken such a knock since Barry died. Mark is all I have and the thought of spending Christmas all alone — because I am alone here really — well, it just breaks my heart. It's not the fact it's Christmas. That's neither here nor there. It's the fact it's Christmas without Mark. Can you understand that? Ever since Mark's father died it's just been the two of us. And now I feel as if I've been abandoned yet again.

Yet again? I hear you ask. I never did tell you what really happened to Barry, did I? Yes, it was a massive heart attack, that was true. But there was so much more to it than that. I've never even told Mark. He used to ask about his father. What was he like? Did Mark take after him at all? Why hadn't I married again? I've always fobbed him off. But if I can't tell you, who can I tell?

I did write to you at the time, just after Barry died, to let you know the devastating news. But the facts were so much worse than you could ever have imagined. It all started that dreadful night in February with a knock on the door. That's the way it so often begins, isn't it? A knock on the door.

I'm sorry Eva, I can't do this now. I thought I could but I'm not ready yet. Soon, I promise. There's so much to tell you but I've got to be in the right frame of mind. What happened to me affected my whole life, everything I did and everything I've become. I will tell you everything. But not just right now.

Yours despondently,

Betty

CHAPTER TEN

Betty returned to her room after breakfast the following day and was surprised to see a piece of paper had been placed on her freshly made bed. She wondered who could have left it there. Intrigued, she picked it up and read the typed sheet;

Come with us to the lovely market town of Narrowby. Its narrow, cobbled streets are home to a wide selection of wonderful independent shops (early Christmas shopping, anyone?) as well as a delightful choice of coffee shops and tea houses. Our minibus leaves on Friday 10am sharp and we'll have you back by 4pm, just in time for afternoon tea. Only £5 per person.

Underneath, someone had scrawled in red; Only 2 places left!

Betty scrunched the paper into a ball and was just about to throw it in the bin when she stopped. Flattening it out, she read it again. She hadn't been out of Friars since she arrived in September so maybe it would do her good to see a bit of the outside world. It would make a nice change, for sure. Yes, she'd have to share the minibus with other people, but once she was there she could do her own thing. And she hadn't been to Narrowby for years. Why not? What had she got to lose? Betty was suddenly excited at the prospect. But what if the remaining places had now gone? What was today? Wednesday. Maybe it was already too late. Her heart sank. But then presumably whoever had left the notice in her room knew there were still seats available. She dialled Reception. Unusually the phone was answered straight away and a voice she didn't recognise confirmed that she had got the last seat on the bus. Betty put the phone down and smiled.

Up until now Betty had been reluctant to join in any of the social events or the activities that were arranged for the residents. Most of the time she ignored the Activity Notice Board which was just outside the Dining Room – she hadn't come here to learn how to arrange flowers or how to spot Saturn in a southern sky. No, there was nothing of interest for her here and the little socialising she did was limited to the Dining Room (although she had an ulterior motive for eating there), and to her daily visits to Lizzie. Occasionally Ephraim would poke his head round her door and, if he wasn't too busy, he'd stop for a chat. He'd even threatened to thrash her at Cribbage one day when he could find the time. But other than that, she kept pretty much to herself. She studiously avoided the Television Lounge, preferring to watch TV in her suite. At least that way there was no arguing as to who wanted to watch what and when. She wasn't even convinced that most of those who sat in front of the TV all day had any idea what they were watching, where they were, or indeed, who they were. So Betty could have hardly described her social life as throbbing. But now all that was about to change. Here she was, about to step out of her comfort zone and face the world again. Betty was terrified at the prospect.

Friday was bright and sunny, if cold. By the time she'd had breakfast and got herself ready, which involved a little bit of mascara and some lipstick (the first she'd worn since she'd arrived at Friars), there was a queue for the minibus and she was last in line. Some of them must have been waiting since dawn, she thought. She vaguely recognised the woman standing in front of her, or at least she recognised the brittle yellow frizz poking out from some woollen monstrosity. There couldn't be more than one woman at Friars with near-fluorescent pubic hair on her head, surely? Ruth? Ruby? Ruby, that was it. The woman turned round and stared at her. It was confirmed. It was that awful gravy-slurping, dyspeptic woman from Melanie's table. She of the startling eyebrows and luminous lipstick.

"Goin', are you?" she asked enigmatically.

Unsure how to respond, Betty thought it safer to just nod. This close to her, Betty was able to study her in all her glory. The woman was a walking Liquorice Allsort. It was evident her eyebrows had been plucked into extinction and replaced by heavy black smears. Her yellow hair was crisp and scraggly, tied back with a My Little Pony ribbon. The bright red lipstick Ruby wore today had clearly been applied with a spatula and the colour had bled into the wrinkles that surrounded her puckered mouth. Her bright orange eye-shadow was already smudged. The woman was a technicoloured disaster. Everything about her was discordant and mismatched. Ruby's woollen coat was of green and yellow checks with red patch pockets – clearly designed by committee (Betty presumed they only worked at night and even then with the lights turned off), and perched on her head was a pink knitted tea cosy. Surely Betty was mistaken. She peered closer. Sadly she was not. Please let me not have to sit next to her, she prayed quietly. Please.

It was a slow process loading everybody aboard. Those of a frailer disposition were assisted up the steps and into their seats by Raoul and Ephraim and there was a lot of jostling and shuffling as people got themselves settled. Finally it was Betty's turn and she climbed the steps unaided.

"Good morning Mrs M." Ephraim smiled broadly. "Good to see you."

Now she knew who'd left the notice on her bed. She should have guessed. She smiled back at him. "Good morning to you too."

There was only one spare seat, right at the back and over the wheel arch, and yes, she saw to her utter dismay, it was next to Ruby. Betty made her way slowly and with difficulty down the aisle to the back of the bus, tripping over handbags and walking sticks. Nobody apologised or made any attempt to move any of the obstacles; they only glared at her in irritation. She didn't recognise any of them. Where had they all been hiding? she wondered. She sat down next to Ruby, exhausted.

A bronzed and even larger Mrs King got on the minibus clutching a clipboard. Betty hadn't seen her since she got back from her holiday, but wherever she'd been, she'd obviously made the most of whatever had been on offer. Betty could imagine her tucking into a gargantuan buffet, filling her plate again and again before collapsing on a sunbed by the pool, umbrellaed cocktail within easy reach.

"Right everyone. Head count. Good. Everyone here. And that's how we want it to be on the way home too. Raoul here is your driver for today and he will park the bus in the main square and leave it there all day. Be back on at 3.30 please. There may be other minibuses so please make sure you get on the right one. You can't miss it. It has Friars Rest on both sides. If you do miss the bus...well, it's been nice knowing you."

There were a few chuckles but most of Betty's fellow passengers looked blank.

"Have a lovely time and don't spend too much money." She closed the door behind her.

Betty leaned back in her seat and tried to stretch her legs but the wheel arch left her nowhere to put them. She sighed loudly. Ruby wriggled in her seat then poked her in the ribs.

"A trip to the lost town of Wherewithall. Not been before. Excited."

"I think we're actually going to Narrowby," said Betty.

Ruby didn't respond but looked out of the window. After a few minutes she poked Betty again.

"We 'ad a car like this," she announced loudly. "'Ad 5 gears it did, but we never used the fifth one. 'Usband couldn't see the point."

Betty closed her eyes. It was going to be a long trip. She must have fallen asleep because the next thing she knew, Ruby was poking her again.

"Can you stop doing that," she said. "It's really annoying."

"I wanna get out," whined Ruby.

Betty was surprised to see that they were the only two left on the bus. Somehow they had arrived, parked, the bus had emptied and she'd slept through the whole lot.

"I'm going to get me a sandwich," announced Ruby. "I fancy one of them LGBGT things. One wi' lots of bacon. Comin'?"

Betty stood with difficulty and willed the blood back into her cramped legs. "No. I've just had breakfast."

"Never too early for food, that's what I always say."

Her knees screaming with pain Betty walked stiffly down the aisle, holding on grimly to the seat backs, and was grateful for Raoul's assistance in getting down the steps.

"You get back early, you get a better seat," he promised her. She smiled her thanks.

Betty was thrilled to see that Narrowby had changed little since she was here last time. The large cobbled square was surrounded on all four sides by splendid sturdy buildings, rolling gorse-clad hills providing a stunning backdrop to the pretty market town. There were shops of every description, pubs, cafes, a convenience store and a newsagent. There was even a small bank. All were solidly constructed from Yorkshire sandstone although most of them were hidden from view by the many market stalls, each with a bright red and blue striped awning. Betty looked round her. It was a pretty picture but it was busy and she could do with a sit-down. But what she really needed was a couple of painkillers, just to take the edge off her aches and pains. She looked in her handbag – usually there was an open pack of Paracetamol lurking in the bottom somewhere but she couldn't find it. Cursing under her breath she looked round for a chemist. There, in the corner of the square, she spotted one. Walking unsteadily across the cobbles she weaved her way through the stalls. Inside, Betty waited patiently as the young male assistant at the counter sorted out her change. She was intrigued by the display of brightly coloured boxes and bottles behind him. What a collection, she thought. A remedy for every disease or ailment under the sun. She tried to guess from the names what the medicines or treatments were for. Zit-Geist? Betty was sure she could guess that one. Something to do with acne surely? Corn-Utopia. No question. Chill-Blame? Not too sure about that one. And then there was Shift Happens. She chuckled. It's got to be a laxative with a name like that. How do they come up with these names? Laxative eh? I know someone who definitely does not want any of that. A thought crossed her mind.

"Sorry, I almost forgot," she whispered as the sales assistant gave her her change. "I need a laxative too. Have you got anything that's really strong." She pointed in a vague downward direction. "Bit congested I am."

"We've got this." He took a box from the display behind him and handed it to her. It was Shift Happens. "It's one of the strongest on the market. You don't have any allergies do you?"

Betty assured him she hadn't. "Just read the instructions carefully. It's pretty potent and quick-acting but has the advantage of no lingering aftertaste."

"Sounds ideal," smiled Betty. "Can I have two boxes? I don't come into town that often."

"Don't see why not."

Once outside, Betty beamed with delight. She needed to find a cafe so she could get a drink and take her Paracetamol but, strangely enough, her knees didn't seem to hurt quite as much now.

The cafe she chose was quiet, despite it being market day. She looked at her watch. Probably a bit too early for the lunch crowd, she thought. It was an old-fashioned place, the sort Betty liked, with waitresses in tidy back dresses with white aprons and flat shoes. The décor was dated but it was warm and comfortable and the service was good. But what Betty liked most of all was than none of her fellow escapees were anywhere to be seen. Tea was served in a proper teapot with a jug of hot water and a strainer and Betty, notwithstanding the fact that she'd not long eaten, chose a Welsh Rarebit from the extensive menu, even treating herself to a small glass of wine. She sat back feeling pleased with herself. She couldn't have explained why she'd bought the laxative – she certainly didn't need it for herself; that had been a little white lie. But she felt strangely empowered just by having it.

Betty ate her lunch slowly, enjoying the view of the hustle and bustle of the market from the warmth and comfort of the cafe. She'd have a wander round the stalls after, maybe get a little something for Lizzie. Some home-made jam or some nice biscuits. And then she'd get back to the minibus in good time so she'd get a good seat, preferably one far, far away from Ruby. But any thought of achieving either was dashed when she saw the queue for the minibus. How long had these people been waiting, for goodness' sake? Didn't they have better things to do? They'd queue for their own funerals, she mused. Loading the minibus took even longer this time as several of the men were clearly wobbly on their feet, having obviously spent a good few hours in one of the several pubs. Once again she had Ruby for company on the way back and, once again, it was torture by wheel arch.

"I got me sandwich," announced Ruby. "'An I 'ad a nice scone. I do like a nice scone." She burped loudly, as if in appreciation of her fine dining experience. Sadly there seemed to be no getting away from her.

"I'm very pleased for you," said Betty, wincing.

She glanced round. Apart from Ruby, everybody was fast asleep before the mimibus had even set off. She closed her eyes, pretending to sleep. The last thing she wanted to do was engage in any sort of conversation with this flatulent, garish parody of a woman. And anyway, she had other things to think about. Laxatives being one.

CHAPTER ELEVEN

Friars Rest
November

Dear Eva,

You would not believe just how outraged I am! Wait till I tell you what happened. But first things first.

I went on a delightful trip to Narrowby – the last time I went there was with Barry. I can't even begin to think how many years ago that was. It was one of our very rare days out together. He always seemed to be working, his business (something to do with computers, I never really did understand it), took up so much of his life. There were always problems for him to sort out at work, staffing issues or contract problems. He seemed to spend all his time at the office, even weekends, would you believe and never seemed to have any time off. So when he suggested a day out together, I was over the moon. I can't remember why we chose Narrowby, we just did. It was lovely. Anyway, that's by-the-by.

The Home had arranged a mini-bus trip and I decided it would be good for me to get out of Friars for a day. I had a lovely lunch, all on my own, and pottered round the market. You'd be surprised what they sell on markets these days. I can remember when all you could buy was vegetables picked that morning at nearby farms, or fresh meat, pork pies and sausages, all locally sourced. Local cheeses and bottles of cordial. But now! I could have bought any amount of racy underwear. Or a time-share in a safari lodge on the Serengeti Plains. Or even a mobile phone, would you believe. I was tempted, Eva, by the phone, I mean. I thought it might be easier to keep in touch with Mark if I could ring him direct. I have to go through the switchboard at Friars if I want to make any outside calls – not that I ever do – who would I ring, apart from my son? - and it costs a small fortune. I asked the man on the stall how much they were but his English was almost incomprehensible. He tried to explain everything the phone could do but I struggled to understand him. This phone got Dating Roma, he kept saying, over and over. I'm not sure what that meant but I doubted that I would ever need it, my courting days being long over. (Also the reason I rejected the racy underwear). Anyway, I decided against buying it. Sorry, I got side-tracked again.

The bus got us back in the afternoon and having had a big lunch not that long after breakfast, I decided to skip dinner and have a quiet evening on my own in my room. I read the paper, played a few games of Patience and decided an early night would do me good. I was just about to get into bed when the door burst open. And who should be standing there? You guessed it! Johnny! I shrieked! Can you believe that! For the first time in my life I actually shrieked!

Johnny! I cried, clutching the neck of my nightie tight in both hands. I had no idea what he was planning to do but I didn't want him getting any ideas. What on earth are you doing here? The man pointed his finger at me. You've done it again, you unfaithful woman!

I'm sure his speech was slurred. What had I done? Stood me up, you did. You weren't there for lunch, Betty Mortimer. Or dinner. Honestly, Eva. I've never heard the like. I didn't have to explain my actions to him but I thought it might calm him down. I've been out if you must know. On a trip to Narrowby in the minibus. Not that it's any business of yours. But you can't come barging in like that! I told him to leave. Johnny's reply? He belched loudly. What is it with flatulence and burping in this place? Did he apologise? Far from it. Oops, he said. The kipper that time forgot! Had one for lunch. It's still with me. And with that he dropped into the armchair. Why are you doing this to me, Betty? Tormenting me so. You would not believe how pathetic he sounded. I assumed he was drunk and told him so. I may have had a glass or two, he conceded. He took his monocle out of his breast pocket and tried to locate his eye, but it was all too difficult and he gave up. Why do you keep abandoning me? he demanded. At that point Eva, I knew I had to be firm and I told him to go before I rang someone. I had no idea who I'd ring but it seemed to work. Or at least I thought it did. He got to his feet with some difficulty and wobbled towards me, arms outstretched, like one of those zombie things you see in late-night horror films. Not that I watch them of course. I don't think he meant to grab me but somehow he tripped over his own feet and lost his balance and lunged towards me. I screamed as loud as I could. I was right in the firing line with nowhere to go so I fell back onto the bed with Johnny on top of me. My eyes were watering at his kippery breath. I tried to scream at him, to tell him to get off me, but it came out as more of a squeak. I was struggling to breathe – a combination of panic and having my lungs squashed. I tried to push him off but he wouldn't or couldn't budge. Just at that moment there was a loud knock on the door and, without waiting for an answer, who should walk in but Mrs King.

I don't think I have ever seen the woman so angry. What's all this noise? she demanded to know. Mrs Mortimer! Betty! What on earth is going on? I would have expected better of you! I gasped for breath. It's not me, I wheezed. It's him! I pointed weakly. He pounced on me. I'm not sure Mrs King believed me but she turned her attention to Johnny. Is that true, Mr Latimer? But she got no response. Johnny Latimer was snoring softly, dead to the world. Mrs King left and returned a few minutes later with Ephraim and Mikey. They helped Johnny to his feet and dragged him unceremoniously from the room.

I lay there, wheezing, clutching my chest dramatically. Are you alright? she asked me. I think she was worried I may have been having a heart attack. I nodded. I think so, I said weakly, but I want a lock on that door. Mrs King shook her head. You know we can't do that. Just in case you need help during the night we'd have to break it down to get to you. I suppose she had a point. I dread to think what would have happened to me if you hadn't turned up when you did, I sobbed. Not much, by the sound of things, the woman pointed out. You were shouting loud enough to wake the dead. And to be honest, I don't think Mr Latimer was capable of very much at all. He's out for the count. I sniffed loudly. You have no idea how upset I was, Eva. She offered to bring me something to calm me down. A nice mug of cocoa perhaps? I declined. Or something stronger? A brandy? I shook my head. Try and get some sleep, she told me. We'll talk about it in the morning and you can decide what you want to do about Mr Latimer. I'm not sure what, exactly, but if you want to make a formal complaint, you can. No, I told her. I want him evicted. That's what I want. I want

53

him sent to another home. I don't know we can go that far, said Mrs King. But there may be some penalty we can invoke. I told her not to bother and you could see how relieved she was. But I had decided on my own punishment for him. Better than anything she could devise. And one that would give her something to think about as well.

I made sure I got down to breakfast the following morning really early. There were a few others there but they ignored me. I sat at the Latimer table and poured a large glass of orange juice. From my handbag I took four sachets of the laxative I'd bought in Narrowby. I hadn't expected to find a use for it so quickly. I stirred the powder into the orange juice and watched it dissolve without trace. Just as I was putting the empty packets back in my bag, Johnny walked in to the Dining Room. He sat down next to me, shame-faced, and apologised immediately. I don't know what came over me last night, he said. Well, actually I do. I allowed my feelings for you to get the better of me. I didn't say anything. I am truly embarrassed, Betty. Can you ever forgive me? Talk about contrition, Eva. The man was positively squirming. Think no more of it, I told him magnanimously. These things happen. Johnny looked at me in amazement. I didn't think you'd be so forgiving. After all, I'd had far too much to drink. I burst into your room. I don't know what was going through my mind. You did scare me quite a bit, you know, I told him. The man could not apologise enough. I am so sorry. It's just the passion I feel for you is…I don't know how to describe it. Profound. Profound? That's one word for it, I thought. He nodded. Profound. There's no reason why somebody of my age, our age, shouldn't have feelings, is there? I thought it best to agree with him. You mean that? he asked but I don't think he quite believed me. I wouldn't have either! I do, I assured him. I'm sorry that I reacted the way I did. I was just a bit shocked, that's all. Then there may be hope for me? The odious man took my hand. With you? I had him hook, line and sinker, Eva. Who knows? I was toying with him now. I gave him what I thought was my Mona Lisa smile and passed him the glass of orange juice. You poured that for me? Johnny was clearly touched. He held the glass to his lips and my heart missed a beat as he drank deeply. I exhaled sharply. You really are a most remarkable woman, Betty Mortimer. Not many women would forgive my behaviour last night. I smiled sweetly at him. Drink your juice and we'll say no more of it. And then, blow me down, if he doesn't shout across the room at Janice. She stopped what she was doing and came over to see what he wanted. That's delicious orange juice, he told her. Is it a new brand? I held my breath. Janice didn't think it was but said she'd check. Why? It just tastes different, that's all. I may have another glass. And, do you know, Eva, he did.

I joined him and his brother for lunch. I was too excited to eat but I wanted to see if the laxative had had any effect yet. The man in the chemist had said it was fast-acting but I didn't know how fast was fast. Johnny and Sinclair bickered throughout the whole meal and this time I was happy to let them. Johnny tried to hold my hand under the tablecloth. Are you alright Betty? he whispered. Your hand is ever so sweaty. What could I tell him, Eva? That I was sitting on tenterhooks waiting for him to clutch his stomach in agony and rush from the room? I just feel a bit warm, I lied smoothly. Johnny winked at me then resumed the conversation he was having with his brother. Not so much of a conversation, *really more a castigation of each of their ex-wives, but it's a typical example, Eva, of the nonsense they both talk. I repeat it here exactly as I heard it to give you a flavour of what the two of them are like when they are in full flow.*

"That wife of yours, though, Jilly, she was something else. What a miserable cow. And ugly too."

Sinclair nodded. "But no more so than your Tessa. My God! How she could nag!"

"Well, that's what wives do, isn't it?"

Sinclair was quick to agree. "That's what they were put on the planet for. Right Betty?"

I claimed not to be paying attention.

"Johnny here, he was saying that the only purpose of a wife is to nag." *He laughed loudly.* "They're nice as pie until they get their feet under the door and then pow! They hit you between the eyes, nag you to death, claim it's you that's driven them to it and then take you for every penny they can."

"Absolutely." *I thought it best to agree.*

Johnny looked at me. "I thought a woman of your spunk would have something to say about that."

You can imagine exactly what I thought about it, Eva, But I'd had enough. I got up to go.

"See you at dinner?" *Johnny was almost begging.*

I nodded and left them to their inane, misogynistic nonsense.

Still no gastric developments by dinner but Johnny did tell me later that Mrs King had asked him to go to her office. Like being summoned to the headmaster's office, he said, without the pleasure of the spanking. She'd given him a good dressing-down about his behaviour last night and told him he was lucky I wasn't going to take it further. He told me he'd been suitably contrite and had apologised to her for his behaviour. He also told her that he'd apologised fulsomely to me and that I had forgiven him, kind woman that I was. I started to feel guilty when he said that. Perhaps I had over-reacted with the laxatives. I only wanted to teach him a lesson but maybe I'd been a bit over-the-top. I wonder what you would have done in the circumstances.

Unusually for me, I was having a nightcap in the Quiet Lounge after dinner, a small Chivas Regal, when Ephraim popped his head round the door. Came to see if you were alright, he said. I thanked him and said I was. You be careful, he warned me. I didn't know what he meant. You just watch yourself with Mr Latimer. Johnny? That's the one. Why? I asked, intrigued. I shouldn't be telling you this, Mrs M, but I don't want to see you hurt. Johnny Latimer's got previous for this sort of thing. Pouncing, you mean? And worse, he said, not smiling. Ephraim leant closer and whispered. I don't know why as we were the only two in the room. One night, a few years ago, according to Ephraim, Johnny crept into Mrs Arbuthnot's room. Game old bird, she was. Up for anything, was how Johnny described her to anyone who would listen. Eva, I was horrified. Would people think the same of me? He spent the night with her and was just about to leave her room early the following morning. When she didn't respond to his 'cheerio', he noticed she wasn't breathing.

55

Silly old bat had only gone and died on me during the night and never said a thing, was how he explained it at dinner that night. She'd choked on her false teeth and Johnny was sitting there, blaming her for her own death. If she'd had her own gnashers, it never would have happened, he'd said. Nothing he could do of course. The old crow was long gone. Liked to think he was responsible for the smile on her face, but he rather thought it was more down to her derailed dentures. I couldn't believe what I was overhearing, Ephraim told me. Johnny had hoped to slide out of the room unnoticed but Mrs King had decided to come in bright and early that day, and there she was, walking down the corridor. She challenged me, she did, the old crow, continued Johnny to his captive audience, just as I'd closed the old trout's door behind me. That's not your room, is it Mr Latimer? He does do a very good imitation of Mrs King, I must admit, does Ephraim. Mrs King had asked Johnny what he was doing in Mrs Arbuthnot's room at this hour of the morning and, of course, he had no answer. She'd knocked on the door, found Mrs Arbuthnot dead in her bed and Johnny just stood there, looking hangdog. Died in her sleep, he told her. The least said about this the better, said Mrs King.

Can you believe it, Eva? But there was worse to come. Ephraim also confided in me that while Johnny was having a dalliance with Mrs A, he was also visiting another lady in her room on occasion. So he was two-timing both of them. Shameless! Now I knew I was right to do what I'd done. But I couldn't understand why Mrs King hadn't told me last night that Johnny Latimer had got a history of this sort of thing. I should have been warned. But it's Ephraim, bless him, who has my welfare at heart, not her. Had I been wrong to give Johnny the laxative? Far from it. Best thing I could have done in view of what Ephraim has just told me, only another dosage, and double what I'd given him this morning, could in any way atone for what he'd done to poor Mrs Arbuthnot, and the other lady, and what he'd been proposing to do to me.

Your loving sister,

Betty

CHAPTER TWELVE

Johnny Latimer was in intensive care for 3 days before he died. Friars Rest was positively hopping with the news. It wasn't that the residents were strangers to death – after all, most of them felt that was the only reason they were there. Tucked away by their relatives, out of sight, out of mind, until the day that the inevitable phone call was made and the ultimate Direct Debit cancelled. Usually the death of a resident was hardly worth a mention, except by Reggie Dawson who covertly ran a sweepstake among a few of his fellow ancients (as well as several helpers, though God help them if Mrs King ever found out) as to who would be next. He hadn't seen Johnny Latimer's demise coming and Reggie was miffed that he would be out of pocket as a result of his unexpected departure. All his money had been on Lizzie Hetherington. She was a dead cert, so to speak. Honestly, you couldn't rely on anybody these days. No, what got the home buzzing was that everyone thought of the Latimers as larger than life. Even those who didn't know them well were convinced they were immortal. They would never die. Except one of them had.

After hours of intense stomach cramps followed by an immoderate dose of what Sinclair had described as 'the squits', an ambulance had been called and Johnny Latimer was taken to the local emergency hospital, Sinclair by his side. Despite numerous attempts to re-hydrate him, tubes going in and out of every orifice in his body according to his brother, Johnny finally succumbed. The hospital was disappointed they'd failed to save him but they simply could not control the diarrhoea. Must have been something he'd eaten or drunk, they surmised. But then he did have underlying bowel problems. And he was in his 80s so maybe it wasn't that surprising. Sinclair, who had stayed with his brother the whole time he was in hospital, sleeping in a visitor's room close to the ICU, returned to Friars exhausted.

There was a strange hush in the Home for several days after the news of Johnny's death broke. Naturally everyone was horrified, some even saddened, but there was the inevitable sigh of relief – it wasn't me! At least not this time. Betty took to her bed for three days and everyone assumed it was grief. There was a consensus on the Latimer table that there had been something special between her and Johnny. She must be so distraught, they muttered to themselves, shaking their heads sadly. Finally, late in life you find someone to love and then look what happens. Nothing could have been further from the truth.

Betty was sick with guilt and worry. She had murdered Johnny Latimer. Death by laxative. And they would trace the laxatives back to her and she would be found guilty and taken off to prison. What would Mark think? His mother. A murderer. She couldn't eat or sleep and the helpers were getting worried. Her meals went untouched and she looked gaunt. Betty lay in bed racked with remorse. She hadn't meant to kill him, she told herself over and over. It was just meant to be a warning shot across the bowels. She grimaced. That was crass indeed. She honestly believed Johnny would recover after a few days' discomfort and that Mrs King wouldn't allow him to come back to Friars because of the incontinence policy. It was only intended to pay him back for his unprovoked attack on her and for his previous lecherous behaviour. She'd only meant to teach him a lesson, never intending for it to end the way it had. That was just unfortunate. Betty tried to look at it positively. On the upside, he wouldn't be misbehaving again. And it would also mean that she would move up the line for the Rose Suite. Betty sat up in bed with a start. Surely that hadn't been her motive? Even subconsciously? She remembered Lizzie saying that people would kill for her room but she'd been talking about Johnny Latimer, surely? She couldn't mean her, Betty? No, Johnny was the sort that could kill, that's what Lizzie had meant. Reassured, she lay back down. What a notion! Okay, her plans had back-fired somewhat and it was very regrettable that he'd died, but there'd been no real malice intended on her part. It was a mistake, that was all. Yes, a bad one and the result, though not good, had produced an outcome which, to be honest, when she thought about it, was not really as dire as she imagined. Finally Betty fell asleep, exhausted but happy.

 She woke the following morning strangely refreshed and, having convinced herself that she had probably done the world a favour in removing from the planet one of the most obnoxious men she had ever met, decided to resume eating with the others. A notice on the Activity Notice Board outside the Dining Room caught her attention. It was a plain piece of white paper with a black border, hand-drawn in felt-tip, announcing the sad passing of Johnny Latimer and providing funeral details for any who wished to attend. It was signed by Mrs King.

 Betty stopped to read the bulletin.

 "Ha! Another one bites the dust."

 She turned to look at the man who had suddenly materialised by her side. She'd seen him before but didn't know his name. He jabbed his finger at the notice. "Poor bugger has passed. But passed what, I hear you ask?"

 "What do you mean?" Betty asked him. "He's dead."

 "But it doesn't actually say that, does it? It says he's passed. Passed what? With flying colours? His cycling proficiency test? Wind?"

 Betty stared at him.

 "They should rename it the In-Activity Notice Board," laughed the man, "I mean, if they're going to tell us about the dead ones, there's not much activity going on then, is there?"

 Betty scowled. "That's in very bad taste," she told him.

 "Well get you!"

Betty tried to walk past him but he was in her way. "Excuse me!" she said pointedly. He stood aside.

"Dried-up old gusset," he muttered as she shouldered past him.

Careful, she thought, I've done it once, I can do it again.

"Oh Betty, I see you've been reading my notice." Mrs King grabbed her elbow and steered her towards Reception.

I'm never going to get any breakfast at this rate, thought Betty.

"I just wanted a quiet word. Sit for a minute if you will." They both sat down in comfy seats next to Reception. Mrs King leaned in to Betty, knees practically touching. "You're probably wondering why the funeral is taking place so quickly."

It hadn't crossed Betty's mind.

"Fortunately the hospital were satisfied that Mr Latimer, Johnny, died of natural causes," she went on. "So no autopsy and there'll be no post mortem or inquest. Which of course is very good news for everybody."

Betty nodded, smiled broadly and, without thinking, clapped her hands. It was brilliant news. For her particularly. It meant she'd got away with it. No arrest. No murder charge. No prison. Mark would be proud. Mrs King was taken aback. What a strange reaction, she thought.

"You seem very pleased?"

"Of course I am. Pleased for Friars," she added quickly. "It wouldn't do it any good to be dragged into an inquest. Not good for your reputation, is it?"

"Quite!"

"And an early funeral means people can move on. I was thinking about poor Sinclair." Nobody was further from Betty's thoughts.

"I did wonder about that unfortunate incident the other night."

"What about it?" Betty was suddenly wary.

"Well, I just wondered if it could have been a factor."

"A factor? What do you mean?"

"In his death. Poor Mr Latimer was taken ill quite soon after."

What was she getting at? Did she know something? Did Mrs King suspect her or was she just fishing? "He had had rather a lot to drink," Betty pointed out.

"Yes. Maybe that had something to do with it." If she knew anything Mrs King wasn't saying.

"Just a coincidence then, wouldn't you say?" Betty looked squarely at her without blinking.

"Almost certainly," said Mrs King.

"It wasn't the first time though, was it?"

"What wasn't?"

"I heard about Mrs Arbuthnot."

Mrs King looked uncomfortable. "Who told you about her?"

59

"I can't divulge my sources," Betty said, somewhat dramatically.

"Ephraim."

"I couldn't possibly say. But Johnny Latimer obviously had a history of seducing women, didn't he?"

"What do you mean?" asked Mrs King.

"Well, she wasn't the only one from what I hear."

"We treat people as adults here," Mrs King reminded her. "Some of the residents may be a bit on the elderly side, but that doesn't mean they don't have...urges."

Urges, thought Betty. Is that what you call them?

"And I understand Mr Latimer's relationship with Mrs Arbuthnot was entirely mutual. And she died from natural causes."

"Choking on her false teeth?"

"Unfortunate, I agree."

"Just as well I've still got my own teeth or I could have been next," said Betty. "I guess I was lucky. But if someone hadn't told me I would never have known." She sat with her hands folded. "Don't you think you should have warned me, after the other night, that Johnny was known for this sort of thing?"

"I don't think you should listen to all this gossip, Betty."

"But if it happened it's not gossip, is it?"

Mrs King dodged the question. "Some things are better left unsaid."

Where had Betty heard that before? "Quite!" she said, staring hard at Mrs King. "Now, why did you want to talk to me?"

Mrs King sat back in her chair. "I just wanted to find out if you wanted to go to the funeral."

Betty shook her head. "I don't think so. I don't like funerals and, to be perfectly honest, I'm not sad he's gone."

"I can understand that." Mrs King stood. "I won't trouble you any more."

No, you won't, thought Betty. But, more importantly, nor will he.

"Go and get your breakfast now. I've kept you long enough." She smiled at Betty sweetly.

By this time the Dining Room was almost full but there was an empty seat next to Sinclair on the Latimer table. Dead man's shoes or something, she thought. Reluctantly she sat down next to the late Johnny's brother.

"I'm very sorry about Johnny," she said.

"No you're not!"

Betty was horrified. And just when she was congratulating herself that she'd gotten away with his removal. 'Death' was too strong a term and 'murder' was entirely out of the question. "I'm sorry. What did you say?"

"I know you're not sorry at all. You didn't like him. I could see you were just putting up with him."

"Well, he wasn't an easy man."

"I know that. He was my brother." Sinclair wiped away an imaginary tear. "The place won't be the same without him."

No, thought Betty. It'll be a whole lot better.

"And anyway, I know what you did." He was waving his finger at her.

Betty dropped the knife she was holding. It clattered onto her plate. She felt her stomach heave.

"What?" It was more of a whisper. "What did I do?"

"You know."

By this time every person round the table had stopped eating and was listening intently to the conversation.

"What did I do?" she repeated.

"You killed him!" he hissed.

Betty could feel the blood rush to her cheeks and she swallowed noisily. She tried to speak but couldn't.

"You know you did. Depraved, that's what you are. Tempting him with your womanly ways. Making him fall in love with you. Loved women, my brother did. Couldn't get enough of them. Not like me. I hate 'em, especially after what my wife did to me. And now I hate you. You killed him, plain and simple."

Betty let out a tentative sigh of relief. No mention of bowels, then.

"That's a dreadful thing to say," she countered. "I did nothing to encourage him. I didn't ask for his attention and I certainly didn't want it."

"No, but you got it. Hussy!"

"Sinclair, please. That is so untrue."

"I know he went up to your room. He told me so. Told me about your planned romantic assignation. His very words."

"Nothing could be further from the truth. I had nothing to do with it. He burst in on me. Unannounced and certainly unwanted."

The rest of the table was agog, hanging on every word. If only something like this happened every day.

"Not the way I heard it. Tormented him to death. Told me you spurned him. Egged him on then rejected him at the last minute. Not good for a chap that. Not good for his ticker nor for any other part of him that doesn't work properly. Sent his bowels into free-fall, you did."

The image was not a pretty one. Betty folded her serviette and placed it by her uneaten breakfast.

"I'm not going to listen to another word of this rubbish. I had nothing to do with his death and your suggestion that something I did caused his stomach upset, well, that is utter tosh!" She looked round at the rest of the diners at the table, their mouths agape as they savoured every thrust and parry. Eyes looked down and eating resumed. She stood up. "You can think what you like, Sinclair, but I know the truth."

61

"Tart!" he called after her as she left the Dining Room. The whole room watched her leave. She would not dignify him with a reply. Her face was grim but only because she was trying hard to suppress a smile. Inside, her heart was turning somersaults. Sinclair had no idea how his brother had died. Mrs King, whilst she may have had her suspicions that something was not quite right, had no idea either. But Betty did. She had well and truly got away with it.

CHAPTER THIRTEEN

Friars Rest
December

Darling Eva,

Well, that's it. I bet you can't guess. I am now a murderer. Or should that be murderess? I meant to check and clean forgot. Whichever, I am confessing, but only to you, Eva, that I am responsible for taking the life of another human being. Although I never thought of him as human. Johnny Latimer was the most unpleasant, ignorant, lecherous, disgusting, most disagreeable man I have ever come across. And me, your one and only sister, Betty, I killed him. What do you say to that, then? Everybody is convinced it was something he ate but I know different. It's taken me quite a few days to come to terms with the fact that I murdered someone. Killed them. Bumped them off. Not words I would usually use but I have to accept it's exactly what I did. I do have a mild preference for the term 'bump off'. It sounds a bit gentler, somehow. Friendlier. Don't get the wrong impression. I'm not proud of what I've done. Well, maybe just a tiny bit. But he really did deserve to die, you know. At first, when it happened, when I realised that I was the cause of his death, I was horrified with myself. How could I do such a thing? I didn't enjoy it, in case you're thinking that. Not one little bit. Honestly! And the brilliant thing is that nobody else really knows, except you. Mark hasn't the faintest. Mrs King is unsettled by the whole affair but she's too polite or too canny to voice any suspicions she may have. Sinclair, Johnny's brother, has accused me of all sorts but I think my biggest crime as far as he's concerned is being a woman. But I was surprised at just how easy it was to accomplish. I only meant to scare him a little but I got carried away. Don't get me wrong, I'm not entirely callous. I do have feelings, Eva, but on this occasion I must have temporarily misplaced them.

Anyway, life goes on. For some at least. Sinclair is now next on the list to move into Rose Suite (sorry, I must remember to call it by its proper name - THE Rose Suite), when Lizzie finally dies. I found out the other day, Ephraim I think it was who told me, that both Sinclair and Johnny Latimer had been on the waiting list. Apparently they'd tossed a coin to see who would be first and Johnny won. Except that he's now no longer in a position to claim his prize, (now that he's dead). So Sinclair gets bumped up the list after Johnny gets bumped off, (by yours truly!) and I need to check with Mrs King who is after him. Me, I hope. I get the impression that not many people here are interested in moving to the Rose Suite, which is good news for me.

I did think about bumping off Lizzie myself. But only for a moment. I have really come to like the old girl and I enjoy my time spent with her. I know I could do it, kill her that is, and it would be so easy, but I don't want to. She's desperately frail but she has this inner strength I admire so much and I feel protective towards her. I want to keep her safe from all those baying hounds who were, and still are, desperate to move into her suite, so I could never dream of hurting her. Mercy gave me the idea how to do it, though. Do you remember Mercy? I think I've mentioned her before. She's from Zimbabwe apparently, and believes that Jesus is hovering in every doorway waiting to scoop us all up to take us to somewhere better. She firmly believes he, or should I say HE, scooped her up and dropped her unexpectedly in North Yorkshire. Anyway, I do seem to digress a lot these days. Rambling, I suppose you'd call it. Well, Mercy sometimes helps out with whoever is in charge of the drugs trolley last thing at night. She's not supposed to, what with her being laundry, but if they're a bit short-handed she mucks in and gives the prescribed medication to whichever ancient requires it. I got chatting to her one night. She told me that they have to be careful as Lizzie has an allergy to Paracetamol and even a couple of tablets could see her off. I don't think she should have told me that, but there you go. She said that Lizzie would just drift off to sleep and slip away quietly without knowing a thing about it. What a delicious way to go, I thought. Unlike Johnny who died in the most appalling distress, so his brother told me, screaming and bent double in buttock-clenching agony and swearing like nobody's business. There's no call for that sort of language. I never swear, as you well know. Well, maybe the odd word if I am really riled. But for him to use some of the words that Sinclair told me? There was no need for that at all, even if he was on his deathbed. Seems people just have no sense of occasion, do they?

Are you horrified by this, Eva? Does the thought that your sister has killed unsettle you? Well, it shouldn't. Nothing has changed. I'm still your sister and I still miss you terribly. But doing what I did, well, it seems to have given me an inner strength too, a bit like Lizzie. I feel empowered. Not quite omnipotent but not far off. Difficult to explain.

Christmas is just round the corner. Another letter from Mark saying he will definitely not be back before the New Year. The tour is still going better than planned yada, yada, yada. Contract under negotiation for a North American tour. Too busy to come and visit his poor old mother. I still miss him dreadfully but I must admit, I have had my distractions. I'm now trying to work out what to do about Sinclair. He's starting to really bug me now. It got to the stage where I couldn't stand his accusations any more so I quit the Latimer table and moved back to the other side of the Dining Room, as far away from him as I could get, to sit with Melanie and the multi-hued Ruby. It's been a while since I sat with them and, to be fair, it's better company, Ruby and Reggie notwithstanding. I'm getting to like Melanie though. She used to work as a journalist on a local paper and has some good stories to tell. Ruby is the same as ever – badly dressed and talking nonsense. She's developed this dew-drop which sits permanently at the end of her nose. Wipe your bloody nose! I want to scream at her, but don't, of course. Because I don't swear, remember? But it just sits there until gravity does its thing and it plops silently into her food. It's so gross and makes me feel quite sick. If only there was something I could do to stop it. One of the men on the table really annoys me too. Actually, they pretty much all annoy me, if I'm perfectly honest. Bit of a theme here, Eva, but most of the people I live with in the Home are instantly dislikeable. But this one, Ashley Robinson, he takes the biscuit. He's got this awful habit of mining the contents of his ears and nose whilst he's eating. Can you imagine! And I know it's not normal to have that much hair in your ears. And don't get me started on his nostrils! There should be a law against tufts like that. He's got this little goatee too. His goat, I call it. Now what's that about? Am I getting a little bit intolerant, do you think? Maybe it's time to try another table. But, wherever I am, I can still feel Sinclair's eyes boring into me all the time. I try to ignore him but don't always succeed. This needs to be sorted.

One thing that is getting me down is the number of visitors that have suddenly appeared. It's as if all the families and friends of the inmates have suddenly remembered that it's Christmas and that they have what they laughingly call a 'loved one' hidden from view, someone who must be visited, taken out for afternoon tea if they're lucky, or a cup of tea from the Beverage Station if they're not, patted on the head and not seen for another twelve months. Unless Mercy's Jesus has anything to do with it. But at least they're getting visitors, which is more than I am. I have nobody to come and visit me, no friends, no family, and do you know how lonely that can feel? Strange that it never seemed to be a problem when I lived on my own. Mark was pretty much my only visitor but that didn't seem to matter. Now I'm surrounded by people, I have never felt so alone in all my life.

The entire place is festooned with Christmas decorations and festive bonhomie – it's almost more than I can bear. I've never really liked Christmas if I'm perfectly honest. It's too brash. I'm playing more Patience now than I have for a while – I think about a lot of things when I play. Probably not good for me. There's a tinsel-covered plastic Christmas tree in every public area, would you believe? Some of the residents even have a small tree in their suites! And there's paper chains all over the place. There's even little, what d'you call them? Those table decoration things. There's one on each table in the Dining Room. They were made by some of the inhabitants during one of the Activity sessions. I saw the notice but decided it wasn't for me. Neither was the Decorate Your Own Christmas Pudding (using nothing but paper doilies and spun sugar – that could be quite incendiary in the wrong hands, I thought). They're pretty crude, these table decorations – a few fir cones, a candle and some glitter – and I know I could have done better but why would I want to?

A notice appeared on the board the other day for a Christmas Riverboat Cruise – An Ouse Booze Cruise they called it, describing it as an evening of dinner, dance and merriment on the river. It's not particularity cheap but I must admit I quite fancy it. Not the dance bit, of course. My dancing days seem as remote as the North Pole and, of course, my knees are very definitely not up to it. And who would I dance with? But I like the idea of a bit of merriment. Whilst I was deciding whether to sign up or not, Ashley, he of the ear, nose and goat, came and stood alongside me. *Why would you pay to go and have a meal out?* he said, jabbing his finger at the notice. *I've already paid to eat here. It's like paying twice for the same thing. It's not quite the point,* I told him. *It's a Christmas thing.* At that point we were joined by Reggie. Have I told you about him? He sits on our table too and burps Ruby, just like you would a baby. There's something about him I really don't like, apart from the way he looks. He's painfully thin and has this sheen to him because he sweats a lot. Very unpleasant. Somebody, I can't remember who, it may have been Ephraim, told me he runs a sweepstake on who's going to die next. Can you imagine that? Have I mentioned this before? I do get a bit confused now and then. Anyway, I couldn't believe it when I heard it but somebody else said it was true, so it must be. Apparently, when Lizzie goes, he stands to make a lot of money. Awful, awful man. Something should be done about it. *Are you going to go?* I asked him. *On the cruise?* He shook his head. *Nah,* he said. *Don't like the water. Can't swim. Then he went on to tell me at some length (yawn, yawn), about an unpleasant childhood experience when he nearly drowned. Shame it was only nearly, I was tempted to say. Ashley had long since wandered off, obviously feeling the need to do some serious excavating on his own. So I added my name to the list and next Thursday I shall book an appointment with the visiting hairdresser, Amy, and get some highlights done. I'll treat myself to a manicure from Anong (she's from Thailand and usually works in the kitchen but has a nice little side-line in mani-padis as she calls them — manicures and pedicures to you and me). She told me her name means bountiful forest — I felt like introducing her to Ashley. Then I'll dig out my best party frock, put some make-up on — that doesn't happen too often — and go out and have some merriment. I shall report how I get along in due course.*

With love, always
Betty

CHAPTER FOURTEEN

Betty looked at herself in the bathroom mirror and, for the first time in years, she wasn't displeased with what she saw. A real picture, even if she did say so herself. She smiled. She still thought she looked her age but she was pleased with what Amy had done with the blond highlights, which somehow softened her features. Betty's face had filled out somewhat and she no longer looked as gaunt as she had when she'd first arrived at Friars. A bit of carefully applied blusher had given her some much-needed colour in her cheeks. She applied some pale blue eyeshadow – the same shade as her dress – and several coats of mascara. Finally lipstick and she was ready. Not bad at all. She turned her head from side to side. But who was she all dressed up for? Only me, she decided, but that's good enough.

Friars had laid on a big coach on this occasion, such was the interest in the cruise, and there was an air of excitement on board, loud chatter and plenty of laughter. Clearly everyone was in a festive mood. Betty's eyes watered as she climbed aboard, cheap perfume and bad after-shave making it hard to breathe. It was a short drive into the town centre and then down to the quayside where the boat was waiting for them. As they got off the bus everyone stopped to admire the riverboat, their breaths condensing in the cold night air. It was bright red, a double-decker affair, with 'Ouse Cruise' painted in gold on the side and decorated with multi-coloured fairy lights. The top deck was open to the elements whilst the bottom deck's enormous picture windows revealed the restaurant inside. One by one the party-goers made their way gingerly on board, down a rickety gangplank bedecked with yet more fairy lights, eager to get into the warmth.

"Welcome aboard," said a pair of smiling, uniformed crew members, one male, one female, standing on either side of the main entrance. They were identically dressed in crisp white shirts with a black tie and gold epaulettes, and black trousers. Each wore a red cap, embossed with the ship's logo, an interlocked O and C in gold. "Welcome to your Ouse Booze Cruise." Mostly they were ignored by the revellers who were keen to get in out of the biting wind, but Betty took time to smile at them both and to thank them. Courtesy costs nothing, she reminded herself. She joined a line of her fellow residents who were struggling out of their coats. "Don't lose that," smiled the young girl, exchanging Betty's coat for a ticket, "or there'll be a bun fight at the end of the evening!" What fun! thought Betty wickedly. Could be the highlight of the whole trip. The group was then herded, slowly, into a small lounge where uniformed waiters passed amongst them offering sparkling wine, orange juice and canapés. She took a glass of wine and something she thought looked like diced spam on toast but turned out to be smoked salmon mousse with chopped egg. Delicious. She helped herself to another one before the waiter disappeared. Looking round the room, Betty realised she still didn't know most of the people there. She recognised Melanie. And Ruby, of course. But she was surprised to see Reggie here, especially after he'd told her he wasn't coming. Afraid of water or something. She wondered idly what had made him change his mind. An announcement came over the tannoy inviting the remaining guests to head to the restaurant. It was like a mini-stampede as people suddenly realised that if they were the remaining guests then their fellow diners had already beaten them to it for the best seats. Shaking her head, Betty stood back so as not to be trampled underfoot. God, considering some of these people were well into their 80s and 90s, they sure could move when they wanted to! A waiter stood nearby, obviously thinking the same thing. He grinned at Betty and offered her the last glass of fizz on his tray. Why not? she thought. It is Christmas.

Betty stood in the doorway of the restaurant. The tables, arranged around a wooden dance floor, all appeared to be full. Where was she to sit? Then she noticed Melanie standing up and beckoning to her. Bless her. She'd saved her a place. Glass in hand, Betty made her way across the dance floor and gratefully sat down in the last remaining seat.

"Ladies and gentlemen!" A tall man dressed in a badly fitting two-piece brown suit and matching toupee stood in the middle of the dance floor, microphone in hand. He tapped it repeatedly until he got everyone's attention. "Ladies and Gentlemen, welcome to the Ouse Booze Cruise. My name is Grant. And I'm here to grant you your every wish. Ha! Ha!" There was no response from his audience. Betty looked round. He'd lost half of them already. "Now, we all know why you're here. You're here to have a good time. But first, Safety First." Betty looked at the others on her table whilst Grant outlined the safety instructions should the boat suddenly decide to sink. Melanie looked very stylish in a fitted, long-sleeved dress, black and white checks. Betty smiled at her and mouthed her thanks. The ubiquitous Ruby was dressed in the most violent shade of green Betty had ever seen. She was in some sort of ball-gown which was covered in flounces and bows. It was off the shoulder and revealed acres of grey, wrinkled, reptilian skin, making her look like a terrapin coming up for air. But what really surprised her was just how muscular Ruby's arms were. Quite surprising for a woman of her age. Along with everything else Ruby's make up was, as usual, discordant, florid, badly-applied and simply wrong. Betty could hardly take her eyes off her. She was surprised to see Ashley was there, in a Tweed jacket with his usual over-abundance of body hair trying to escape from his nose and ears. He'd told her he wasn't going to go but had obviously changed his mind. But there was no sign of Reggie. Must be at another table, she thought. Betty didn't recognise any of the others at the table: a small, untidy man who never said a word all night; a bearded man dressed formally in a dinner jacket, dress shirt and pink cummerbund; a quiet mousy woman who happily played with her food, arranging and re-arranging it on her plate whilst singing quietly to herself (Betty wanted to reach over and smack her hard); and a nondescript man who introduced himself as Larry.

"So now you know where to find the lifebelts and how to use them," continued Grant, in no doubt that not a single one of them had been paying him the slightest bit of attention, "I don't want any of you practising mouth-to-mouth until we start the party games!" Not a murmur. Grant went on as if he was used to it. "Now the captain has told me we're just about to cast off, up anchor and do whatever else is needed to set sail on the high seas. Or the River Ouse, as we call it. So batten down your hatches and splice the mainbrace, all ashore who's going ashore." Still nothing. "Everything's included so eat and drink as much as you want. And for those of you able to stand at the end of the meal, we'll have some fun. What d'you think about a bit of dancing?" Clearly not much. "Or some party games?" Even less. Ye gods, this was a tough lot. "Right then, Bonny Appetite, as they say somewhere foreign. Or Fill Yer Boots, as we say here in Yorkshire!" He switched off the microphone and headed to the bar where he downed in one gulp what he considered was a well-deserved, very large whisky. He knew when he was beaten.

Waiters and waitresses started scurrying about, plates balanced all the way up their arms, serving the food quickly and efficiently. Betty was impressed. Her champagne flute had been whisked away and now she was enjoying a very smooth red wine which tasted slightly of blackcurrants. As soon as her glass was empty it was replenished immediately with great flourish by a smiling waitress whose sole job it was to dispense large quantities of alcohol as quickly as she could. And she was quick. It was all Betty could do to keep up. The meal was delicious – and even Ashley, sitting opposite her and still mining for buried treasure while he ate, did not manage to put her off her food. The melon and prawn cocktail was tangy and the roast beef was cooked just the way she liked it. There was plenty of gravy and they brought round seconds of vegetables for those who wanted them. Betty approved of that. She opted for a dessert called a Christmas pudding ice cream, wanting something light to finish with. Even so, when she finally stopped eating, Betty was stuffed and more than a bit light-headed with all the wine she'd drunk. But she still decided that a cup of coffee and several chocolate truffles would round the meal off nicely. She leant back in her chair.

"Phew!" she said.

"Phew indeed!" agreed Melanie. "That was quite some meal."

"I don't think I'll eat again," quipped Betty. "Think I need a turn round the deck before the fun starts. Clear my head a bit." She stood up, wobbled and sat down again quickly. "Another coffee needed I think!"

"Do you want me to get you another one?" asked Melanie, as Grant meandered out onto the dance floor again, clutching his microphone.

"Maybe later thanks. I don't think I'm ready to face all this jollity just yet," Betty said, "I won't be long." She stood up, slower this time and very carefully headed for the exit. After a brief visit to the Ladies to splash some water on her wrists (it never worked in her younger days and it didn't work now), and to re-apply her lipstick, she slowly climbed the stairs to the upper deck, holding tight to the rail. Betty opened the door, stepped out into the fresh air and breathed deeply. The wind had dropped but it was still bitterly cold. She shivered, wondering whether this was a good idea after all but it was so refreshing after the stuffy restaurant below. It had recently rained and the deck was slippery underfoot. She tentatively made her way to the back of the boat. In the far distance she could make out a line of lights. She leaned against the railing, peering out beyond the boat's wake. Must be the town, she thought. Or a town. She actually had no idea where they were or how far they'd come but she was aware of just how dark it was. Countryside, but whether it was forest or farmland she couldn't tell. Betty thought she was on her own but suddenly Ruby materialised next to her. Now where had she come from?

"You made me jump, Ruby. You shouldn't come creeping up on people like that. Nearly gave me a heart attack, you did."

"Is it the same?" asked Ruby.

"Is what the same?"

"The sea. Is it the same on both sides of the boat."

"We're on a river, Ruby. Not the sea," explained Betty.

"Alright then. Is the water the same on both sides of the boat?"

"Why would it not be?"

"That's why I'm asking."

"No Ruby. On the left side it's yellow and full of fish. On the right side, it's pink and full of cabbages!"

Ruby nodded wisely. "Just as I thought." And with that she left Betty and returned to the restaurant.

"God, but you're a nasty piece of work." A man's voice, coming from the shadows. Betty's heart missed a beat. She turned and grimaced as Reggie appeared from behind a stack of plastic chairs, cigarette in hand. Was there anybody who wasn't up here?

"I thought you weren't going to come."

"Changed my mind, didn't I? Glad I did, too. Got to see you as you really are."

"What do you mean?"

"Come up here for a quiet smoke and what do I get? You being a right bitch to that poor woman!"

"What?" Betty was outraged.

"What has she ever done to you?" demanded Reggie. "Lovely lady she is." Really? Betty cast her mind back to when she first met them both, when

Reggie was kindly burping Ruby. She hadn't thought anything about it at the time but it was obviously a very intimate thing to do. There must be something going on between the two of them.

"I...nothing. I was just teasing her, that's all." She wished she hadn't had quite so much to drink.

"Teasing? Mocking, more like. I suppose that's your idea of fun."

Betty didn't know what to do. She decided to ignore him and go back downstairs but he moved closer to her until she could smell his rancid breath. She tried to get away from him, leaning back, hard against the metal railing.

"I've been watching you." He exhaled cigarette smoke in her face. Betty coughed. "And I don't like what I see."

"Like I care. And anyway, I've heard all about you," she said in retaliation.

"What? What have you heard about me?" He leaned towards her. "Gossip, no doubt." Betty tried to turn her head but he was right in her face. "Go on, tell me. What have you heard about me?" Reggie gripped her chin with one hand.

"I've heard about your sweepstake." Betty's voice sounded garbled, a combination of terror and not being able to open her mouth properly making it difficult to speak. For such a skinny man, he was incredibly strong.

"What? What did you say?" He loosened his grip on her chin.

"I said I've heard about your sweepstake. Betting on who's going to die next. It's obscene!"

He laughed. "You stupid old cow. That's only a piece of fun."

"Fun!"

"Yes, fun. Where's your sense of humour, you ugly, fat trollop?" He leaned closer still. The railing was now cutting in to her back. She was struggling to breathe. But Betty was incensed. You bastard! I am not fat! Or ugly! You have just signed your own death warrant.

His body was hard up against hers now, pushing, pushing. What was he trying to do? Push her overboard? Squash all the air out of her? Betty's feet started to slide under her. It flashed through her mind that she should have worn more sensible shoes. Is that really going to be my last thought? I'm going to die and I wish I'd worn more appropriate footwear? With a strength she didn't know she possessed, she pushed against him with both hands, trying to find space to breathe. At the same time she brought her right knee up sharply, as hard as she could, contacting with something soft. Reggie screamed in agony and let her go. Betty elbowed him hard in the chest then dropped to her knees, scrambling away from him as quickly as she could, on all fours, breathing hard. Catching her breath she staggered to her feet and stumbled towards the door to the lower deck. Without a backward glance, she pulled it open wide and flung herself inside. Taking several deep breaths Betty tottered down the stairs, her legs weak, and dashed back into the Ladies. That was where Melanie found her twenty minutes later, unconscious on the floor.

CHAPTER FIFTEEN

Friars Rest
December

Can you believe it, Eva? We've had another death at the home. Well, not actually at the home but on a boat. Or off a boat, to be exact. Sorry, this is gibberish but there's just so much to tell you and I don't know where to start.

It was the night of the river cruise. Apparently this is an annual Christmas event organised by the Home and I felt in need of a bit of fun so I signed up for it. But never in my wildest imagination could I have ever dreamt it would turn into an absolute nightmare. You may think I'm being a bit melodramatic here, but wait until you hear what I have to tell you.
It all started off innocuously enough. A lovely dinner with probably a lot more wine than I'm used to. It was when they were about to start what the MC described as the 'fun' part that I decided I needed to clear my head with a bit of fresh air. I decided the upper deck was the best place – away from all the noise and partying. But no sooner had I got there than I was attacked! Yes, attacked! By that awful man Reggie. I swear he was trying to kill me but I really have no idea why. I've hardly spoken more than half a dozen words to him since I arrived at Friars but it seems he doesn't – or didn't – like the way I talked to Ruby. I think they may have been an item, I believe that's the phrase these days. But that's no reason to squash all the air out of me and try and throw me overboard. The man was mad, I tell you, bent on doing me harm. Anyway I managed to get away from him and the next thing I know I'm back at the Home, tucked up in bed, a worried Mrs King sitting beside me rubbing my hands (no doubt more concerned about another death at the Home). Apparently Melanie found me on the floor of the Ladies – I shudder when I think of it. When was it last truly disinfected, I wonder? Melanie told me later she thought I'd passed out from too much drink, so she decided it was best to alert the crew. They decided against calling an ambulance, thank goodness – imagine how embarrassing that would have been. They thought it was the drink too, would you believe, but as I was showing signs of coming round they called for a taxi to take me home. Melanie, bless her, offered to come back with me but I insisted I was fine (I have no memory of that conversation at all). Mrs King and Mercy put me to bed (I don't remember that either). What I only found out the next day, when I was sitting up in bed eating a few spoonfuls of delicious cream of tomato soup with the most marvellous garlic croutons, was that I wasn't the only person who didn't come back on the bus last night. Apparently there were two empty seats on the bus but in the chaos and confusion of the boat crew getting me home in a taxi and, later, loading everybody else on to the coach (some of them very much the worse for wear, so Ephraim told me when he popped in to see how I was doing), nobody did a proper head count and the coach returned to Friars with two spare places which nobody noticed. One was mine of course, but guess who else didn't make it home, Eva? Yes, it was Reggie. My attacker. It was only when he didn't appear for breakfast the following morning (not many of them did, I understand –

some monumental hangovers kept lots of the revellers in their beds), and when he failed to appear for lunch as well (never a man to miss his food, so Melanie told me), they decided to check his room and do you know what? His bed hadn't been slept in. Of course, that was when the panic set in as it became clear that he hadn't come back last night with everybody else. Ephraim, bless him, kept me up to date with developments over the next few days.

Reggie's body was found two days later by a man out walking his dog. I don't know if it's the same with you in Canada but we owe such a debt of gratitude to dog-walkers in this country. If it wasn't for them, so many missing bodies would go undiscovered, a lot of murders wouldn't be solved and very few murderers would be brought to justice. I don't even like to think about it. Reggie's body had washed ashore ten miles, yes, ten miles, down river, close to a tiny little hamlet called Laxmire-under-Water, the sort of place where nothing ever happens. Well, it's on the map now. Lead item on the local news – reporters swarming all over the place. It was such a pretty place once, delightful little cottages overlooking the river, and occasionally, when the river bursts its banks, under it. But now it was completely spoiled by a fleet of ambulances and Police cars. There was some sort of rubber river rescue boat as well, one that had been searching the Ouse when it was discovered that Reggie was missing. Fortunately for Mrs King there was no mention of Friars Rest in the news. She's been in a constant tizz, poor woman – two deaths in the Home, or directly connected with it, in as many months.

There has been no other topic of conversation at mealtimes, Eva, with everyone speculating as to whether the man had simply had too much to drink and fallen overboard or whether there had been, dare they say it? Foul Play. It certainly has livened things up around here and provides even the quietest with something to talk about.

The Police came here and everyone who was on the cruise was interviewed, me included. It really was quite good fun. Ever such a nice young pair of constables. So smart and respectful. Incredibly polite too, which is something I've always liked. But I was in a quandary. I know that I was the last person to see Reggie alive. And if the Police suspected that that was the case, then maybe they would think I had something to do with his death. Oh, I didn't tell you, the cause of death was not drowning apparently, which surprised us all. Although to my mind, there would have been a certain felicity (is that the right word?) if he had drowned, seeing as he was so afraid of water. No, he hit his head when he went overboard, smacking it against the railing on the deck below as he fell. That was where the kitchens are – or galleries, I think they call them when they're on a boat – but none of the crew saw or heard anything. Too busy I expect, clearing up after that wonderful meal they put on for us to look out of the window for falling bodies. And it was wonderful food. For mass catering, I really was most impressed. But did he fall or was he pushed? is what everyone is asking. Nobody has suggested that he might have slipped. After all, it had rained and the deck was wet. I know I struggled with my shoes. I haven't mentioned it in case they ask me how I know. And that's my dilemma, Eva. I know how he died but I can't share it with anybody. Except you.

To cut a long story short, the Police left us to our speculations and doubts – I thought it safest to keep my thoughts to myself and made no mention to anyone, least of all the Police, that I had been on the upper deck taking the air, or that the awful man had tried to kill

73

me. I doubted whether Ruby would remember anything – she's always on a different planet – and a few days later the same two constables returned and told Mrs King that they were pretty much satisfied that Reggie had fallen to his death, having consumed an excess of alcohol. (All of us who'd been interviewed confirmed he had been drinking very heavily all night). Ephraim told me that one of the policemen had mentioned to him they found some strange bruising to Reggie's testicles (not a word I use every day) at the autopsy, or was it the post mortem? I can't remember. But they thought it must have happened somehow as he went over the side. Anyway, they aren't going to pursue it and, best of all, they're not expecting any nasty surprises at the inquest. All things being equal they consider the matter closed and they don't expect to be bothering us again. Not everyone is happy though, as Mrs King has said there'll be no more river cruises, which is a great shame. I certainly would have enjoyed it much more if the man hadn't tried to kill me and would love to go on another one. But she has decreed that they are too dangerous. There were mutterings the other morning from Ashley at breakfast about some people not being able to hold their drink and spoiling it for everyone else. That's rich, I thought, considering he'd told me clearly he wasn't going to go, not wanting to pay for a meal twice. I think he was having a dig at me, coming home in a taxi, but maybe he meant Reggie. But I don't see how he can blame me! Either way, I ignored him. I'm delighted with the outcome. I don't suppose Reggie is over the moon about it but then he got what he deserved. I wonder what odds he would have given himself on being next in line in his sweepstake. Very long ones, I should think. But at least it has put an end to that horrid little practice of his.

I've been thinking back on that night, Eva, despite trying very hard not to do so. I've never seen the point in going over old ground as it achieves absolutely nothing. The man's dead and that's that. But recently I haven't been able to stop myself, just every now and again, trying to remember exactly what happened. Guilty conscience? I hear you asking. No. Definitely not. I've tried to push it to the back of my mind, pretend it never happened. That's the easiest way to deal with things like that. It feels like it was ages ago but, for some reason, some of it still seems so fresh in my mind. It would give me nightmares if I let it but I'm made of stronger stuff. I'm the only one who really knows how he died – I know because I killed him – and that makes me feel...tingly. It was an accident, of course, just like Johnny. I could never set out to kill someone deliberately, you know that. But it was his fault however you look at it. He chose to come on the cruise even though he was afraid of water, so he had to accept the consequences. Live by the sword, die by the sword, Dad used to say. Do you remember? Not too sure that's got anything to do with how Reggie died, but you get my drift. He attacked me, unprovoked, but it was when he called me fat and ugly. Well, that did it for me. That was so uncalled for. I think if he hadn't said that I may have been happy with just kneeing him in his most sensitive bits, but I was so angry I put everything I could into elbowing him in the ribs. Took all the wind out of his sails, I can tell you. I'm still a bit hazy as to exactly what happened next. I remember dropping to my knees then crawling to get away from him. But I have this image of me going back towards him, picking up one of his feet as he was bent double, still clutching his wobbly bits and swearing at me – honestly, Eva! Such language! Yes, I vaguely remember picking up a foot *and heaving with all my might. Not that it took much. The man was all skin and bones. Not an ounce of fat on him. I'd love to know how he kept the weight off so successfully. A scream, a dull klunky sort of sound and then a splash as he hit the water. Or maybe I'm imagining that bit. But somehow I don't think I am. Deep down, I know I did it but I don't think I had any choice. It was him or me. If I hadn't dealt with this problem there and then I'd have to spend the rest of my life looking over my shoulder, waiting for him to find another opportunity to murder me. So I believe it was nothing less than self-defence. So no harm done, eh? Anyway, it's all water under the bridge now. Floating bodies too.*

Yours, only a little guiltily,

Betty

CHAPTER SIXTEEN

Betty had been dreading Christmas Day. It would mean she'd been at Friars now for over a quarter of a year but there were days when it seemed like a lifetime. One day just merged into another and, apart from the excitement over the deaths of Johnny and Reggie, nothing much had happened. Still no more news from Mark. It wasn't as if she expected a present or anything from him but a Christmas card or, even better, a phone call, would have been nice. She turned her face to the wall. There was a knock at the door and in breezed Priti.

"Happy Christmas Mrs Mortimer! Rise and shine!"

"Go away!"

Priti ignored her and put a glass of Buck's Fizz down on the bedside table. "Come on! It's Christmas. Everybody loves Christmas."

"I don't."

"But you have to."

Betty rolled over to face her. "Why?"

"Because everybody does."

"Priti, can I let you into a secret?"

The girl nodded.

"I hate it even more than I hate anything else in the world."

Priti ignored her. These old people could be so silly at times. She opened Betty's wardrobe. "Now what are you going to wear today? Got to look your best. What about this one?" She pulled out the blue dress Betty had worn on the river cruise.

"Not that one!" Betty sat up in bed.

"Why not? It's lovely. It's so you."

So me? Betty was horrified as she remembered what she'd been doing the last time she wore it. How could she ever wear it again?

"Alright. What about this one?" Priti pulled out a knee-length pale grey woollen dress with a cowl neck. "This is beautiful. Is it cashmere?"

Betty sighed and got out of bed. "Okay, you win." There was no way Priti was going to leave until she was up and showing every sign of getting dressed.

Priti smiled at her and hung the dress on the back of the door. "Have a lovely day, Mrs Mortimer. Happy Christmas." Priti stretched up and gave her a peck on the cheek. Betty was dumbfounded. When did someone last do that? It was Mark, when he left her. But he was her son. Nobody else outside the family had ever done it. It only made her feel even more depressed and alone.

The Dining Room was still only half full but there was an excited buzz in the air. Betty steeled herself as she made her way to Melanie's table, nodding greetings to one or two friendly faces as she passed by.

"Happy Christmas Betty," said Melanie.

"You too."

"It's Christmas!" yelled Ruby, dressed, as far as Betty could make out, like an elf, in a red and green trouser suit with Christmas Tree earrings and a black, pointed witch's hat with a bell on the end. She had green tinsel draped round her neck. "It's so exciting."

It is if you're a four year old, thought Betty. Or maybe Ruby, and all the others, were simply regressing, returning to a misremembered childhood, far distant and candy-coated.

Ruby was tucking into a hearty breakfast, her plate piled high with bacon and sausages. Was that three fried eggs Betty counted? Clearly the untimely death of her burper, Reggie, had not affected her appetite at all.

"Look! Look! It's Mrs Claus!" squealed Ruby, squirming in her seat. If she gets any more excited, thought Betty, she'd going to wet herself. Ruby pointed excitedly to the doorway, where Mrs King stood, dressed in what appeared to be a very well-padded red and white onesie. Is that meant to be a Mrs Santa costume? Betty wondered. It looked like a giant, over-inflated Babygro. Except it's not padded, decided Betty. That's all her. Mrs King continued to smile at everyone, opening her arms wide as if to embrace the entire room.

"Happy Christmas everybody!" she beamed. God help us, thought Betty.

"Happy Christmas Mrs Santa!" shouted Ruby and half a dozen others. God help us, thought Betty. This goes from bad to worse.

Wobbling into the room on her usual vertiginous stilettos, Mrs King laid a hand on a shoulder here, a pat on a head there, as if granting a beneficence to a chosen few. She finally made it to the centre of the Dining Room where she came to a stop. In her hand she held a clipboard.

"Now, before I let you know about our plans for the day, I just wanted to tell you that we've got nearly a full house for Christmas as only three of our residents have chosen to go home for the holiday. Everybody else has decided to stay because you all know how much fun we have here. Don't we?" (That's one way of interpreting it, thought Betty. More like the rest of us have nowhere else to go). Ignoring the blank faces staring at her, Mrs King continued. "Just a few details about today, ladies and gentlemen. After breakfast, we'll all adjourn to the Television Lounge next door where guess who? Yes, Santa is waiting for us. Imagine that!" (I can't, said Betty to herself. I really can't). "The television will be off, I'm afraid," (That's a first), "but I know that Mr Claus has got a sackful of lovely presents for us all." (Let mine be an AK47 please). "Then you can do whatever you like but lunch is at one o'clock, here in the Dining Room, where yours truly," here she actually bowed, "will be helping our helpers serve you a traditional Christmas lunch with all the trimmings." Betty waited, along with Mrs King, for the oohs and aahs. There were none. "I know Geraldo, our wonderful chef, is going to excel himself this time. There's plenty of time to eat up before we go and watch the Queen's speech." (Tell me it's not compulsory). "Then we have Christmas Bingo," (Nooo!) "with some pretty spectacular prizes, I can tell you. That's also in the Television Lounge." (I think I'd rather stick pins in my eyes). "There'll be an evening buffet in the Dining Room for anyone who's still got a little bit of room after all these Christmas goodies," (Oh, there'll be takers for that, you can bet your bottom dollar), "and in the evening there's to be a good old-fashioned sing-song with one of Santa's little helpers, Mrs Frobisher, better known to you as Marge from housekeeping, on the piano." (Let me die now, begged Betty). "Doesn't that sound wonderful?" (No, it does not). "Now enjoy your breakfast everybody and Mr Claus and I will see you in the lounge." (Not if I see you first).

The room emptied quickly after Mrs King's announcement, breakfasts wolfed down so as not to miss Santa. Betty took her time, savouring the peace and quiet.

"Not tempted to go and see Santa?" asked Melanie.

"I think I can live without that," replied Betty.

"Good presents, that's one thing about Mrs King. She is generous at this time of year. I got a bottle of port last year. And not your cheap stuff either."

"What about those people stuck in their rooms?" Betty was thinking about Lizzie.

"Oh, our Santa's very mobile. He'll visit everyone who wants to see him. Nobody'll be forgotten. Still not tempted?"

"I don't think so. See you later."

As she left, Betty grabbed Janice who was busy clearing the tables in preparation for lunch.

"Can I have a glass of fizz to take up to Lizzie please?"

"Of course you can. Would you like another one for yourself too?"

"Why not? Thank you."

There was a queue waiting to go into the Television Lounge, everyone chattering excitedly. They were going to see Santa! Glasses in hand, Betty waited for the lift but no-one paid her any attention. She couldn't get away from this near-hysteria quickly enough. At least with Lizzie she could spend some time with somebody sane.

Lizzie lay in bed, dozing. Betty put the glasses down quietly and went to sit on the window seat. Outside it was grey, heavy clouds spitting rain. Weather to suit my mood, she thought, dark and gloomy. She closed her eyes. Why was this such a lonely time of year?

"How are you doing?" Lizzie was awake. Betty helped her sit up and fluffed up her pillows.

"I'm fine. It's madness downstairs so I'm seeking refuge with you."

"Don't tell me," said Lizzie. "Mrs King dressed up in that ridiculous costume distributing largesse as if we over-charged residents hadn't already paid for it in our exorbitant fees? More mince pies than you would care to see in a life-time? Ruby looking as if she'd just stepped out of Santa's workshop? She could crack a walnut in the crook of her arm, that one." Lizzie laughed. "And was there cheap Buck's Fizz for breakfast?"

"Speaking of which," Betty got up and handed Lizzie a glass, "I got this for you."

"Thank you my dear, that's so kind. I shouldn't really but I'm sure a few sips won't do me any harm. Cheers!"

"Cheers and a happy Christmas. Aren't you supposed to drink alcohol?"

"Not with all the medication I'm on, but it is Christmas. Mmm. Lovely. Now, tell me what you've got planned for the rest of the day."

"Not much really. I've managed to avoid Santa and I shall certainly give the bingo and sing-song a miss. I can't imagine anything worse."

"Don't go in the TV Lounge after lunch," warned Lizzie. "Wall to wall farts, I can tell you. All that rich food. It sets one of them off and they all follow suit. 'Rank' is not the word!"

Betty laughed uproariously. "Consider me warned."

"Anything interesting going on?"

"Nothing I can think of. Same old same old. One day is pretty much like another."

"Tell me about it! Wait till you've been here decades. But at least there's been a bit of excitement since you arrived, Betty."

"What do you mean?"

"You know. First Johnny Latimer with his death by diarrhoea. Made me laugh, that did. Then Reggie throwing himself overboard on that river cruise. Before you came we hadn't had a death in two years. Must be something about you." Betty smiled awkwardly. "Who's next I wonder? Got anybody else in mind?"

"Lizzie! I can't believe you just said that! You can't possibly think that those deaths have got anything to do with me!" She was mortified that Lizzie could even think that of her.

"Just kidding. But things have got interesting since you arrived, you must admit. No bad thing, though. We needed a bit of a shake-up here. Getting complacent we were. Forgetting the reason we're all here."

"What do you mean?" But Betty knew the answer.

"We're here to die, girl. This is a retirement home. It's not for the young and healthy. It's for the old and unwanted who have nowhere else to go. Somewhere to park us until it's time to move on. Depressing but true."

Betty's mood sank even lower. It's what she'd said to herself on many an occasion since she'd arrived. Hearing it out loud was another matter altogether.

"Don't worry about it, Betty. Look at me! You could have years left. I know I have. I don't plan on going anytime soon."

Betty was glad to hear it but the thought of the years stretching out ahead of her – it was almost more than she could bear. There was a knock at the door and in walked Santa.

"Ho, ho, ho!" came a familiar voice. "I thought I'd find you up here."

Betty burst out laughing. Ephraim. Dressed in a red Santa suit badly padded out with pillows and sporting a cotton wool beard, he carried a black bin bag over his shoulder. He looked ridiculous and she told him so.

"You should hear what they're saying downstairs! I never knew Santa was black!" He mimicked Ashley perfectly. "Never was when I was growing up. We always had a white Santa in Harrogate. You tink all de Santas in de world be white? I asked him. He didn't know where to put himself! Glad to get away from them for five minutes, I can tell you. I need a bit of sanity." He sat down in Lizzie's armchair and produced a hip flask from his pocket. "Drink anyone?" he asked. "Best Jamaican rum this side of the Pennines."

"I don't mind if I do," said Lizzie.

"Do you think you should?" asked Betty. "You've had a glass of fizz already. You said you shouldn't have alcohol."

"Gnat's piss, that stuff," said Lizzie. "Mrs King buys it by the tanker load and rolls it out for what she calls Special Occasions, this being one of them. No, it's Christmas and I'm going to have a real drink for once." Ephraim passed her his flask and she took a good long swig. She offered it to Betty.

"Too early for me. I'll stick with the gnat's!"

"I looked for you downstairs, Mrs M," said Ephraim. "Was going to offer you the chance to sit on my knee! Tell Santa if you'd been a good girl or not! Missed out there, you did."

Betty grinned at him. "Yes," she agreed, "my loss." She was enjoying this flirting business.

"Anyway, somewhere in here," he rummaged in his bin bag, "I have gifts for you good ladies." He handed them each a present wrapped in festive paper. Lizzie unwrapped a jar of expensive-looking bath salts; Betty, a box of dark chocolate violet and rose creams. "Don't tell anyone, but I chose these myself."

"Thank you," said Betty, "that is so kind." She was genuinely touched.

Ephraim stood up. "Now, sadly dis Santa be a busy man and still got de presents for de most crumbly." He tucked in an escaping pillow. "So I'll bid you lovely ladies a fond farewell for the time being. See you at lunch, Betty?" She nodded. "Good stuff." He tucked his hip flask away, shouldered the near-empty bag and blew them both a kiss as he closed the door.

"Lovely man," said Lizzie. "Ah, if only I was forty years younger!"

"Wicked woman!" laughed Betty.

"I tell you what, I could go another glass of fizz. Would you mind going to get me one?"

"Are you sure? What about your medication?"

"Oh, to hell with that. One more drink won't hurt me."
"If you're sure..."
"I am. Now stop nagging and off you go."

There was a tray of Buck's Fizz at the Beverage Station so Betty took two glasses and headed back upstairs. She couldn't have been gone more that ten minutes. "Here we are, Lizzie, but I think you ought to call it a day after this one. Lizzie? Lizzie?"

Lizzie was still propped up in bed but her head was tilted to one side, her chin on her chest and eyes were wide open. Betty rushed to her and touched her cheek. It was still warm but Lizzie had clearly left sooner than she'd planned. A single thought flashed through Betty's mind, "It wasn't me!"

CHAPTER SEVENTEEN

Friars Rest
Boxing Day

Dearest Eva,

A very happy Christmas to you. But I'm sad to say it wasn't happy for me at all. I had a fearful day. My good friend, Lizzie, she of The Rose Suite, died yesterday. I know what you may be thinking but, hand on heart, I can tell you in all honesty it was nothing to do with me. It seems alcohol and medication just don't mix. I think I may have known that but I'm not too sure. Whatever, Mrs King seems to hold me personally responsible for Lizzie's demise, as well as being guilty of trying to spoil her Christmas. Mrs King's that is. Not Lizzie's. Hers was already ruined.

Once I realised Lizzie was dead I rang Reception but there was no answer – everybody joining in the festivities. So I went downstairs and found Mrs King enjoying a quiet ten minutes in her office. She returned with me to The Rose Suite and confirmed what I'd already told her. What do you know about it? she demanded. I told her that Lizzie had had a couple of glasses of Buck's Fizz (I didn't mention Ephraim's hip flask – don't want to get him into trouble, lovely man that he is). Then she harangued me for a good five minutes. Didn't I know Mrs Hetherington was on medication? Didn't I know she shouldn't drink? Didn't I know it could kill her? She made it out totally to be my fault. Oh Eva, I am heartbroken. I didn't want her to die. Lizzie was my friend. I thought I was making her happy, getting her a drink. And now I've killed the one person I really liked. Mrs King warned me not to say anything, to leave Lizzie where she was and she would sort it out. Christmas would go ahead and no-one would be any the wiser. Cruel, cruel woman, Mrs King, accusing me of poisoning Lizzie with alcohol. Devastated, I returned to my room and sobbed my heart out. I have not felt this crushed since Barry died. I remember writing to you soon after he died and I tried to tell you about it a little while back but I didn't feel strong enough at the time. I suppose now is as good a time as any.

It all started with a knock on the door. I'd already put Mark down for the night – such a good sleeper he was. Never had any problems with him going right through the night. I was in the kitchen getting dinner ready and waiting for Barry to get back from work. I'd made him his favourite. Fancy me remembering that. It was a lamb stew I make with beer. Delicious. I'll have to give you the recipe one day. I was just about to start mashing the potatoes when my life fell apart. There was a knock at the front door. Forgotten his door key, I thought. But no. Standing there were a man and a woman. Police people, as it turned out, (neither was in uniform), holding up identification badges, looking grim. Mrs Mortimer? the man asked. I'm Detective Sergeant Pervaiz and this is Detective Constable Dyer. Can we come in? I knew then it was bad news, the worst possible sort. I took them into the lounge and they suggested I may like to sit down. What a cheek! I thought at the time. Telling me to take a seat in my own home. But I did as I was told. The woman took up the story. Barry had suffered a massive heart attack and had died in the ambulance on *the way to hospital. I looked at her, disbelieving. Not my Barry, I thought. He was right as rain when he left for work this morning. The usual peck on the cheek before he left. Teasing me, telling me not to work too hard. No, they'd got it wrong. It couldn't be Barry. It had to be a mistake. I sat there saying nothing. Can I get you a cup of tea? asked the Policeman. I nodded. Can I go and see him? In hospital? The bringers of bad news exchanged glances. Yes, you can. We'll take you there shortly but there are some things you need to know which you might find quite upsetting. As if I wasn't upset enough already. Things I need to know? Like what? The Policewoman, DC Dryer, was it? took a deep breath and examined her fingernails closely before she spoke. Your husband, Barry Mortimer, she said, not looking at me, was with someone else when he was taken ill. Of course he was! I shouted at her. He was at work. She shook her head. There's no easy way to tell you this. You will find out sooner or later so we think it's best you hear it from us in your own home. If it gets into the local papers, and I think it certainly will, we want you to be prepared. He wasn't at work, your husband. If he wasn't at work, then where was he? I demanded. At that moment, Detective Pervaiz returned carrying three mugs of tea on a tray. I found some biscuits, he said. Thought you might like one. I don't want a bloody biscuit! I shouted. I want to know what happened to my husband. Well, Eva, the long and short of it was that Barry had been visiting a well-known, how shall I put it? Woman? I won't say 'lady', of ill repute. Known locally, although I'd never heard of her, as Madame Cutlass. (I believe the emphasis was on the ass, if you get my drift). More about her later. Your husband was found by the paramedics, Mrs Mortimer, dressed in – here the lady policewoman took another deep breath before she continued – dressed in unusual clothing. Unusual? He was dressed as Little Miss Pirate, explained the Detective chap as he helped himself to another Hobnob. What? I screamed. What's a Little Miss Pirate? I was dumbfounded, Eva. What a sheltered life I'd led. It seems that Little Miss Pirate is a costume that people, no, men, should I say, wear. It involves stockings and suspenders (you remember those awful things we used to wear? Dreadfully uncomfortable and breezy round the thighs?) Well, so I was duly informed, some men get a thrill out of wearing them. But that's not all. There's also a patch over one eye, a spotted bandanna round the neck, a bandolier and very large bloomers. I couldn't quite work out how they fitted in but it was part of the package apparently. They also have a little wooden sword (I make no comment here at all), which they tuck into a wide black leather belt, and sometimes brandish it threateningly whilst saying such nonsense as 'Avast me hearties'. This is, or rather was, the cue, I'm reliably informed, for Madame Cutlass to get out her trusty cutlass from its scabbard and spank them hard on the bottom. Have you ever heard the like? I knew our love life wasn't terribly exciting, Eva, but this? What I found very hard to digest, though, was that part of the attraction was tattoos. Pirates always had tattoos. So Madame Cutlass, for a small extra fee, would draw tattoos on the naked chests of her clients, skulls and treasure maps, in felt-tip pen. Do you know how difficult it is to get felt-tip out of a white cotton shirt? I used to ask Barry about it when I did the laundry and all he would say was that he had a problem with leaky pens. I never thought anything more of it. Well, you wouldn't, would you?*

Madame Cutlass had realised that Barry was in difficulty when, somewhat ironically, he stopped saying Piece of Eight! Pieces of Eight! Apparently this is yet another signal, but this time it's to tell Mrs Cutlass to spank even harder. This was something Barry particularly enjoyed I found out later. So when he stopped asking for more pain, she got worried. His face had turned blue and he was gasping for breath. The woman had done a First Aid course (I think that's something to be encouraged in her line of work) and she knew to stop the spanking immediately. She began mouth to mouth regurgitation and when she realised that wasn't working, she phoned for an ambulance. And that was that. Barry died in the ambulance, still dressed in his Little Miss Pirate uniform. I understand that one of the paramedics had been kind enough to pull up Barry's bloomers from round his ankles, trying to make him look a bit more decent. Some people can be so thoughtful, can't they?

The Police were ever so kind too. They drove me to the hospital – I'd called in a neighbour to look after Mark who had slept through the end of my life as I knew it – and I was taken in to see Barry. It wasn't terribly edifying, I can tell you. My husband, lying in the morgue, still dressed in his finery, his lipstick smudged. I didn't mention the make up, did I? I'll leave you to imagine that for yourself. I took his hand but it was cold. You utter arse, I told him.

The next few weeks were a blur. I blamed myself of course. If Barry had been happy at home, had got all he needed from me, maybe he wouldn't have turned to that dreadful woman. Why had I not been more imaginative in the bedroom department? More colourful? I would have done anything for him. Maybe even spanked him, if only he'd asked. But he never did. The papers got hold of it, as the Police said they would. Too good a story not to print. Front page of the Stratton-on-Ouse Oracle. Any details the Police had missed were provided by all the local newspapers, lurid stories covering the front pages, titillating their readers for weeks on end. I thought about sending you some press cuttings so you could have a cheap laugh at my expense. But there were more than enough people doing that already and I knew you wouldn't have found it in the slightest bit amusing. I was the laughing stock of the town, as you can imagine. Couldn't leave the house without people pointing and laughing at me. I was just so relieved that Mark was a baby – too young to know anything about it. So now you can understand why I've never told him anything about his father in all these years. What could I say? That Barry liked dressing up as a lady pirate and being spanked? I was too humiliated to tell him, even when he was older. And somehow, luckily, by the time he was old enough to understand, everybody had moved on. Except me, of course. I don't think I ever did. Barry Mortimer and his piratic adventures were part of me. And what was his legacy to me? Enough humiliation to last me a lifetime.

The funeral was difficult. I didn't want to go but thought I ought. The Police had somehow managed to keep the details out of the papers so it was a discreet affair. Just me. And Madame Cutlass. Oh yes, she came. Turned out she wasn't just your common or garden bottom-beater. She catered to and for all sorts. Barry, in his naiveté, thought she was exclusive to him. But no. She traded her wares far and wide, so I found out later.

So there we were, at the crematorium. Had the place to ourselves. Just the three of us, Madame Cutlass sobbing on one side, me, dry-eyed on the other and Barry, lying in the middle between us. I'd chosen the cheapest, most basic coffin in the catalogue – MDF I think they call it. One up from cardboard but a bit stiffer. Oops! Probably not the best *word to use in the circumstances. If I hadn't known about Madame Cutlass, and I'd genuinely believed I was saying goodbye to the man I'd loved with all my heart and who I though had loved me equally, I would have chosen something more elaborate and expensive. But now I knew everything, or thought I did – Madame Cutlass still had one or two surprises in store for me that day – cheap and nasty summed it up perfectly. It was a Humanist ceremony, very short and simple. The MC, (I think that's what they call them), said a few words. But what could she say about the man who had stolen my trust? Who had lied to me over the years. After all, he couldn't really have loved me, could he? Not if he had to go looking for happiness elsewhere and found it in the arms of a cutlass-wielding pirate captain lady person. He broke my heart, Eva.*

At the end of the ceremony, if you could call it that, she came over to me, still crying her eyes out. What I couldn't get over was how ordinary she was. Plain, drab even. Please don't hate me, she said. I was only helping him to explore his inner self. Took a long time finding it, I told her. He was good to me, was Barry, she informed me. You don't know how happy that makes me, I replied but the sarcasm was lost on her. But you need to know he never stopped loving you. Fuck off! I said. God, that felt good. (Sorry, Eva. It's not the sort of language I usually use but I was quite upset). But there is just one small thing, she said. I looked at her. The house I live in. Barry bought it for me but it's in his name. He was going to transfer it over to me but never got round to it. Will you be able to do it? Please? If you don't, I'm homeless. I have nowhere to go. Fuck off! I said it again and walked away. Please, she cried, running after me. He wanted me to have it. He said so. Go and find someone else's memories to ruin, I told her. And I walked out of her life forever. At least I thought I did. You didn't know I could be so heartless, did you, Eva? Neither did I. But she took my husband away from me so I took her home away from her. That was the price she paid. Seemed like a fair deal to me.

There was an inquest of course. I didn't attend that. The Detective who ate all my Hobnobs advised against it. The press would be there clamouring for a picture, a quote. How does it feel, Mrs Mortimer, to find out that your husband liked dressing up and having his botty walloped? More smut for the masses. I couldn't face yet more humiliation so I stayed at home, the curtains drawn. I'd been the laughing stock of the town once. I didn't need to be again.

And that was it, Eva. That's how Barry died. I hope you're not too shocked. I was. I died then and now with Lizzie, I feel like I've died again.

Yours in sorrow,

Betty.

CHAPTER EIGHTEEN

Lizzie Hetherington had finally and permanently vacated the Rose Suite and Sinclair Latimer moved in. Mrs King put a notice of her demise up on the Activity Notice Board, saying that Lizzie had passed away peacefully in her sleep. She was worried that these deaths were now becoming a bit too frequent for her liking. And wasn't it funny how Betty Mortimer was always somewhere in the background? Mrs King had confirmed to a delighted Betty that she was indeed next on the list for the favoured suite, but Betty would have much rather Lizzie hadn't died. Now that her friend was gone she realised just how much she missed her. Lizzie had been Betty's oasis in a sea of chaos, even if only for half an hour each day and now even that had been taken away from her. Betty said she wanted to go to the funeral. It would be the first funeral she'd gone to since Barry's and she wasn't looking forward to it but she wanted to be there.

"I don't see why not," said Mrs King. "It's not as if she had any family. I can't see anyone else wanting to go. Except Ephraim. He was quite fond of the old lady. I'll go, of course. I always do. One or two others might decide to come. We'll see."

But it turned out to be just the three of them. Mrs King drove them to the crematorium in her brand new dark blue Lexus. She wore a sombre navy blue suit which matched the car exactly. Betty and Ephraim sat in the back, not saying a word.

"You two stay here whilst I pop in and see if we're ready," Mrs King told them as she parked the car across two parking bays. "Won't be long."

Ephraim looked across at Betty. "Thank you," he said.

"For what?"

"For not telling Mrs King that I'd given Lizzie a drink. I'd have lost my job."

"There's no need to thank me. You didn't do anything that I hadn't already done. I got her the first glass of sparkling wine and had gone down to get her another. I didn't know it wouldn't mix with her medication. How was I to know?"

"I knew," said Ephraim sombrely. "I just didn't think, that's all."

"It's not your fault. Really."

"I feel guilty. I feel as if I'd killed her."

Betty smiled inwardly. If only you knew, she thought. She'd killed three now, if you included Lizzie, but none of them had been deliberate. She was the reason they'd all died, not that she felt any responsibility for their deaths. Nor any guilt, for that matter, except maybe a bit for Lizzie. But Betty would put it to the back of her mind. And Ephraim should too. She took his hand in hers.

"You did not kill her or have anything to do with her death, Ephraim. It was an accident, pure and simple."

"You're kind Mrs M. But I shouldn't have had that rum on me. Mrs King does not allow any drinking on the premises as far as staff are concerned. It's immediate dismissal. But it was Christmas and I knew it was going to be a very long day, so I thought, why not?"

"In your shoes, I would have done the same thing. I mean, how were you to get through the day being Santa for a bunch of rickety, over-excited wrinklies who are behaving like four year-olds? I think I'd have needed a lot more than rum. I really don't know how you do it. I don't have any patience with the old codgers. Most of them drive me up the wall. To my mind, you're a saint." She squeezed his hand. "So let's say no more about it, shall we?"

"I don't know. I still feel responsible."

This man needed to toughen up.

"How about we call it partners in crime and leave it at that?" suggested Betty. "We can both take the blame if it makes you feel any better. What do you think?"

Ephraim thought about it for a few seconds then nodded his head in agreement, "Okay Mrs M, partners in crime it is."

Good. That was sorted. They shook on it.

"But I still owe you one," said Ephraim.

"For what?"

"Not grassing on me. I need this job."

She smiled at him. Why not? Maybe it wouldn't do any harm to have someone owing you a favour. You never knew when you might just need it.

Sinclair Latimer was now even more insufferable. He had got what he and his brother had both wanted; the Rose Suite. Every opportunity he could, he gloated. He gloated to anyone who would listen and to those who wouldn't. Everyone was heartily sick of him going on about how he'd finally got the best suite in the Home. Of course, it should have been Johnny's but since he'd now gone, it was, by rights, his. It was no more than he deserved, he told anyone who wasn't quick enough to escape him – that included all of the residents and most of the helpers – since he'd always been used to the finer things in life. It was his due. It's only a room, someone dared to suggest to him.

"Only a room!" he'd exploded. "That's like saying that caviar is only fish eggs! Where on earth were you brought up, man?"

The poor man, terrified, muttered something about Chipping Sodbury and fled, close to tears.

But, more than anyone, the person Sinclair really wanted to lord it over, was Betty. He knew she was the next in line to inherit the suite but he was going to make sure she waited a very long time, and in the meantime he was going to remind her every day of what she was missing. He hated the woman with a vengeance, convinced she alone was responsible for his brother's death. Ever since Johnny had died in such agony, whenever Sinclair spoke to Betty he had made it clear to her that the blame rested solely on her shoulders. He had a goal now, and that was to make her life at Friars as unpleasant as possible. Standing at the Beverage Station making herself a cup of coffee the afternoon of Lizzie's funeral, Sinclair sidled up to her.

"Wonderful room, that Rose Suite."

"I'm so happy for you," she replied through gritted teeth. Betty found it difficult to be civil to the man.

"No, I mean it. It's an utter delight. So much space. Lovely views too. And a bath. What more could you want?"

Betty busied herself with choosing a biscuit.

"Of course, Johnny would have loved it." Betty didn't reply. "And it should have been his. Shame he's not here to enjoy it."

"Yes. Isn't it." A chocolate digestive.

"I still hold you responsible, you know."

"Don't talk rot, Sinclair. Your brother died because he had gastric problems. Nothing to do with me."

"Oh, I still don't believe that. You can protest as much as you like but I know it was your fault."

Was this man ever going to let up? She tried to walk away but he gripped her arm, spilling some of her coffee.

She glared at him. "Look Sinclair. I was at Lizzie's funeral this morning. I'm not in the mood for this rubbish. For once and for all, I'm sorry your brother is dead. But his dying had nothing at all to do with me. Now can you please let me go before I scream blue murder."

"Murder. Yes, you said it. Murder, that's what you did. The more I think about it, the more I'm convinced you killed him. I haven't worked out how exactly but I will."

"Oh, don't talk such nonsense."

Still Sinclair would not let her go.

"It's not nonsense and you know it. He lusted after you, did Johnny."

"That was hardly my fault!"

"You're a wanton, that's what you are!" A wanton? she thought. What a strange thing to call someone. "A hussy, that's what you are! A tart!"

That was enough. Betty wrenched her hand away and threw what was left of her coffee over him. His crisp white shirt was ruined.

"Aargh! You've scalded me, you bitch!"

"I'll do more than that if you don't stop harassing me."

Sinclair's screams had attracted attention. Out of nowhere, it seemed, Mrs King suddenly appeared, her face like thunder, several helpers by her side.

Then residents began to pile out of the Television Lounge, attracted by the noise.

"What is going on?" she demanded, hands on hips.

"She's burnt me, the whore!"

"Mr Latimer, I will not have language like that in Friars! Please go to your room and I will send one of the helpers with a First Aid kit."

"The coffee was barely warm," said Betty. "Stop over-reacting."

"My shirt! You've ruined it. I'll sue you, you hellhag!"

Hellhag? Wanton? Where did he get these outrageous names from? Betty wondered.

"Mr Latimer! I won't ask you again!"

"You haven't heard the last of this, Betty Mortimer." He jabbed his finger at her. "Nor you, Mrs King, for allowing such a...a...she-devil to live here. You have no idea what you unleashed when you allowed this...woman, and I use the word loosely, to move in!" He turned and stomped off, muttering under his breath, thrusting onlookers aside.

"Nothing to see, everyone, nothing to see," said Mrs King to the growing band of spectators. "Off you all go. Back to the TV." There were tuts of disappointment but the crowd slowly dispersed. "Are you alright Betty?"

"I think so," she replied but she was trembling.

"What on earth was that all about?" She took Betty's elbow and steered her towards her office. "Come in and tell me what's going on."

"There's nothing to tell," Betty told her when she was seated, a fresh cup of coffee in front of her. "The man hates me, that's all."

"But why? What have you done to upset him?"

Betty took a sip. "He's convinced I killed his brother."

Mrs King stared at her long and hard before speaking. Whilst she'd never put such a thought into words, there were certainly times when she herself had mused on the fact that there had been a series of unusual deaths since Betty had arrived. Even as recently as a couple of days ago, when she pinned yet another Notice of Passing – as she preferred to call them – on the Activity Notice Board, the thought had again crossed her mind. Prior to Betty's arrival there hadn't been a single death for two years. Now, in four months, there had been three. Of course, the residents here were elderly – look at Lizzie. 96 when she died. Some of the guests were frail, certainly, but there had been nothing wrong with either Johnny or Reggie. For their age they were both in pretty good shape and she'd been very surprised at them dying so suddenly. But in both cases, as unexpected as their deaths may have been, there was nothing untoward. Johnny had died of natural causes – he'd always been susceptible to stomach disorders; and the Coroner had been satisfied that Reggie's death was an accident as a result of him having fallen overboard from the cruise boat after drinking to excess. And now Lizzie. She had died from an unfortunately lethal combination of alcohol and medication. Mrs

King tried to keep her ear to the ground about what was going on between the residents, getting little titbits of information from the helpers and sometimes the residents themselves. So she was well aware that Betty had become quite close to Lizzie and she also knew that Betty got on quite well with Johnny, even sitting at the same table as him and his brother. But nobody had said anything about Betty and Reggie. So it had to be a coincidence, didn't it? The fact that Betty was close to two of the deceased. But then so were a lot of people here in Friars, helpers included. What other explanation could there be? It was just a fluke, pure and simple.

"Do you want to make a formal complaint against Mr Latimer?"

Betty shook her head. She would think of other ways to deal with him. "I don't think so. He's obviously very excitable."

"Fair enough. But I think you should give him a wide berth, don't you? It's important we don't have scenes like earlier repeated. It upsets the residents."

"Absolutely. Can I ask you, Mrs King, considering what Mr Latimer accused me of, do you think he's quite right in the head? I mean, if he's a bit mentally unbalanced or something like that, is this the right place for him?"

"What are you saying?"

"Well, if he's prone to such mood swings and to threatening people, shouldn't he be somewhere more…secure?"

"I don't think it's come to that, Betty. Sinclair Latimer has lived here happily for many years. I think what we have is simply a clash of personalities. Nothing more."

"I just worry that he might be a bit dangerous, that's all. I'm really scared he might try to harm me."

"I don't think that's very likely." Mrs King tried to reassure her. "He's still grieving for his brother, of course. He misses him dreadfully. They were very close. I don't think he intends you any harm."

"Yes, I'm sure you're right. But I'll do what you say and steer well clear of him."

Mrs King watched Betty leave. If anyone ever told her that running a retirement home was easy, well, all they had to do was come to Friars for a day!

CHAPTER NINETEEN

Friars
January

Well here we are, Eva. Another year over and a new one begun. The Christmas decorations have been taken down and put away – I wonder if I'll be here to see them next year. Although I really don't like Christmas, as you know, now that the decorations are down the place looks as if there's something missing. It feels empty somehow. But isn't it frightening how time flies by? I didn't see the New Year in – I can't remember the last time I did. I was in bed by 1030. Never been much of a fan, even in my younger days. Why celebrate the passing of time? Some of the oldies stayed up to say goodbye to the old year, Priti told me. Gathered round the television they were, watching the fireworks and Big Ben strike twelve, half of them fast asleep. Mrs King had laid on some more Buck's Fizz and the kitchen had provided some late night nibbles. So I don't think I missed out on anything. To be honest, I don't care if I never see another glass of Buck's in my life. Strange, isn't it, how something so innocuous can have such unpleasant associations?

Speaking of which, I'm missing my friend Lizzie so much already. Her death has really hit me hard. It does mean, though, that I move up the list for her much sought-after suite. But I have still to wait for the awful Sinclair Latimer, brother of the recently deceased Johnny, to shuffle off this mortal coil or otherwise move on, before I can finally move in. He's been absolutely hateful to me since his brother died – calling me all sorts of names. He actually called me a wanton the other day. I always thought that was a type of Chinese dumpling. And just this morning, as I was going into breakfast, he was coming out. I will have my revenge, he hissed at me as he walked past. Can you imagine? Quite put me off my porridge it did.

He cornered me in the Games Room a few weeks ago, Sinclair. I was trying to find something to read that didn't involve steamy bedroom scenes and long lost cousins. Do you like yourself? he hissed in my ear. I was trapped between the Fiction and the Travel sections and couldn't go anywhere. I looked at him blankly. What sort of question is that? I asked him. A simple one, he replied. Do you like yourself? I couldn't think of an answer. Because no-one else here does, he told me. So at least if you like yourself, you've got one friend. Wasn't that an awful thing to say? To be told that everyone dislikes you, especially if it's not true. It says so much about the man, doesn't it? But what if it is true? I told you when I first arrived that I thought people were laughing at me. Especially the helpers. That they were all being far too nice. But I thought that was just me being insecure. Some people here are genuinely kind and I really believe they do like me. Look at Ephraim. And Priti. Janice too. I'm not so sure about some of the others. Mrs King, for example. But there's Melanie. She's always been very pleasant to me. And I had a lovely game of draughts (do you call it Checkers in Canada like they do in America?) with a delightful lady called Frances just the other day. So when Sinclair said this dreadful thing to me, that everybody hated me, I was so upset. Horrid, horrid man. I walked past him in the corridor this evening, ignoring him completely.

And he's been accusing me of all sorts too. He said I murdered his brother and he's going to discover how. He frightens me awfully, Eva, but I don't let on. Certainly not to him. He's got no proof I killed Johnny – and I keep telling myself I didn't really, you know that. It was an accident, same as Reggie. And Lizzie. Oh, did I tell you about Lizzie? I can't remember. That was an accident too. I don't feel any remorse about any of their deaths, apart from Lizzie's. I didn't plan on that one happening. But none of them were my fault. But I do wish Sinclair would somehow just disappear. Not just because I'd finally get the Rose Suite, although that would be nice, but because I really, really dislike the man. I suggested to Mrs King that maybe he was mentally unstable, calling me a murderer – he actually used that word, can you believe it! You killed him, he said. Those were his exact words. I told her that I feared for my safety and asked if he wouldn't be better off in another sort of establishment. Preferably one far, far away. She didn't agree. Probably worried that if she tried to move him, he'd sue her. He blames her for allowing me to move into Friars in the first place. I think she'd like it if he was gone but she won't ask him to leave. We had a real humdinger, Sinclair and me, at the Beverage Station, in front of half of the residents the other day. Mrs King doesn't like that sort of thing. I still don't like her, you know. Never did from day one. There's something about her, I can't quite put my finger on it, but you know how you can take an instant dislike to someone? Lizzie felt the same. And I'm sure Mrs King feels the same way about me. I sometimes catch her looking at me askance – almost as if she's wondering what I'm thinking. It's as if she suspects me of something. I can't think what, but I don't like it. One thing that amuses me is what she calls me. When I first arrived at Friars, she asked me what I would like to be called, Betty or Mrs Mortimer? I didn't express an opinion but I notice that when all's right with the world and she's happy with me, then I'm Betty. But if there's any question about something I may have done or said that doesn't meet with her approval, or there's some serious issue to talk about (Sinclair Latimer for example), then I'm Mrs Mortimer. Do you remember, when we were kids and we'd done something wrong? What a pair we were! Always getting into trouble. Twins are always double trouble, Mum used to say. And when she told us off I was always Elizabeth, never Betty, and you were, well, you were still just Eva. It's like that. It's like being a child all over again.

That set me thinking, about being a child again. I can so clearly remember us as kids playing together in the back garden of our house on Pollard Street. Do you remember? And Barker, our puppy. It seems like it was only days ago. Then all of a sudden we were teenagers, fighting over the same boys, the same lipstick, the same dreams. You were the first to get married. I remember when you first brought Alan home to meet Mum and Dad. They were so impressed. A bank clerk. Although I don't think they call them that these days, do they? Financial advisor, or some other grandiose title. Good solid job, I remember Dad telling him, you could go far. And you did. All the way to Canada. Some sort of overseas recruitment programme, wasn't it? For the bank's foreign division. Alan did well to be selected. Mum was heart-broken when you told her you were going to live in Toronto.

Not the other side of the world but not far off. You're too young, she said. Remember? I vividly recall her saying she might never see you again. Why ever not? you asked. What's to stop you getting on a plane and coming over to visit? You too, Betty. All of you can come. And we'll be back to see you. Of course we will. But it wasn't to be, was it? The years passed. Alan positively thrived in his job and got promotion after promotion, while Dad's health deteriorated. Then Mum got ill too and they died within weeks of one another. It was a shame you never made it home for their funerals but I don't hold it against you, Eva. I probably would have done the same in your shoes. I just think it's a shame they never saw their grandchildren, though, Emily and Jasper. I still have the photos you sent me, when they were what? Three, four years old? Playing in the snow in a park. Or was it your garden? Such gorgeous children. I remember being so envious when you had your two. One straight after the other I seem to remember. That must have been so exhausting for you. Barry and I were married by then. I gave up work after we were married. He wanted me to be at home, meal on the table as he walked through the door. To be honest, at first I was happy to do that – the jobs I'd had were pretty unexciting and didn't pay very well – but what I didn't realise at the time was how much independence they gave me. And then along came Mark.

We'd tried for years to have children and I'd pretty much given up. And then, out of the blue, this little bundle of joy entered our lives. Such a cliché, I know, but so true. We were unbelievably happy. A perfect family, I thought. I'd mentioned to Barry on several occasions that I'd like to go back to work, get a job once Mark was a bit older. I didn't want to turn into one of those women whose only topic of conversation was babies. But he dismissed the idea flat out, insisting it was my role to look after our son. So I gave up any thought of looking for a job and concentrated on raising our baby boy. I did as he asked and have regretted it to this day. Don't get me wrong, Eva. It wasn't a chore. I loved looking after Mark. But Barry had insisted that my role in life was in the home. From the beginning he told me that I didn't need to work. It wasn't as if we needed the money – his business thrived from the start. I only realised much later how utterly selfish my husband had been but by then it was too late.

You never worked either, did you, Eva? Your husband was successful as well. But did you want to? Maybe it was different with two children to look after. But I always wished I had. If I'd gone out to work, had my own life, things might have been very different. I wouldn't find myself without real friends so late in life. But then, as you know, Barry died and my life fell apart.

I tried a bit of volunteering work once. Barry had been dead nearly five years and Mark had started school. One day a week in a charity shop but it didn't last. Bit too impatient with people, I was told. You'll laugh, but I remember once this old woman came up to me at the counter with a cardigan in her hand. It was £1 but it had a hole in the sleeve. Or should I say it had a small hole in the sleeve but it was only £1. It's got a hole, she pointed out to me. Yes, I said, I know. That's why it's only £1. This is a charity shop, you know. But it's got a hole, she repeated. Are you deaf? I asked her. What? She actually yelled at me, Eva. I am not deaf! Nor am I made of money. Now reduce the price or else! I took the woman by the elbow and guided her outside the shop. You see that sign? I asked her, *pointing to the yellow and blue painted sign which stretched the length of the shop front. The one that reads Assistance Dogs for the Anxious? Well, we're thinking of changing it to Thinking Dogs for the Inordinately Stupid. I think you could well be our first beneficiary. The woman looked at me with a face like thunder. So did the manageress. I was sent home that day. No, patience was never my strong point.*

I really do believe that if I'd continued working after I'd married Barry, things might have turned out differently, but who knows. I'm not going over old ground again. We can't change what happened. None of us can. We just have to be thankful for what we've still got.

Truth to tell, Eva, apart from Sinclair being an absolute pain in the whatnot, I don't think I've been this happy for as long as I can remember. I like to think I have a few friends here now, even if Sinclair says otherwise. But even a few friends is more than I had when I was on my own. I didn't like it here at first, you know that, but I've become used to it and I wouldn't want to move now. I quite like the place and some of the people, and it does have its moments. But Mr Latimer is certainly a fly in the ointment. He is spoiling it for me in a big way. I think if he wasn't here things would be, if not perfect, then not too far off. Somebody needs to do something.

Oh, before I forget, Eva, a very happy New Year to you and all your family. To Alan and Jasper and dear sweet little Emily. I do miss you, you know. So very much.

With all my love, as always,

Betty.

CHAPTER TWENTY

A notice from Mrs King went up on the Activity Notice Board announcing to all residents that the annual spring clean of the entire establishment would take place early this year. All suites and public areas, as well as kitchens, staff areas and anywhere else you could think of would be subject to a deep clean. Any disruption caused would be kept to a minimum and residents were asked to be patient and understanding.

"You know why it's so early, don't you?" Ephraim was standing next to Betty as she read the bulletin.

"I didn't know we had a deep clean at all," she replied, "although I suppose I should have guessed."

"We usually have it in March."

"So why now, then? What's different?"

"Mrs King has got the heebie-jeebies."

Betty looked at him. "Can't she get a cream for that?"

"Oh Mrs M, you kill me! No, she's in a real flap-doodle."

"Ephraim, what are you trying to say?"

"The woman's in a panic. Hitting the old sweet sherry a bit hard."

"I didn't know she liked a tipple."

"Between you and me," said Ephraim leaning closer, "loses it a bit, does our Mrs King, when things get a bit difficult. Then out comes the Bristol Cream."

"I would have thought that running a place like this would have kept her permanently under the table! What is it this time?"

"She's worried that Friars Rest is attracting attention for all the wrong reasons. Got the health people coming round," replied Ephraim.

"The health people? Who are they?"

"Inspectors from the Care Quality Commission. They check up on places like this. Make sure everything's as it should be."

"Why wouldn't it be?" Betty asked.

Ephraim steered her away from the notice board just in case they could be overheard. "Rumour has it that they are a bit concerned at the recent number of deaths here. They monitor that sort of thing."

"But surely they can expect deaths in a place like this?"

"Yes, but a little bird told me that they are really worried. Want to come and see for themselves what's going on. Want to see what we've all been up to and why Mrs King is bumping off so many oldsters."

"You shouldn't say things like that, Ephraim. You know it's not true."

"I know it's not but she has to convince them. They seem to think something odd might be going on. Too many coincidences for their liking."

"How do you know all this?"

Ephraim pulled his ear lobe. "I keep me ears to da ground."

"What will they do? Interview all the residents?" Betty was starting to get worried.

"No. I shouldn't think so. But if they have real concerns about a place they can close it down by taking away the licence. Means Mrs King could no longer run Friars as a retirement home. And I'd be out of a job."

"And I'd be homeless." Now she was truly alarmed.

"I don't suppose for a minute it would come to that," said Ephraim, noting the look of concern on her face. "They'll already have seen the various death certificates and the Coroner's report so I expect they'll just turn up, give the place a quick once-over, then leave us alone for another couple of years. It's more about them being seen to be doing something. I don't really think we have anything to worry about."

"When are they coming?"

"We're never told. They like to surprise us. But Mrs King has got wind of the visit, hence the spring clean now. She wants to make sure that the place is looking its best when they arrive."

"Well, let's hope nobody else dies in the meantime." Betty was serious. The last thing she wanted to do was up sticks and move to another home and she imagined that all the other residents would feel the same way. She'd hated Friars when she'd first arrived but then she would have hated anywhere. Now she was used to the place and the people. It had become her home, something she never thought she'd find herself saying. No, there would be no more accidents in the foreseeable future. Sinclair was safe for the time being.

"And speaking of surprises," said Ephraim, handing Betty a small bunch of fresh flowers. "Happy Birthday!"

"What?" She had clean forgotten. "That is so kind of you. But how did you know? I hadn't even remembered."

"It's on your Admission Record. Mrs King likes to make sure we don't forget things like that. It's important, she keeps telling us."

"Well, that's very sweet of you. But, to be honest, the fact that I'm now 76 is no cause for celebration."

Ephraim smiled. "It's still better than the alternative. And, anyway, you don't look a day over 75."

"Thank you Ephraim. But at least you remembered. Which is more than my son did."

"Don't be too harsh on him."

"No, you're right. He's busy out there forging his new career. Probably got other things on his mind."

Betty was worried about the Inspectors' surprise visit but she wasn't going to let that spoil her day. It was her birthday, something that had completely slipped her mind. Not only had she got flowers from Ephraim but there was a bottle of champagne waiting for her in her room along with a small box of dark chocolate truffles. A small card read 'Happy Birthday from everyone at Friars.' Betty was delighted and decided that she was going to make a real effort today and try to be nice to everyone. Even Sinclair. It was to prove harder than she thought.

She wandered down to the Television Lounge. Half a dozen residents sat in front of the TV, several of them snoring quietly. Betty recognised one or two but there was nobody with whom she wished to spend any time. Anyway, they were too engrossed in whatever was on television at 1030 in the morning to pay her any attention. She left them to it. There were a few more folk in the Games Room. A loud and argumentative game of bridge was underway at one of the tables; at another, several residents were busily engaged with colouring books. Betty sighed. This was hardly her idea of fun. She'd have a look in the Quiet Lounge and if there was no-one there, she'd go for a walk round the gardens. The only person in the lounge was Ruby. Betty hesitated. Did she really want to sit and talk to Ruby? She told herself she'd promised to be nice to people today and, after all, she'd never had a real conversation with that woman. But maybe there was a reason for that. She turned to leave but it was too late. Ruby had spotted her.

"Oi! Betty! Over 'ere."

Betty attempted to smile. It wasn't easy. Ruby patted the seat on the sofa next to her. "Sit!" she commanded. Betty sat. Ruby was dressed in what appeared to be full-length crushed-velvet dress of the deepest purple, collar and cuffs trimmed with yellow rabbit fur. Sequinned satin slippers peeped out from under the hem. Betty reminded herself to ask Ruby where she got her clothes from and then to avoid it like the plague. Ruby had a huge tangled mass of wool in her lap.

"Are you knitting, Ruby?"

"I will when I can find the end." She turned the fur ball over and over, prodding it with her finger.

"It's a pretty colour." It wasn't. It was yellow with orange flecks and Betty thought it looked like sick. The yarn was seriously frayed; it had clearly been a knitted garment of some description in a previous life.

"What are you going to make?" Betty was trying really hard. She surreptitiously looked at her watch. How soon before she could decently leave?

"I'm going to make an 'at."

"An 'at?" Betty repeated.

"For Ashley."

"How lovely." She tried to sound as if she meant it. "Was it something else before?" Betty pointed to the hairball. "Are you recycling?"

Ruby stopped what she was doing and looked at her. "No. Not cyclin'. Knittin'."

97

God, this woman was hard work. "It just looks like it was a jumper or something. One that's been unpicked and you're re-using the wool. To make an 'at."

"It was."

"Was what?" This was proving to be a very long and completely futile conversation.

"It was socks. Belonged to Reggie, they did. I know cos I knitted 'em. But now 'es gone, I'm turning it into something for my Ashley." Ruby stopped what she was doing and looked hard at Betty. "Miss 'im I do."

"I'm sure you do."

"Like that, we were," said Ruby, clicking her fingers together. Betty wasn't quite sure what Ruby meant but she made a sympathetic clucking sound. It was the most Ruby had ever spoken to her since she'd arrived in Friars and it would probably keep Betty going for a good while yet.

"I'm truly sorry for your loss," said Betty trying to stand up, but Ruby put a hand on her arm. She was so strong that Betty was forced to sit down again.

"Never could work it out."

"What?"

"'ow my Reggie fell overboard on that ship."

Betty swallowed. "What do you mean?"

"'e was a strong bugger. An' them railings was high."

"I understand he'd had quite a lot to drink," said Betty, wondering what Ruby was getting at.

"'e always 'ad 'ad quite a lot to drink. Wasn't a problem till that night."

Betty said nothing.

"'an you was the last one to see 'im alive, wasn't you?" The hand on her arm gripped tighter. God, the woman was strong.

"What are you suggesting?" she asked, trying to pull her arm away. Did Ruby suspect her? And, more importantly, had she told anyone else what she suspected?

"I think you know more than what you're sayin'."

"I told the Police everything I know. We all did."

Ruby gripped harder. "I'm not sure as I believe you."

"Please, Ruby, you're hurting me. You don't know your own strength." Ruby let her go and Betty rolled up her sleeve, horrified to see red marks on her arm. "Look! Look what you've done."

"Farmer's daughter, farmer's widow. You don't get muscles like mine without tossing a few sacks of fertiliser around."

Betty stood up, shaking. She'd tried to be nice to someone and look where it had got her.

"If I ever find out that you were involved in my Reggie's death," Ruby warned her, "I'll 'ave your 'ed on a plate, I will."

Ed? I don't know anybody called Ed, thought Betty. Who's she talking about? Then the penny dropped. This woman was threatening her. Okay, if that's how she wanted to play it, Betty had ways of dealing with people she didn't like. But she'd have to be careful with this one. The woman was strong. And whilst she might appear not to be the sharpest knife in the drawer, Ruby had clearly decided that Betty had somehow been involved in her darling Reggie's death.

"If it was you, if you killed 'im, I'll 'ave me revenge."

Not if I get to you first, thought Betty. She left the lounge, leaving Ruby to continue trying to unravel her ball of wool. Well, that was a complete failure. So much for trying to be nice to people. She was going to revert to type and keep her distance. Especially from Ruby.

But that was the second person who had spoken to Betty of revenge. Sinclair had said exactly the same thing. But revenge for what? What could the woman possibly suspect her of? Ruby clearly hadn't seen anything the night of the cruise or she would have told the Police. Or Mrs King at least. No, it was only a suspicion on her part, based simply on the fact that she, Betty, was the last one to see Reggie alive. She had no proof of anything. No, Betty decided, she had nothing to worry about, but she'd keep an eye on her, just in case. Anyway, her hands were tied, at least until the Inspectors had been and gone.

CHAPTER TWENTY - ONE

Friars Rest
January

Perhaps I was wrong to offload all that on you about Barry, Eva, and if I've upset you, I'm sorry. But I feel so much better for having got it all off my chest. No-one really knows what I went through. I do still miss him, despite everything. You're probably wondering why I never married again. I suppose, at the end of the day, I really couldn't be bothered. All that angst – it's for kids. And I'd been let down so badly, how could I ever trust anyone again? Cynical? Absolutely. But I really don't know which was worse, losing Barry or losing his love. Could I have forgiven him if he hadn't had the heart attack and he'd given up Madame Cutlass? I've asked myself that a thousand times and to this day I still don't know the answer. Once the trust has gone, that's the very foundation of a marriage out of the window. I'd like to think I was big-hearted enough to forgive and forget but I know, deep down, I'm not. So I didn't remarry, I raised Mark and I watched the years gallop by. Not much of a life, I hear you say. But it was enough. For me.

But I did get the most wonderful surprise a few days ago! Guess who came to visit me? Yes, Mark of course. I have never been so thrilled. I'd just finished lunch – Ruby had been regaling the table, again, with tales of her Christmas lunch. How many times had I heard it now? How there'd been paper hats and crackers, turkey and trimmings. Those Dogs in Blankets she liked so much. What was she talking about? Christmas Pudding with holly on top. Had she mentioned Dogs in Blankets? she asked me. How could I have missed Christmas lunch? Best meal she'd ever eaten! I didn't mention I'd been with Lizzie – I doubt that anything I said would have registered with her. If she told me once about those bloody Pigs in Blankets, (that's what they were), she told me a dozen times. Ruby said she was going to ask Geraldo, our chef, if we could have them every day at breakfast. Something really needs to be done about that woman. Anyway, side-tracked again. As I was saying, I was just finishing my pudding – a lovely fresh fruit salad, so delightful after all that rich fare we've been having – and they put bananas in it. I'd never have thought to do that – you know how quickly they go brown – but it works a treat. Back to the story! Mikey came in to the Dining Room to tell me that I had a visitor. Somebody was waiting for me in Reception. I couldn't think who it could be. I hadn't had a single visitor since I moved in here and I was totally flummoxed. Isn't that a lovely word? And who was there but my son! I could have died with happiness. He looked very different from when I last saw him. Mark was never what you'd call handsome. He had a sort of lived-in face but that had now gone. Clearly his new life was suiting him down to the ground. He'd lost quite a bit of weight and looked the better for it. He'd always had a tendency to a bit of a gut, just like his father, but that had disappeared. Now Mark was sun-tanned and he had a sparkle to him. He'd grown a pony-tail, for some reason – not sure about that, Eva. Pony tails are for little girls and horses. And I noticed he had an ear-ring too. Least said. But he was still my son. We hugged, I stood back to look at him, and then we hugged again. My heart was bursting, I can tell you.

Can't stay too long, he told me. Off to the States tomorrow so this is only a fleeting visit. You've got time for a cuppa with your old mother, haven't you? Of course he had. So I made us a cup of tea each at the Beverage Station. He wanted green tea, would you believe. Green tea? I asked. Been drinking nothing else in Korea and Japan. They don't really do milk over there. You should try it. It's good for you. I'll pass on that. Like my Yorkshire tea, I do. If it's good enough for builders, it's good enough for me. Mark liked my room. I remember these, he said, pointing to the watercolours I'd brought with me. They look good here. How are you liking it? I told him it was okay but that nothing much ever happened – I didn't mention Johnny or Reggie. Or Lizzie. But what was his news?

Well, the tour in the Far East had been a huge success and they had released two albums on the back of it. Albums? You know, records. Oh. And now they were off to Washington to start their next tour. County Durham? I asked. You know what I mean, Mum. US of A. We've finally broken into the States. That worried me, Eva. Don't want two criminals in the family. We got the contract we wanted and me and the lads will be touring for two solid months. Brilliant eh? I agreed it was, even though it meant I wouldn't see him for such a long time. But I was happy for him. Truly. And after America? Who knows? Maybe a couple of months off doing nothing then off to South America. Or back to the Far East. They'd have to wait and see but at the moment things could not be going better.

He handed me a beautifully wrapped parcel. I brought you a present, he said. From Korea. For your birthday. He hadn't forgotten after all. It was a green pot with holes in it. It's lovely, I told him. What is it? A Buddhist incense burner. Lovely, I said, wondering where I was going to get Buddhist incense in Nether Rising. But it's the thought that counts.

Isn't it wonderful to see your children happy? Mark had waited a long time for this and I couldn't have been more pleased for him. Growing up without a father can't have been easy. I was always tempted to smother him as a child. After all, he was all I had. But I didn't – I let him have pretty much a free rein and he turned out to be an independent little so and so. Like mother, like son, eh Eva? I'd like to think I did my best for him. He left school without a single qualification. It's not that he wasn't bright. Far from it. Too clever, I always said, but Mark just couldn't apply himself to anything. So very different from his father, but then the least said about that, the better. I feared for him at the time, Eva, Mark that is, with no qualifications and no prospects, but he got a job in a hardware store in town, a place called Bobbit's. (Now that did have an apostrophe!). It's a family-run establishment in Stratton-on-Ouse selling everything you'll ever need and stuff you never thought you'd want but end up buying anyway. Hammers and nails, bird feeders, paint, teapots, slug pellets – you get my drift. Everything under the sun under one roof. It didn't pay terribly well but he was happy there and liked the people he worked with. Plus he got 20% off everything so that was really handy when we needed some rawl plugs or a new washing-up brush. But Mark was content and that was all that mattered to me.

He taught himself to play the mouth organ, of all things. I don't think it could have taken him very long. I mean, how difficult could it be? There's nothing to them, is there?

He got together with some friends, three other lads, and several times a week they would play in local pubs for pin money and all the real beer they could drink. Ale, Mum, he would say. It's Real Ale. I knew that. They called themselves the Cornflour Blues. Nice boys they were; Marty played the banjo, Steve had a saxophone, Ben played a caustic guitar (I think that's what he called it), and my Mark had his mouth organ. I went to listen to them one night, wanting to hear what their music sounded like. They were surprisingly good. What do you call that sort of music? I asked Marty in the intermission. It's Blues, he told me. Hence the name of the band. I'm sure you know the type of music, Eva. "Woke up this morning. Glad that I did. Because it's better than not. Waking, that is." Happy stuff. I made those lyrics up but you get my gist.

This had been going on for years, then last spring they were asked by a manager to play in his pub, The Dartford Funnel, quite a rowdy establishment in the town centre, down near the river. There was a group of Koreans in the pub that night, enjoying (if that's the right word), an authentic English experience (warm beer and twice-cooked chips). They were here for some sort of conference and wanted to explore Stratton to see what the natives did for fun. They all loved the music the boys were playing and one of the Koreans said he knew somebody who knew somebody else. You know how it is. The boys didn't think too much of it at the time but a couple of months later, Ben got a phone call from one of the Koreans who was back home by then, and the next thing you know, they've got a tour booked. Mark was over the moon. I've never seen him so excited.

It was a mixed blessing for me. It was wonderful to see him so happy and excited but it meant change. What with him going abroad and me having a couple of falls at home, the die was cast, and it was into a home for me. We never did get to the bottom of what caused the falls – Dr Gupta thought it was more than just tripping over a rug but I had a few tests and they didn't show anything untoward. I suppose I let Mark persuade me – I could have stood my ground and insisted on staying in my own house, but I never liked arguing with Mark so this time I did as I was told. And he was right of course. I'm getting used to being here, in Friars, and I eat far better than I ever did at home. Plus I am very well looked after. To be honest, I think if I'd stayed where I was I might not be in as good shape as I am today.

I've often wondered if Mark is gay. Not that it would matter, of course, but I always liked the idea of grandchildren. He used to bring the odd girlfriend home (I don't really mean odd. Some of them were quite nice). But none of them seemed to last and there was certainly never any mention of engagements let alone marriage. Don't you ever want to get married? I asked him one day. Have children? Maybe, he said. If I find the right person. Don't leave it too late, I warned him. You don't want to wake up one day and find that life has passed you by. Is that what happened to you? he asked me. I stroked his face, quite taken aback. It happens to everybody, I told him. Didn't know you had a philosophical sister, did you, Eva? You see, I can still surprise people, even at my age.

Anyway, it was so wonderful to see him, even for such a short time. I'm really proud of him and what he's doing. He promised he'd try harder at keeping in touch but I know he won't. He's a busy man now, forging a new path for himself. And I'm not included. Good luck to him, I say. But at the end of the day, he's still my little boy.

They're always part of you, aren't they? Your children. No matter what they do, no matter how old they are, at the end of the day they're still your children.

Yours, happier,

Lovingly, Betty.

CHAPTER TWENTY - TWO

It was February now and still no sign of the Inspectors. Betty had forgotten all about them. She had other things on her mind. She'd had a postcard from Mark and couldn't have been happier. He was in Seattle now and they were heading south to Portland. New dates and venues were coming up all the time. All of the band were were exhausted but they loving every minute of it. Betty knew it would be a long time before she saw her son again but that was not what was worrying her. No, the smokers were back under her window.

She wasn't sure when they'd returned. The weather throughout December and January had been pretty foul and Betty had been more than happy to keep her window in Violet Suite closed. But yesterday had been glorious – one of those rare winter days with clear blue skies and almost a feel of spring in the air. She'd opened her window wide, taken a deep breath and that's when she'd smelled it. Looking down she saw two of the handymen leaning in an open doorway directly below her, smoking away, without a care in the world. If there was one thing Betty hated it was the smell of cigarette smoke. She was livid. Mrs King had told them to stop and they had – for a while. Now they were back, flagrantly doing what they had specifically been told not to do. It simply wasn't good enough. No point bothering Mrs King with this – they'd ignored her once, they'd do so again. No, Betty would teach them a lesson. They would not ignore her. Now all she had to do was to think of a way of sorting it out.

Betty spent a pleasant afternoon with Melanie in the Quiet Lounge. They'd taken a jigsaw from the Games Room and had laid out all the pieces on one of the low coffee tables. A fanciful scene of snow-capped mountains and green meadows with fat black and white cows and a manic Heidi look-alike standing in front of a preposterously perfect wooden chalet, was slowly emerging. The blue sky and blazing sunshine depicted in the jigsaw was a complete contrast to the weather outside. It had not stopped raining all day.

"My goodness," said Melanie. "You should have heard Sinclair Latimer mouthing off at lunchtime. I swear the whole room could have heard him. You'd think he owned the place. Going on about how he now enjoys a pre-dinner soak in his wonderful bath. Only suite with a bath in the entire Home, he delighted in reminding us all. As if we didn't know."

Betty had skipped lunch that day, preferring a sandwich in her room whilst she wrote to Eva.

"He's unbelievable, isn't he?" Betty said. She found a piece of Heidi's face, a rictus of unnaturally gleaming white teeth, and added it to the growing picture.

"He was telling everybody how he likes to lie there, covered in bubbles, a port and lemon on the side, listening to the radio. Then he leisurely gets dressed and comes down to grace us lesser mortals with his presence. He didn't actual say the last bit but you could tell it's what he means. We're so beneath him, all of us. Honestly. Moving into the Rose Suite has given him such airs and graces you would think he was bloody royalty. I know he does."

"He'll get his come-uppance one day," said Betty. "His sort always does. I just try and ignore him."

"He really doesn't like you, does he?" said Melanie.

"No. But the feeling is entirely mutual."

"I can't imagine why he's taken against you so."

Betty sat back, stretching. "Got backache now, doing this wretched jigsaw. Think I'll go for a stroll round the garden. The rain seems to have stopped and I haven't been out in the fresh air in ages. Do me good. See you later."

Betty stood looking out of the window but changed her mind about going out. It was still wet underfoot and now a wind had sprung up. There was fresh air and there was fresh air! But this was a bit too fresh for her. Plus could she really be bothered to change her shoes and put her coat on? No, she'd save it for another day.

"Have you seen the notice about the Valentine's Day dinner and dance?" Melanie asked her at dinner.

Betty shook her head. "I must have missed that one."

"One of Mrs King's ideas. Special buffet and then a dance in the TV Lounge. Fancy it?"

"Tell me you're not asking me to be your Valentine," laughed Betty.

"No. But it could be a bit of a giggle. And a chance to dress up."

"I think my romancing days are long since over but I don't mind the dressing up bit. Can't see many of this lot doing any dancing, though."

"Me neither. There's only thirty places. Give it a go?"

"I think I'll pass. But thanks for asking."

That night Betty thought about the dinner/dance. Why not give it a go? The last social event she'd been to was the disastrous river cruise almost two months ago. It would be good to put a dress on and a bit of lippy. And watching some of these rickety old pensioners take to the dance floor would be a laugh. She'd see Melanie and tell her she'd changed her mind. Betty thought about what she'd wear. Not the blue dress – her Reggie-cide dress, she called it. Too many memories with that one. She really must remember to ask Priti to throw it out. It was not as if she could ever wear it again. Maybe the black dress with the flattering wrap-over skirt. The neckline was a bit low for her liking but she had a lovely gold necklace she could wear with it. Matching earrings too. Yes, why not?

The following morning at breakfast she told Melanie she'd changed her mind and would go to the ball after all! She returned to her room feeling quite excited. After Barry's death there had been virtually no opportunity to dress up, to go out and have a good time. At least being here in Friars had provided her with a bit of a social life. She took her dress from the wardrobe – it would need ironing. Then Betty opened her jewellery box looking for the pieces she was thinking of wearing. The box was solid, hand-crafted by a lady in Leeds, and it was her pride and joy. Made from old timber beams, it was a work of art. And with an ornate brass padlock, it meant she could lock away her treasures. Not that she had anything of real value but, to Betty, everything inside was priceless – her 14 carat gold necklace and earrings, a few bits of costume jewellery inherited from her mother, some letters from Barry from their early times together, Mark's first baby bootees, a few photos of Eva and her children, and that was about it. It was more a box of memories than anything else and it was one of the very few pieces she had insisted on bringing with her to Friars. Being made from solid wood, it was too heavy to lift from where she'd struggled to put it on the day she first arrived, on the window ledge, so she unlocked it in situ. She carried the contents of the box to the bed. It was like a trip down memory lane. Betty smiled as she buried her face in the tiny woollen booties, convincing herself that they still had that magical baby smell. A friend, she couldn't remember who, had knitted them for Mark. They were so small and delicate. Hard to reconcile them with the big strapping man her baby had become. Betty was just about to open one of the letters from Barry, written to her when he was away on a lengthy business trip somewhere, when she heard laughter. It sounded as if it was coming from outside her window. She opened it wide and peered down. Those bloody smokers! She poked her head out as far as she dared, intent on giving them a piece of her mind, but as she leaned forward she started to lose her balance. Instinctively putting a hand out, she tried to steady herself against the window frame. But somehow she misjudged it and ended up trying to brace herself against the box. Her whole weight behind it, the wooden box tumbled out and down. Out and down and straight on to the head of one of the smokers. He was dead before his body hit the ground.

Fortunately Dr Chatterji was already on site, dealing with a nasty case of Athlete's Foot in one of the helpers, but there was not much he could do. The man, Roberto, his spattered name-tag read, was well and truly dead. He examined him cursorily but it was pretty conclusive. Both head and the wooden box lay smashed although the box had fared slightly better. Dr Chatterji called an ambulance but told them not to hurry. Whilst he was waiting for the ambulance to arrive, Mrs King asked him to have a look in on Betty.

"She's clearly distraught," Mrs King told the doctor (though Betty was nowhere near as distraught as the poor man who'd been standing next to the handyman she'd just killed – he'd have to change his overalls, if nothing else.

He'd stood there, looking at his friend's body, hands tightly clenched in prayer in front of his blood-flecked face, then turned to one side and vomited). Mrs King was upset too. Yet another death at Friars and Betty Mortimer was clearly responsible this time. She mentally calculated how many forms she'd have to complete for this one.

The doctor gave Betty a sedative and they left her to rest.

"I need to call the Police too," he said, when they were sitting in Mrs King's office.

"Must we?"

"We must. They'll want to interview that woman. What's her name?"

"Mrs Mortimer. Betty Mortimer."

Dr Chatterji nodded. "Yes, they'll have to speak to her, find out what happened. But I've given her a strong sedative and I doubt she'll wake for a good few hours. But in the meantime they'll need to examine the crime scene."

"Crime scene?" Mrs King was positively pale. This was starting to spiral out of control. "But it was an accident, surely? She may have been responsible but she can't have intended to kill the poor man."

"I'm sure you're right. But there are protocols, you know. And even if it was an accident, which I'm sure it was, there'll have to be an inquest."

"Not another bloody inquest!"

"What do you mean?" the doctor asked her.

"We had to have one when Reggie died. Fell overboard from the boat. It doesn't do the Home any good. Why do we have to have an inquest? You know the cause of death."

"I do. There's no doubt about it. He died from a massive brain injury caused when a very heavy object landed on his head. There's no disputing that. But how the heavy object got there in the first place is a matter for conjecture. The Police's, not mine. Now, can we find a tarpaulin to cover the body? I think it's going to rain again."

Mrs King checked in on Betty shortly after the doctor had left but she appeared to be sound asleep. She stood there a while, watching, before quietly closing the door behind her. Betty opened her eyes and breathed a sigh of relief. She could feel Mrs King's eyes boring into her as she lay there, convinced she could hear the woman's mind buzzing, trying to work out exactly what had happened. But Betty was in no mood to talk to anyone at the moment, not before she'd done some serious thinking. Even with Dr Chatterji's chemical intervention, she couldn't have slept if she'd tried. Despite the strength of the sedative, which would have probably put a carthorse out for a week, she lay in her bed chewing on a corner of the duvet, going over and over in her mind what had happened. It wasn't pleasant. The man she had squashed, by accident, was a helper. Not one of the residents this time. He was someone who'd contributed, albeit indirectly, to making her life here at Friars more pleasant. At least, that was the theory. In fact this man, this helper, had been a thorn in her side. Disrupting her sanctuary with his endless chatter and his awful cigarettes. Maybe he got what he deserved. Betty was momentarily ashamed of herself. This man had been part of the very fabric of the Home, dedicated to the well-being of all the residents, and look how she'd repaid him. But if he hadn't smoked, she argued, none of this would have happened. Wrong place wrong time, but both of his choosing. So she couldn't be to blame, could she?

CHAPTER TWENTY - THREE

Friars
February

Dearest Eva,

I think I've gone and done it again. I've killed another one. Accidentally of course. You must believe me when I say that I never really mean to kill anyone. But it was death by jewellery box this time. That's a first, I hear you say. Well, I'm nothing if not imaginative. But I am devastated, Eva. My beautiful jewellery box is quite beyond repair.

I must admit, I am worried about how things are starting to escalate. I'd be tempted to say that things are getting out of hand but that's a bit of an exaggeration, although I do sometimes feel as if things are closing in, like I'm being stifled. I am still in control but I hadn't intended for there to be any more accidents for the moment because I know the Inspectors are coming soon, although nobody knows when. You see, that's another thing. If I knew exactly when they were coming, I could plan accordingly. I knew if there was another death in the Home they'd just get all excited about it, and according to my friend Ephraim they're already agitated enough. So there's no point getting them even more worked up. That's why I'd decided that Sinclair was safe for the time being, and Ruby too. I've mentioned Ruby to you before. Awful woman, but now she seems to think I had something to do with Reggie's death. So that's two of them now, Sinclair and Ruby, who are both convinced I'm involved in their loved one's deaths. See what I mean about things starting to feel claustrophobic? I don't like it one little bit. She's a bit of a femme fatale, that Ruby, though I can't think why. She's got a face like a clap of thunder and dresses appallingly. Melanie once told me that it wasn't just food Ruby liked in abundance, if you get my meaning. I know for a fact that as soon as Reggie died she latched herself on to Ashley (the ear and nose-mining engineer. I'm sure I told you about him). So there's no standing still for that one! Shameful, if you ask me. But, once again, I digress.

There's going to be an inquest (not about my box, of course) but about the poor man on whose head it landed. Roberto, he was the man who died, and the man who was standing next to him at the time, shouldn't have been here at all. In the country, I mean, not just at Friars. They were both here illegally, so Ephraim told me. Shouldn't have been here and shouldn't have been working. Poor Mrs King. She's going to be in even more trouble, employing people with dodgy papers. So maybe by getting rid of one of them I might actually have done her a favour. The other chap, who witnessed the whole dreadful event, he's disappeared. Gone. His locker in the staff room has been cleared out and all his possessions have gone. So not only is Friars Rest a hotspot for accidental deaths but it's at the heart of illegal immigration too. And I thought this was going to be a quiet place when I moved in.

I was interviewed by the Police – two of them again. They always seem to come in pairs, have you noticed? But it did break up a dull day. We sat up in my room – they did like my Korean incense burner and the lovely landscapes I brought from home. Reminds me of a holiday I once had, said the younger constable. Devon, is it? pointing to one of them. I had no idea. A beach is a beach, but this one was very well painted I must admit, and the way

109

the light dances on the incoming tide is quite enchanting. They asked me to tell them exactly what had happened, so I showed them where my box used to sit and where the window frame still was. Explaining how I'd misjudged one for the other, I was in tears the whole time and they were ever so nice about it. Seems to have been an unfortunate accident, they told me. But who knew a wooden box could be so heavy? (I did). Not the best place to have kept it, on the window sill, was it? I could only agree. With hindsight, I said, sighing deeply. Mrs Mortimer, the older one said, these things happen. Did the poor man have a family? I asked, clutching one of those fine hand-embroidered cotton hankies you bought for me years ago. Do you remember? You posted them to me from Canada one Christmas. Tiny purple violets and delicate buttercups. Hard to imagine anyone doing such detailed, painstaking embroidery. So pretty and they've stood the test of time. Not like much these days. Where was I? Oh yes. Did the man who took on my jewellery box and lost have any family? (I didn't say that, of course. Not the bit about my box). None that they knew of, the Police told me. All they knew was his name and, to be honest, they weren't even sure it was for real. What a shame, I said. I'd have liked to have sent them a little something. That's a lovely thought, said the young officer. Very kind of you, echoed the other. But if there is no-one, not much I can do, is there? They both agreed there wasn't. But again, it's the thought that counts.

I've thought about this recent incident a lot, as you can tell. But I blame him entirely. Roberto. The simple fact of the matter is that he and his friend shouldn't have been smoking under my window. Mrs King had told them off about it before. They chose to ignore her and now they have to live with the consequences. Well, Roberto won't, of course. But the other one will. I always knew smoking was bad for your health and so it has been proved. Perhaps it will persuade the other man, the one who's disappeared, to give up smoking altogether. So some good may come out of this, you just never know.

I watched a programme on the television the other night. About serial killers. A bit macabre, I know, but it was fascinating. I learned so much. Did you know you only have to kill two people to qualify? Although some argue with that and say it has to be three. But, either way, it's not many is it? And the other thing you need is a cooling-off period, but it never explained exactly what that meant. I wonder if it's like the 14 day cooling-off period that the insurance companies give you when you renew your house insurance. You have 14 days to regret what you did, or confirm it was the right thing to do, before you start all over again. Never did quite get my head round that bit. And animals don't count, apparently. So if you kill a family of, say, five, and their dog and cat, you can only count the people. That'll have the animal activists up in arms I shouldn't wonder. Every animal has a life! How can you not include them? Well, you can't. The programme was called Serial Killers and Their Kittens. I think they were trying to show that even these killers can have a softer side. Which made for a good, unbiased, documentary, which is the way it should be. So based on numbers alone, your sister is a serial killer. What d'you think to that? There was this chap in Meltontoft. That's just up the road from here. I vaguely remember reading something about it in the paper at the time. He decided he didn't like his wife. Or her mother. Took against his neighbours too. On both sides. A total of eleven people. Eleven people! Can you believe it? He poisoned all of them, chopped the bodies up, burned some of the bits on his barbecue. Last summer, it was. We'd had a beautiful June – non-stop sunshine for three solid weeks – my lawn took a hammering, I can tell you. And there was a dog too, I recall. One of the neighbours had this horrible little yappy thing. He got rid of that too, but as I said, that didn't count towards his total. And what better way to get rid of the evidence than barbecue, he thought? Who's going to question a barbecue in summer? Everybody was doing it. I suppose inviting your neighbours, assuming you still have any, round for a steak on the barbie takes on a whole new meaning, doesn't it! Any bits left over he dissolved in acid in the bath. Now, to my mind, that was sheer stupidity. That would have taken the shine off the enamel more than somewhat I would have thought. Anyway, the only way they discovered what he'd done was because he confessed. Realised he'd quite liked his wife after all but, more to the point, he missed her cooking. Apparently her sausage casserole was to die for. I won't make any bad jokes here, Eva, but you'd think he'd have thought of that beforehand. But still he had no regrets about her mother. Or the neighbours. Odd, some people, aren't they? But the thing that struck me most of all, and something that the programme was at great pains to point out, was that this serial killer had a pet. A kitten called Mitten. How sweet is that? So despite the fact he had murdered, chopped up and grilled or dissolved some eleven people, underneath it all he had a heart of gold. Obviously he wasn't a dog lover, but I don't think that's relevant. But it gets you thinking, doesn't it?

But as I was saying, on numbers alone I qualify as a serial killer. That's quite something, don't you think? They've all been accidental deaths, I've told you that before, but what am I up to? Four now, is it, since I arrived at Friars? Nowhere near the eleven that man did. The fact that I didn't like any of the ones that died, except for Lizzie, that may have had something to do with my efforts. Did I want them gone simply because they were obnoxious? But that could apply to almost everybody in the Home, so I think there's got to be more to it than that. I wonder if they'll make a programme about me one day. I do hope not. I'd be so embarrassed. And what would Mark think if he got to see it? But it does seem an incredibly small number to me. Only two. Or three. There could be grades of serial killers, couldn't there? Something like;

1. Just Trying.
2. Room for Improvement.
3. Getting there.
4. Now you're being serious.
5. Houston we have a problem. (Wonderful film, that. Have you seen it? And Tom Banks? My favourite actor of all time)

What do you think, Eva?

Of course, if you look at it from Mercy's perspective, I'm Jesus' little helper. Not quite a sunbeam, but the next best thing. If he's really waiting round every corner, hiding under the

111

stairs or readying himself to jump out from the wardrobe to gather us up into his tender embrace, then I'm giving him a helping hand, aren't I? Doing my bit to send his little lambs to heaven. I deserve some recognition for that, surely? I must ask Mercy about it one day. See what she thinks.

And it does beg the question as to whether someone can be an accidental serial killer. Because that is how I think of myself. If I didn't mean to kill, and on every occasion I didn't, do I still qualify for the title? It's a deep question and one which occasionally, but not too often fortunately as I do like a good night's sleep, keeps me awake at night. I did tell you I was becoming quite a philosopher in my old age. I would love to know what you think about it all, Eva. You know Lizzie was purely an accident. She was my friend. How was I to know about mixing drugs and alcohol? And all I ever meant to do with Johnny was give him a bit of a scare. I certainly did that. Reggie? Yes, that's a difficult one, I admit. I didn't like the man and he was very rude to me. But my mind seems to have blanked out parts of that night on the riverboat so I'm fortunate that I can't clearly remember everything that happened. And as for Roberto, the poor man under my window. Wrong place wrong time. If Reggie and Roberto were deliberate, does that make me a mass murderer? And is it the same thing as being a serial killer? Which sounds worse? I wonder. Something I will have to ponder on.

Baffled, your loving sister,

Betty

CHAPTER TWENTY - FOUR

Something else Betty would have to ponder on was Sinclair. Wherever she went she could feel his eyes following her. Across the Dining Room, he stared. In the Quiet Lounge, he stared. In the Games Room, he stared. She'd even seem him staring at her from his suite window as she walked in the gardens. He seemed to watch her, wherever she went, whatever she did and it was getting so Betty was afraid to leave her room. But enough was enough. He was making her life intolerable and it had to stop. And she knew exactly how she was going to do it. It was just a question of when.

There was a knock on her door. "You're spending a lot of time up here." It was Ephraim. He sat down in her armchair. "Having your meals up here, aren't you? And not eating much of them from what I hear. What's going on, Mrs M?" What could she say? "Is it that man? Sinclair Latimer? Is he upsetting you?"

She nodded. "A little."

"I've seen the way he looks at you. And Janice told me some of the things he's said to you. Doesn't miss much, that girl. Do you want me to do something?"

"What do you mean?"

"Would you like me to do something about Mr Latimer?"

"What can you do?"

"I could have a quiet word with him. Tell him if he doesn't leave you alone, me will box him in de big hairy coconuts!"

Betty burst out laughing. What would she do without this man? "You wouldn't."

Ephraim shrugged his shoulders. "Probably not but I'd like to. Don't like anyone upsetting my favourite crumbly."

"Well, thank you for the very kind offer, Ephraim. If I ever need anyone boxed in the coconuts you'll be the first person I think of. But don't worry. I'm going to have a one to one with him. See if I can clear the air. If that doesn't work, well. We'll have to see. "

"Okay lady. But the offer's there."

"You really are a sweet gentleman, you know that?"

Ephraim's face lit up. "Yes actually, Mrs M, I do." He opened the door to leave. "Oh, and by the way, the Inspectors are coming this evening."

"This evening?" Betty looked alarmed.

"So I'm told. Why?"

"I...I thought they'd come during the day time, that all."

"They can come any time they choose. It is supposed to be a surprise visit, after all."

"And you're sure they won't want to interview me? I mean, us. The residents."

"No, I don't think that's the plan. It's the boss under the spotlight here. They'll have a chat with her and maybe a look around the Home."

Betty felt momentarily sorry for Mrs King. After all, none of this was the woman's fault, was it? "What time did you say they were coming?"

"Sometime this evening. Why?"

"Oh, no reason." But Betty was thinking. Instead of the Inspectors' visit being a problem, it might just work to her advantage. What better distraction could she have for dealing with the Sinclair dilemma than a host of officials wandering around the premises? Everybody would be so focused on them that they wouldn't pay any attention to what she was up to. It might just be a blessing in disguise.

"See you at dinner then?" asked Ephraim.

Betty nodded. Suddenly she'd got her appetite back.

Betty knew that Sinclair could always be found in his room in the early evening, just before dinner. It was common knowledge – he'd told enough people about it. Enjoying a leisurely preprandial port and lemon whilst wallowing in his bath. She intended to visit him in his room, have a face to face talk with him about why he was persecuting her and ask him to stop it. She was going to be totally reasonable – was she ever anything else? Surely as a rational, sensible man, he could only agree that his behaviour was unacceptable and that from now on, he would leave her alone. She felt happier than she had in a long time and settled down to write another letter to Eva.

Betty was feeling confident as she opened her door, pleased to see that the corridor was empty. Being seen entering – or leaving – Sinclair's suite was probably not a good idea. She tiptoed across the corridor. I'm being over-cautious, she thought. It's carpeted, so no-one can hear and there was nobody about anyway. She knocked tentatively on the door of the Rose Suite. There was no answer. Putting her ear to the door she could hear music. Must be the radio Melanie had told her about. It sounded like Radio Three but she couldn't be too sure. Betty knocked again. Quietly. Still no response from inside. She turned the handle. Wafts of scented steam (lavender?) greeted her along with the soaring crescendos of some Italian opera. Could be Verdi, she thought. She stood still, listening. Yes, Verdi, but she was blowed if she could put a name to it. Of Sinclair there was no sign.

The suite had been altered since Lizzie had vacated it. Sinclair had had it painted – a duck-egg blue which Betty quite liked. He'd got new curtains too, dark blue velvet to replace the floral chintz that his predecessor had favoured. There was now a smart roll-top desk in one corner and a large oil painting of a storm-tossed ship in distress hung over the bed. Betty would never have credited Sinclair with being a man of any taste at all yet, looking round the room, she approved enormously. Now all she had to do was have a chat with him, sort out this misapprehension of his about Johnny's death and get him to leave her alone. What could be more simple? But where was he? There was only one place he could be. The bathroom door was ajar and, even over the music, she could hear the sound of splashing. Pushing the door open she spied Sinclair in all his glory. He was lying in his bath, glasses steamed up, a bath foaming with sweet-smelling salts (surely they weren't the same bath salts that Ephraim had given Lizzie for Christmas? Not even he would stoop so low), smacking the water with his hands in time, more or less, to the music. No wonder he hadn't heard her knocking. Betty stepped into the bathroom, careful to avoid the cable connecting the radio, which was sitting on the side of the bath next to an empty tumbler, to a plug next to his desk in the bedroom. Suddenly Sinclair opened his eyes and took his glasses off.

"My God, woman! What d'you think you're doing in here?" He sat up quickly, scooping up armfuls of foam to cover his naked chest. "You can't come in here. Get out! Get out, I say!"

"I just want a quick word, Sinclair, then I'll go." Betty folded her arms to show she wasn't moving.

"Can't it wait, damn you? I'm having a bath, in case you hadn't noticed."

"I did knock. Several times in fact, but there was no answer."

"Well, you can just get out! Invading a man's privacy like this. Who do you think you are?" He noticed that having covered his top half in foam, the rest of him was starting to appear below the water line. Betty averted her gaze. "Please, go!" he begged.

"Not until I've said what I want to."

Sinclair let out a long, explosive sigh. "At least let me get out of this bath and put something on."

Betty shook her head. No, she was determined. Sinclair was a captive audience and she wasn't going to let him go until she'd spoken her piece.

"At least pass me a towel," he begged.

Betty could do that; she wasn't entirety without sensitivity. Taking a small navy blue towel, the same shade as the curtains in the bedroom, off the heated rail, she dropped it into the bath. He clutched it to his middle parts with both hands.

Emboldened now that his dignity was partially restored, Sinclair was angry, "Now, you dreadful woman, what is it you want to say? What is it that can't wait five minutes for me to get out of this bath and put some clothes on?"

Betty perched on the edge of the bath, knocking the tumbler to the floor. Ignoring it, she found the volume dial on the radio and turned it down. Puccini now. She was never a fan.

"What I want to say, Sinclair Latimer, is that you and your brother are, and were, the most obnoxious and unpleasant men I have ever come across. No wonder your wives left you. I'm surprised you found anyone to marry you in the first place."

He looked at her in amazement. "You barge in to my bathroom to tell me that?"

"Oh no, there's more."

Sinclair shivered. "At least permit me to top up my bath. The water's getting cold."

Betty watched him as he sat up, careful to keep the towel covering his modesty, and turned the hot water tap on full.

"You're making my life a misery at the moment, what with your petty insinuations and your threats. I want you to stop!"

Sinclair turned off the tap. "You want me to stop?"

"I do. I did not kill your brother, whatever you may think. He died from tummy troubles."

"Tummy troubles. Is that what you call it? My poor brother died from dehydration caused by excessive diarrhoea. That's a bit more than tummy troubles, if you ask me. And I still think you had a hand in it."

"I did not have a hand in your brother's diarrhoea." Betty did a double take. What an unpleasant thought! But it wasn't so much what she'd said as the fact that she believed it herself. Almost.

"Well, somebody did. He was always careful what he ate. The slightest thing could upset his stomach but he never had any problems till you arrived."

"You're never going to believe me, are you?"

"In a word, no." Sinclair was about to fold his arms but then thought better of it.

"In that case, there's nothing more to say. I'm wasting my breath. Johnny got what he deserved and no doubt you will too."

"What do you mean?" Sinclair did not like the look in her eye. "What are you saying? Johnny got what he deserved?"

"He was awful to me," said Betty simply. "And I didn't like it. So he paid the price. And you will too." She toyed with the radio cable at her feet.

"Paid the price?" He did not like the way this was going. Betty, on the other hand, was enjoying herself enormously. She'd never really had the opportunity to talk to someone like this and she was finding it strangely cathartic, as if she was clearing the way for what came next. Plus it was great fun. She did like to see Sinclair squirm.

"Oh yes. Your brother was a lecherous, hateful man who not only attacked me but attacked and killed poor Mrs Arbuthnot."

"Who?" What was this woman going on about?

"Yes, who indeed? A nobody to you." Betty turned the radio up loud. Wagner now. Her absolute favourite. And for one glorious moment as Brunnhilde, golden haired and no doubt sporting a rather fetching winged helmet, belted out her song for deceived women everywhere, including Mrs Arbuthnot, Betty **was** her heroine.

Sinclair brought her back down to earth with a bump. "Look, Mrs Mortimer. Betty. I don't know what you're trying to say, I don't know what you're accusing my brother of, but I think you should leave now." He wanted to stand up but that would require both hands on the grab rails on either side of the bath, and one hand was already fully occupied. Betty stood up and stared down at him, contempt written all over her face.

"Alright, I'm going."

The man breathed a sigh of relief. Thank God that was over. Now he could finish his bath in peace. And he'd certainly need another port and lemon to calm his nerves before dinner. "What?" he said as Betty continued to stand there. "I thought you were going."

"Goodbye, Sinclair."

He looked perplexed. Goodbye? He'd be seeing the awful woman at dinner, more's the pity. What a strange woman she was. Betty turned to go, a small smile on her lips and, as she did so, she caught her foot in the cable that ran across the floor and tripped. As she fell, she yanked the radio off the edge of the bath and into the water. Immediately, all the lights went out with a bang. Betty hadn't expected that. She stood there, frozen, in total darkness. All she could hear was a strange gurgling sound and there was a slight smell of pork scratchings in the air. Then a generator or something kicked in somewhere and both the bathroom and the bedroom were bathed in an other-worldly green glow. The ghostly light was nothing more than the fire exit signs above the doors coming on but it terrified Betty. Not daring to look at the body in the bath she slowly stumbled her way into the bedroom. Then, as she stepped out of the Rose Suite and into the corridor, all the lights came back on. She blinked and took several deep breaths. Out of the corner of her eye, Betty noticed someone coming out of the Quiet Lounge and rushing towards the stairs but she couldn't make out who it was. Had they seen her? She stumbled into her suite and into her bathroom where she promptly threw up all over the floor. Going down to dinner was the last thing on her mind.

CHAPTER TWENTY - FIVE

Friars
March

Well, I've really gone and done it this time, Eva. I have finally killed someone deliberately. Sinclair! And do you know, it feels so good. Of course, everyone is saying it's another dreadful accident. And that's the way I planned it. And now that the dreadful man has gone, the way is clear at last for me to move into the Rose Suite, the room I'd set my heart on from when I first saw it in September last year. It's taken a lot of sorting but I'm finally there. I'm so excited, you have no idea. I've already started thinking about what colour scheme I'll have but, to be honest, the way the last occupant had it done was surprisingly elegant so I may just leave it as it is. Do you know, sometimes I feel positively giddy when I think just how much has happened since I arrived here at Friars – and there was me expecting a quiet life.

But let me tell you about Sinclair. Word on the street, as they say, (I've taken to watching American Police shows for some inexplicable reason. I should say Cops, shouldn't I? I've always liked a good British Police Detective show but I've suddenly discovered American ones can be just as entertaining but, honestly, it's a different language. I expect you'd understand it. I mean, Canada and the US are pretty much one and the same country, aren't they? I think Mark would understand it too. He's in California now, I believe). What was I saying? Oh yes. Back to Sinclair. The word on the street is that the poor man was electrified, so Ruby told me. I'm not sure that's quite the right word but I got the gist. She mentioned it at breakfast the day after but Ephraim had a much more coherent account of what exactly had gone on.

There'd been blind panic when all the lights went out, something that had never happened here before. One or two of the residents thought their time had finally come and one was convinced he'd died. Ephraim told me their names but I don't think I know them. The one who thought he'd died, a Mr Porterhouse, had been making himself a cup of tea at the Beverage Station and when the lights went, he fainted. It was Mercy who got to him first. I wonder if she thought he was another one for Jesus' growing collection. Poor girl. The man was incoherent when he came to, trying to push her off, telling her she couldn't have his soul. Who are you? he kept demanding. Where are you taking me? I'm Mercy, she said. Mercy? Mercy? He was shouting now. Then you must be an angel? I'm no angel, she tried to tell him. If you're not a heavenly angel then you must be one of the Angels of Darkness, he insisted, come to carry me off. Poor Mercy was distraught. I'm no angel, I tell you. Of any sort. I'm just Mercy, bless you. Mercy. From Laundry. But you just blessed me, he said, his face lighting up. So you are an angel! Does that mean I'm in heaven? She shook her head. No, sweetie, you in Friars Rest. Rest? I'm at rest? So I have died. The man sighed and lay back on the floor, his hands folded neatly on his chest. If only he'd known it would all be so painless. A bit scary, but they'd sent an angel for him. What service! Just as the lights came back on Ephraim turned up and helped the undeceased to his feet and into the lounge, trying to convince him that he wasn't dead. The poor man was even more distraught now.

Death and resurrection in one day. He died, gone to heaven and then been brought back. Why? Did Someone have a mission for him? Down here on earth? He clutched at Ephraim's shirt. Have I been chosen? he asked in a whisper. Does someone up there, and here he nodded towards the first floor, have something in mind for me? Ephraim told me it was all he could do to keep a straight face. He assured poor Mr Porterhouse that he'd only fainted and that he was fine. But nothing Ephraim said or did would convince him that Mercy wasn't an angel. I do feel sorry for her, though. She's got a friend for life now, whether she wants it or not.

But what I had forgotten was that the Inspectors were here at the time. I mentioned them, didn't I? Two of them from the Council or something, come to see why so many people were dying here at Friars. But one person had just been brought back to life too, so it can't all be bad. They were having a cup of tea with Mrs King in her office when the lights went out. She was so on edge that she leaped up, spilled her tea over one of the visitors and dashed into the corridor to see Mercy rolling round on the floor with one of the residents, thrashing about. What was she trying to do? Murder the man? Another dead body was the last thing Mrs King wanted. Apparently it was all too much for the poor woman and she fainted too, falling into the arms of the recently moistened Inspector.

Oh, I wish I could have seen it, Eva. What a farce! Things calmed down after that. The undead man was finally despatched to his suite with a large restorative brandy and the assistance of Mercy (he insisted she accompany him), leaning in to her soft, majestic bosom; and Mrs King was helped back into her office by both Inspectors and propped up on one of the sofas. Ephraim brought her a sweet sherry from the bar and she soon recovered. She was closeted with the officials for a very long time after that, over two hours, talking about the accidental deaths here. She kept ringing for more coffee and refreshments for the three of them and Ephraim was happy to oblige. Of course, he didn't hear everything that was said, just picked up snippets as he went in and out of her office. Mrs King invited the Inspectors to dine with her and some of the residents in the Dining Room, so they could see for themselves what a happy, contented place Friars was. Being true public servants they jumped at the chance of a free meal, with a complimentary glass or two of wine. Geraldo had done himself proud – Lobster Ravioli followed by Poached Pear with Crème Anglaise. And there's me upstairs in my room, barfing away, as they say on the cop shows. The Dining Room had been pretty full, everyone wanting to get together to talk about the power outage. Really Eva, I do find it quite incredible that something as insignificant as a power cut can cause such excitement. These people really do need to get a life.

Mrs King and the visitors had shared a table with Melanie and Co. There were obviously spare places as I wasn't there. Nor was Reggie, of course. Ruby was there, Ashley doing his best to burp her. With such rich fare he had his work cut out for him. But it's fascinating how he's seamlessly filled Reggie's shoes. She doesn't stand still that one. Ruby, I mean. At least one person on the table could be relied upon to be a voice of reason and common sense and, according to Ephraim, Mrs King was all smiles throughout the meal, delighted with the way Melanie sung the praises of the Home. At the end of the meal, Mrs King asked the Inspectors if they would like a tour of the premises before they joined other guests in one of the lounges. One of them, the one over whom she'd tossed her tea earlier, had never been to

Friars before and was keen to see what the place looked like. The other was an old hand I'm told. Been here several times before. Recognised a lot of the helpers by name and some of the residents, which I thought was rather nice. Mrs King gave the pair of them the Grand Tour, similar to the one Mark and I had when we were first scouting out the place. Good word eh? Scouting.

I was lying quietly on my bed, minding my own business, when I heard a loud knock on the door of the Rose Suite. I'd stopped tossing my cookies by then (that's another American phrase I got from the Cop Show. Sounds rather nice, don't you think!), and had cleared up my own mess. I thought if I called for someone to come and clean it up for me it would only draw attention to me. I sat up, feeling sick again. But for a different reason this time. As quietly as I could I opened the door to my room and peered out. There were the three of them standing in the corridor, their backs to me, Mrs King and the two Inspectors. I'd assumed the visitors had long since gone, not realising they still had the Grand Tour to come. Unusual for this gentleman to miss his dinner, I heard Mrs King say. He does like his food and as you've seen, there's plenty to like. I was praying they would go away. Think he was asleep and leave him alone. But no. Mrs King knocked again. This is the best suite in the establishment, she said. It's the finest and most spacious we have to offer and, if you've not seen it before, you'll be very pleasantly surprised. She turned the handle and pushed the door open. One of the Inspectors sniffed deeply. Unusual smell, he commented. Mr Latimer? Sinclair? Mrs King shrilled. Can we come in? And when there was no reply – well, there wouldn't be, would there? – in she walked, into the bedroom. I wonder where he can be, I heard her say. Mr Latimer? This was followed by a loud scream then a heavy thud. She'd found him. The poor Inspectors, like moths to a flame, followed her into the bathroom.

The younger of the two men, apparently having spied a somewhat charred Sinclair still in his bath, managed to make it to the toilet before he threw up but the older man was not so temperate. He was sick on the bedroom carpet. Poor Mercy was once again called into action, so Ephraim told me, this time to mop up after the visitors. I did feel sorry for her. After all, it's not really her job, you know, but she does help out when she can. A real treasure that one. And what a busy day she'd had! But throwing up on the carpet! Can you believe that? It'll have to go. I'm not moving into the Rose Suite with a puked-on carpet. You can never get that smell out of soft furnishings. I remember Mark once... No, sorry, Eva. I'll go on with the story. Mrs King had fainted again – you must have guessed that. Ephraim and Mikey took her back down to her office and Mikey was sent off for another sweet sherry. The two Inspectors, both pale around the gills, joined her after they'd cleaned themselves up. The poor young man. Not only did he have tea down the front of his trousers, but his lovely white shirt was spattered with recycled lobster ravioli. I did feel sorry for them both. I don't know what Sinclair looked like, a bit singed I should think, but it can't have been pretty. And I should imagine that that image would stay with those poor men for the rest of their lives. But I suppose you could argue it was their choice to look at his burnt body. Once they'd seen Mrs King faint they should have known something was wrong and turned round and walked out. But no. Curiosity got the better of them and they paid the price. I don't want to know how Sinclair looked – no reason I should give myself nightmares. The little I know about electrocution is that it won't have been a very pleasant sight. I looked it up on the computer – did I tell you we have a computer in the Games Room? On one of the very few occasions when I've been able to get on it, I goggled (I think that's the word) Electrocution and it was so interesting. You can find out all sorts on a computer, but then I expect you know that, Eva. It's such a helpful device.

I'm glad I didn't see Sinclair's body but I do regret not having seen his face when he knew his number was up. I would like to think that in his final moments he realised what I had done. Whether there was time for him to put two and two together and realise that I had also dealt with his brother in my own inimitable way, I don't know. It's not that I wanted to gloat or anything. I just wanted him to appreciate the efforts I'd gone to. Somehow, though, I doubt there was time enough for that. But at least I have the satisfaction of knowing that I dealt with the pair of them fairly and equitably. And that's important to me. And I also know that Friars will be a much pleasanter place without them.

There's only one slight fly in the ointment, Eva. I was seen leaving Sinclair's suite. I'd been so careful not to be seen going into his room, but when I came out, I was all a-tizzy. Sinclair had just fried to death and all the lights had blown. I wanted to get out of there as quickly as possible. I was vaguely aware of somebody at the other end of the corridor heading for the stairs but I didn't think he'd noticed me. But he had. And guess what? I'm pretty sure it was Ephraim. I do hope this is not going to be a problem.

It's all a bit grim, I know, but now that the last impediment to me moving into the Rose Suite has been removed, (I think), I'm sure my next letter will a much happier one.

Yours, as always,

Betty

CHAPTER TWENTY - SIX

Betty knew that the first thing she had to do was to talk to Ephraim. If he had seen her coming out of the Rose Suite just as the lights came back on, she was in deep trouble. She knew Ephraim always kept an eye out for her, making sure she was alright, and she was grateful to him for that. But how far did his concern for her really extend? Would he feel obliged to tell Mrs King what he'd seen? Or even worse, the Police? She'd seen the Police car in the car park last night – couldn't keep away from the place, it seemed. And it was only a question of time before they'd be back, wanting to talk to everybody. She had to speak to Ephraim urgently but it wasn't until late the following morning that she found him in the Quiet Lounge, alone. He was tidying up after what had clearly been an acrimonious game of Bingo, muttering loudly to himself. Torn Bingo cards and broken pencils had been tossed on the floor. Shredded serviettes and broken biscuits littered the tables. There was even a stain on the wall where a glass of red wine had been thrown. There'd been some sore losers here. Must give it a go one day, she thought. Looks like a whole lot of fun!

"What's the matter?" she asked him.

Ephraim was on his knees carefully picking up the shards from the broken glass. He stopped what he was doing and looked up. "Bloody old farts! Why can't they clean up after themselves?"

She'd never seen him in a bad mood before. "You're cross, I can tell. Not like you. What's the matter?"

"I sometimes get fed up, that's all." He would not look her in the eye.

"No you don't. You never get fed up. Something is bothering you." Betty knew what it was. "Want to tell me about it?" The sooner they cleared the air, the better.

Ephraim examined the contents of his dustpan. "I don't know how to say this, Mrs M."

She was right. He knew about her and Sinclair. Oh dear. She did hope this wasn't going to complicate things. She liked Ephraim. He'd been good to her from the very first day she moved in and she would hate to lose his friendship. "Tell me. We've known each other long enough, Ephraim. Just tell me." Betty sat down on a chair close to him.

"I saw you. I saw you coming out of Mr Latimer's room. Just as the lights came on." Betty nodded. It was as she feared. "I was here in the Quiet Lounge when the lights went out. I rushed out to find out what was going on and I saw you. I had to help out with Mr Porterhouse downstairs, so I didn't give it any thought at the time." He sighed deeply. "Do you know what my first thought was?" Betty could imagine. "But then I thought, no. You wouldn't. I knew how much you disliked the man. So when I heard that he'd been electrocuted in his bath, well, I assumed the worst."

"You thought I killed him?" she asked simply.

Ephraim sighed deeply. "Yes." He put his dustpan down.

"Have you told Mrs King?"

The man looked startled. "No. No, I haven't."

"Are you going to?"

Ephraim didn't respond.

"What about the Police? If they want to speak to you, what will you tell them?"

"I don't know," he replied quietly.

Betty put her hand on his. "I did not kill him, Ephraim. I went to Sinclair's room to see if I could persuade him to stop being so unpleasant to me. That was the only reason I was there. He was in the bath, listening to his radio."

"You talked to him while he was having a bath?"

"Not the ideal situation for a conversation, I admit, but there were things that needed saying. He wouldn't listen of course. His sort never does. So I gave up and was going to leave, but, and you must believe me, Ephraim, I got my foot caught in the extension cable. The one connecting the radio to the socket in the bedroom. I tripped and the radio fell into the bath."

"It was an accident then, as they said?"

"Absolutely. And it was an accident waiting to happen. Everyone knows water and electricity don't mix. He was asking for trouble, using an extension cable like that."

"Is that really how it happened, Mrs M?"

"Cross my heart. I could never have done the man harm. Oh Ephraim, how could you ever have doubted me?" Betty burst into tears, surprised at how easily she could cry. She was getting good at this. Taking her hand away from his, she searched up her sleeve for a hankie.

Ephraim sat, still on the floor, curiously unmoved by this display of emotion. Could he believe her? He liked Mrs Mortimer, there was no doubt about that. She was one of the brighter, more intelligent of the residents, here at Friars. They got on well and enjoyed each other's company. But could he ignore the rumours about Johnny and Reggie? Not to mention poor Roberto. Was she capable of doing what some suspected her of? He didn't want to think so, but after he'd seen her coming out of the Rose Suite he didn't know what to believe. Betty sobbed even louder.

"You have to admit, Betty, Mrs Mortimer, that it is mightily strange that we've never had so many people dying until you got here." Mikey had taken to calling her the Angel of Death but he didn't think she'd appreciate being told that.

"Oh, how could you think that I've had anything to do with these deaths? Cruel, cruel man! And I thought you were my friend."

"I am," he reassured her. "It's just you can't help thinking."

"Thinking what?"

123

"I don't know," he admitted.

"Well, if you believe gossip and rumours, you're not the man I thought you were. How could you even begin to think I could harm someone? Do you think I meant to hurt Lizzie?" Betty looked him squarely in the face. I wondered when you'd bring up Lizzie, Ephraim thought to himself. "After all, you were there the whole time, weren't you? You know exactly what happened." He couldn't deny it. "I only gave her a glass of fizz." Her crying had stopped. He knew what she was going to say next. "You let her have something much stronger. Rum, wasn't it?" He didn't respond. "And how could I have known that alcohol and medicine don't mix. After all, I'm not a care-worker, am I?" Betty paused to let that sink in. "I think, at the end of the day," she continued, "the less said about any of this the better. After all, we're still partners in crime, aren't we?"

That was the moment he knew their beautiful friendship had come to an end. "Partners in crime," he repeated quietly. He struggled to his feet, and with an almost inaudible "Excuse me," Ephraim left her sitting there.

Betty was heartbroken. It seemed everywhere she went, Ephraim was there. Clearing tables in the Dining Room, putting away board games in the Games Room, delivering mail to residents. But things were different now. He was unfailingly polite to her but distant. This wasn't how she wanted it to be. The man had been her friend and she'd wanted to keep it that way. She hadn't wanted to bring up the subject of Lizzie but what choice did she have? It was a question of self-preservation. Betty had thought she could trust him not to say anything about his suspicions concerning Sinclair's death, but she suddenly, and very unexpectedly, found herself having to tell the same story first to Mrs King, and now to the Police, as they interviewed her. Ephraim! The duplicitous, lying, two-faced swine! Wait till she got her hands on him! He'd pay for this, big time.

"It was a dreadful accident, pure and simple. I will have to live with the fact that I killed a man, every day for the rest of my life," Betty told the woman who was taking down her statement. "Can you imagine that?" Mrs King had offered the Police the use of her office for the interview and here they were, Betty and the Police officer sitting opposite one another at her desk.

"It wouldn't be the first time, would it?" the officer had said.

Betty looked confused. "I'm not sure what you mean Miss..?"

"Inspector Connelly."

Betty was getting worried. She knew enough from all the Police shows she watched that it was a high-ranking officer who was interviewing her and she was writing it all down, every word. Betty was going to have to be very careful indeed.

"I knew a Connelly once. She ran a small pet shop in Stratton. Specialised in gerbils I think it was. Looked like small rats to me. I don't suppose you're related?"

"Mrs Mortimer, can you just let me ask the questions please?"

"Oh, I am sorry. I get so easily side-tracked these days."

The Inspector examined a file in front of her.

"From what I understand, there have been others."

"Others? What do you mean?"

"Other accidents."

"I know. It's awful, isn't it!"

"You seem to have known everyone who died."

"You could say that of everyone in Friars. Are you accusing me of something, Officer Cromarty?"

"Connelly. It's Connelly."

"What is?"

"My name is."

"Your name is what?" asked Betty innocently.

Inspector Connelly straightened her file. Was this woman being particularly difficult or was she just stupid? "My name is Connelly," she repeated very slowly. "Inspector Connelly. Now, I want you to tell me everything you can remember."

"Do I need a lawyer?"

"Do you think you do?"

"I don't know. I'm asking you. Do I? On all the cops and robbers shows I watch on television, that's the first thing they ask for. That and a phone call. But I don't know anybody to ring."

"You can have a lawyer if you like but all I'm trying to do at the moment is to ascertain what you can tell me about the deaths of certain residents here. Starting with Johnny Latimer."

Betty's chin started to wobble. "Lovely man, and a good friend," she sniffed. "Had tummy issues. I think his bowels exploded or something. That's all I know. Can I have a cup of tea?" Tears were rolling down her cheeks as Betty remembered her bosom pal, Johnny.

Inspector Connelly got them both a cup of tea from the Beverage Station. No biscuit, noted Betty.

"Thank you for the brew. Isn't that what you call it? They do on Dixon of Dock Green."

"I call it a cup of tea. Now can we continue?"

And continue they did. For the next two and a half hours, with numerous tea and comfort breaks (my bladder is not what it was, Betty confided to her inquisitor), Inspector Connelly asked about Johnny Latimer, Reggie Dawson, Lizzie Hetherington, Roberto and Sinclair Latimer. She told them what little she knew and how devastated she was to have been nearby each one of them when they died.

"I guess I was unlucky in that respect," said Betty.

Not as unlucky as they were, thought the Inspector. But Betty's accounts of what had happened were consistent and, try as she might, the Inspector could not get Betty to admit to being anything other than an unfortunate bystander, in the wrong place at the wrong time, when the accidents occurred.

"Are we done?" asked Betty, looking at her watch. "It's dinner time."

Inspector Connelly closed her file and sat back in her chair. There was more to Betty Mortimer than met the eye, she knew it. Something was not right but she had no evidence. She had no proof that each and every incident was something more than the accident it appeared to be. The only thing she knew for certain was that she would not not put her ageing mother into Friars.

"I think so." She stood up. "Thank you for all your help, Mrs Mortimer."

"Oh, you're so welcome. I have enjoyed meeting you, Inspector Cromwelly. Will I see you again?"

Not if I can help it, the Inspector muttered under her breath. "No, I don't think that'll be necessary. It appears that this last accident was just that. I can't see there being any more enquiries."

"Well, that's good to hear. Not that I mind aiding and abetting the Police, you understand. It helps pass the time." She shook the woman's hand. "Goodbye then."

"Goodbye." Betty opened the door. "Oh, and Mrs Mortimer,"

"Yes?"

"You will take care, won't you?"

"What do you mean?"

"People here in Friars Rest seem to be awfully accident prone, that's all I'm saying." She smiled at Betty. "Goodbye."

There was a spring in Betty's step as she headed into the Dining Room. She'd got away with it again. Those Police were so easy to fool. But this time there'd been a heavy price to pay. She'd lost her friend, Ephraim, into the bargain. She was hurt that he'd lied to her and that he'd reneged on his promise not to tell anyone about his suspicions. Betty would think of some way of repaying his betrayal.

CHAPTER TWENTY - SEVEN

Friars
March

Oh Eva, I am so upset. That dreadful man, Ephraim, I can't begin to tell you what he's done. And I thought he was my friend. He's only gone and dropped me in it, that's what. Fortunately, I've managed to extricate myself, so all is not lost but it was a close run thing I can tell you. In fact, though I say it myself, I really think I've been quite clever. So much so that after Sinclair's death, I feel invincible. But it's all over between Ephraim and me now. I can never forgive him for what he did and I will have my revenge. I just don't know what it is yet. I'll let you know what I decide.

Meanwhile, I never told you about Madame Cutlass, did I? I thought I'd seen the last of her at Barry's funeral but several months later I got a letter from her. Of course, that wasn't her real name. Turned out to be Peggy Blythe. How ordinary is that? Totally out of the blue it was, the letter I mean. New address – she'd had to move out of her den of depravity after I'd sold the house. My house. She was now living in rented accommodation in Cowthorpe. I'd never been to that part of town but I knew where it was. Seedy. Not a nice area at all but it was no more than she deserved. She'd still be able to continue her strange practices, earn her living doing the only thing she was good at. It was an odd letter. Half apology, half begging. She said she was struggling to make ends meet. Her flat was so small it didn't allow her to offer her full range of services and, because it wasn't in such a nice area, she couldn't charge as much. As if I cared. But any thought I may have had of lending her a helping hand, financial or otherwise, was knocked into touch (I believe that's a football term), by what she wrote next. She told me, Eva, that Barry had said that now he had a son, he was going to be a good father and that this would be their last pirate session together. A valedictory spanking, if you like. One for the road. Or should that have been one for the bottom, bearing in mind what they got up to? The mere fact that she'd mentioned Mark, my son, in the same breath as her despicable sexual activities, well, that was it for me. I would rather have seen her dead than offer her any kind of help. But I was intrigued. I wanted to get a feel for what this woman was really like. To find out what she had given my husband that I couldn't. I can hear you saying what a bad idea it was, but it was something I had to do. So I went to see her one last time.

I took a taxi to the house. The street was as unpleasant as you could imagine. Terraced housing which had seen better days. What were once gardens had long since been concreted over to provide parking spaces, or final resting places more like, for cars. There was an abandoned mattress and a three-wheeled pushchair in the middle of the road. Madame Cutlass had the ground floor flat in No 27. The windows were heavily netted so I couldn't see in. I rang the doorbell. It was a good few minutes before the woman herself answered. There she stood, in a garish, lime-green kimono, open sufficiently to show that she had very little on underneath. The look of surprise on her face was a picture!

I didn't expect you to come here, she stammered. *Then why did you write to me?* I asked. *I just wanted you to know the truth*, she said. *Bit late for that*, I pointed out. *Can I come in?* Reluctantly she stood aside to let me in. *You can't stay long*, she told me. *I'm between clients*. *Literally?* I asked her. Yet another of her deviant sexual perversions, no doubt. My first impression was an overpowering smell of cheap perfume and bleach. The hall was tiny, the wallpaper faded and peeling and I could see patches of damp just above the skirting board. Madame Cutlass, (I can't think of her as a Peggy somehow), ushered me into her front room. The greying nets at the window made it dark even though it was a bright sunny day outside. It was all a bit nondescript and cheap, a bit like her. Catty, I know, but sometimes I can't help myself. A small brown velour sofa and one matching armchair. A coffee table covered in dirty dishes and a large flat screen tv in the corner. I wondered where she entertained her pirate friends.

I wanted to see where you live, I told her. She looked round the room in despair. *It's not much but it's all I can afford*. Do you know, Eva, for a moment I felt really sorry for the woman. I'd never seen the house where she'd previously plied her trade. The one Barry had bought and she'd expected to inherit. I didn't want to see it. But I know it must have been something pretty special because it made a prodigious amount of money when I sold it. I knew it was in the suburbs, leafy lanes and flagellation. And now she was reduced to this.

You'll have to go soon, she told me. *I've got a client coming*. I wasn't ready to leave yet so I offered to pay her if she cancelled her client. *I'll pay you for your time*, I suggested to her. Just like he was going to do. I assumed it was a 'he' but you never know these days, do you? You read about all sorts in the papers. Madame Cutlass was surprised. *You'd give me money just so you can stay and do what? Talk?* I nodded. It seemed a totally reasonable offer to me. *£20 okay?* she asked me. I don't know what she'd had planned with her client but it sounded awfully cheap to me. I handed her the money. She left the room to make a quick phone call and I sat, perched on the edge of the sofa – you never know what she might have got up to on there – waiting for her return.

What do you want to talk about? I really didn't know. *I'm just trying to understand what my husband saw in you*, I said. *Why he felt the need for your...services*. *Oh, don't take it personally*, she replied glibly. Was there any other way to take it? I wondered. *Just because men come to me doesn't mean they don't love their wives or girlfriends. They just want something a bit different. Something their partner isn't willing or able to give them.* *Like spanking?* I asked. *Among other things.* *Other things?* I cannot believe how blasé she was about it all, Eva. And it begged the question, what else had she got up to with Barry? I was afraid to ask. *Is this where you do it?* I asked her. *In this room?* Madame Cutlass was horrified at the thought. *Oh no! This is my space. I keep my personal affairs separate from my business side of things.* *Wise*, I agreed. *So where do you, you know, do it? The spanking and other things?* *In the shed.* Eva, I nearly fell off the sofa. *You've got a shed?* Images of semi-naked men dressed like Little Miss Pirates or goodness knows what else being chased around a tiny garden shed by Madame here, wielding her cutlass high in search of some bare bottom to smack, dodging rakes and hoes and tripping over bags of potting compost. *It's not like a normal shed*, she went on to explain. I didn't think it would be. *Come on, I'll show you.*

Madame Cutlass led me down the narrow hall past several closed doors and out through the kitchen door into a white-washed back yard. A small, windowless potting shed occupied most of the space. I bought the shed from B&Q when I took on the lease and fitted it out the way I wanted, she explained. She opened the door, turned a light on and I stepped inside. It was not at all as I'd imagined. Actually, I'm not sure what I'd expected but it wasn't this. It's so small, I exclaimed. You could hardly swing a cat in here. Madame Cutlass laughed. Not a cat, maybe, but you could a Cat O' Nine Tails! I think she was trying to be funny, Eva, but I wasn't amused. There was a chair right in the centre of the shed — you know the sort, Eva, like an office chair, padded with armrests and on castors, the type that's got good lumbar support — and it stood on a wooden platform three feet square and about two feet off the ground. Metal rings were screwed in to the wooden walls and ceiling, from which ropes of varying thickness and leather straps with large brass buckles hung. It wasn't what I expected a den of iniquity to look like, but then I'd never been in one before. I couldn't stop myself shivering. Are you cold? She asked me. It can get a bit chilly in here. I'll turn the fire on. There was a small 2 bar electric fire standing in a corner. What do you think? She sounded so proud. What are the ropes for? I asked her, somewhat naively. Did pirates like that sort of thing or was it just there to remind them of the rigging on a ship? Some men like to be tied up, she informed me. Barry? I wanted to ask, but didn't. What else do they like? Well, the ones who are really into the pirate thing, they like to walk the plank. I did a double take. Walk the plank? But I can't do that here, she went on. Don't have the space or the pool. Pool? Well, not quite a pool. More of a pond. Yes, Eva, I kid you not. Madame Cutlass had had a pond dug in the back garden of the other house. (The estate agent had recommended I have it filled in before I could put the house on the market — it could have put off potential buyers, but as it happened, the pond was stiff with Crackerjack Toads or some other rare beastie, and if I'd done as the estate agent had said I'd have been committing some awful crime. Imagine that! Your sister, a criminal!). The enterprising Madame Cutlass had got some planks (B&Q again. So reliable.), and had somehow rigged up a rickety gangplank along which those who chose to (and paid extra for the privilege), could walk, with her prodding them with her cutlass from behind. You'll have to use your imagination, she told me. Wasn't it dangerous? I asked her. Oh no, the pond was only two feet deep. Biggest risk was hypothermia. I tried to imagine Barry, dressed in his Little Miss Pirate costume, tentatively edging out along the plank, mindful not to get splinters in his feet and falling head first into a pool of brackish water. The problem was, I could see it all too easily.

I was keen to know what sort of other things her clients liked and Madame Cutlass was more than happy to tell me. A lot of them like to be tied up and one or two, the more daring ones, like to go a bit further. What do you mean? They like to be hung from the yardarm. The yardarm? I always thought that was something to do with the first gin and tonic of the day. You're right, she nodded. That's where the phrase comes from. It's a horizontal spar mounted on the masts of ships. The sails hang from them and when the sun reaches a certain angle it means it's late in the day and then you can have a drink. I didn't understand that bit — you can have a drink at any time of the day, surely? — but I let her continue. But they weren't just used to hang sails. They were good for hanging men too.

Sailors, if they were guilty of mutiny, or pirates. Anybody, in fact. And one or two of my men, they liked me to pretend I'm going to hang them. Put a rope round their neck and pull tight. Not too tight, of course. Just enough to make them gasp. This was proving to be so educational, Eva. Not only learning about what sexual proclivities some men had but getting a bit of maritime history thrown in too.

Let me get this clear, I said to her, some of your customers like to be hanged? Or very nearly. She nodded. But how on earth could you manage that in this tiny shed? You don't have a yardarm here, so what do you do instead? I'll show you. My client would sit here – she climbed up onto the plinth and sat down on the chair – and I would tie them up with these ropes. Tie them to the chair first and then put this noose – and yes, there was a noose hanging on the wall – round their neck. You can see it's connected to a small pulley and if I turn that handle, that one over there, it tightens up. You're so clever, I told her, to think all this up. Madame Cutlass fair beamed at me. So let me get this right, I said, as I struggled to climb up next to her on the platform. These ropes are used to secure your wrists? I tied her wrists to the armrests. She smiled encouragingly. Nice and tight now, she told me. I did as I was bidden. Then I reached over for the noose. This one? I asked her. That's the one. I put it over her head and pulled the slip knot tight. How clever is that! And you say that men like this? Oh, they love it. Her voice was raspy. The tighter the better? I asked. Within reason. I was struggling to understand what she was saying. Just enough to make them gasp. Ah. Got it. I bet you were good at that, I said to her. Making men gasp. I turned the handle attached to the pulley another full circle. Madame Cutlass did not look good. Her face was flushed and she was sweating. Her hands gripped the armrests and she tried to speak. Hot? I asked her. Are you too hot? I'll turn that heater down for you. As I turned to step off the platform I lost my balance and I must have somehow kicked one of the wheels on the chair. Before I could do anything, it had slid off the plinth and onto the floor, Madame Cutlass still seated and the noose in situ. What a noise! I don't know what upset me more, the crash of the chair hitting the floor or the snap of Madame's neck as the noose did what it was supposed to. Well, it made me gasp, Eva, I can tell you, so she was absolutely right in that respect. But it didn't have quite the same effect on the woman who ruined my marriage. Madame Cutlass never made a sound.

Put yourself in my shoes, Eva. Here I was in what appeared to be an ordinary garden shed which had been kitted out so that the fantasies of grown men, my dead husband included, could be played out, in quiet, without the neighbours having any idea what was going on. Fantasies which included dressing up as a pirate or a piratess (I think I've just invented a new word, Eva), being made to walk the plank (in better, and more roomy, days), and being hanged from the yardarm. And here was the woman who had arranged it all. Dead. Accidentally, of course. But nevertheless dead. What could I do? I'd done a first aid course years ago, St John's, I think it was. Night classes at the Town Hall. But one look at her told me she was beyond help. I did what I thought best. I untied her hands and fled.

There was a small article in the paper a few days later. Auto-erotic Asphyxiation was the cause of death, so the Police said. AA, for shorthand. I had to look that one up. Died *by her own hand (or neck, it should have read, if they wanted to be completely accurate). And although Peggy Blythe was engaged in a profession of a questionable nature, and many different men had been seen toing and froing (I liked that phrase) from the premises, the Police were not looking for anyone else. What amused me enormously, Eva, was the fact that on the same page as the article about Madame Cutlass was an advert for the Automobile Association. Never would I have thought that being a member of the AA could be so deadly! Should I add her to my tally, do you think?*

Yours, as always,

Betty

CHAPTER TWENTY - EIGHT

Betty was in. The Rose Suite was hers and there was nobody who could take it away from her. It hadn't been easy, she'd be the first to admit, but here she was. The rooms were just as wonderful as she knew they would be. When Mrs King had informed Sinclair's relatives of his demise, she had asked them if they wanted any of his effects. They told her no, and she wasn't surprised that they weren't interested. From what she knew of his family they'd already bled him dry a long time ago. So Betty had been allowed to keep Sinclair's lovely roll-top desk and his new curtains. Even the painting of the drowning ship remained where it was; a fine allegory for life, Betty decided. So when Betty moved in it was pretty much the way Sinclair had left it, and she couldn't have been happier; although, reluctantly, she'd had to accept that the carpet would not be replaced. Mrs King had agreed to have it shampooed but replacing it entirely was out of the question.

"You won't be able to smell anything," she told Betty, impatiently. "I've had it professionally cleaned and disinfected."

Betty wasn't convinced but she'd give her the benefit of the doubt.

One new addition to Betty's possessions was a small box that Ephraim had given her to replace her beloved jewellery box that had caused such catastrophic destruction. She had decided she was going to ignore him completely after what he'd done, telling Mrs King about her going to see Sinclair in his room the night he got electrocuted, but here he was, box in hand.

"Consider it an apology," he told her.

Betty examined the box. It was gorgeous. It was the size of a shoe box and, like her last one, was made from wood. Judging by the weight, Betty thought it was pine or maybe deal. It had been painted pale blue and decorated with with pink and red roses. "Did you make it?"

He nodded. "I'm so sorry I had to tell Mrs King that I'd seen you coming out of the Rose Suite that night, but I had no choice. You see I wasn't the only one to have seen you. I'd been in the Quiet Lounge, tidying up after a game of Indoor Golf and one of the residents had been giving me a hand. As I headed downstairs I told her to stay where she was and wait until the lights came on. I'm afraid she saw you leave Mr Latimer's suite and head into your room. So put yourself in my shoes, Mrs M, if I hadn't told Mrs King she would have done and then I would have got into trouble. You know how much I need this job."

Betty looked at him. So your job is more important than my friendship? she thought. "Who was the resident?" she asked.

"It doesn't matter who it was," replied Ephraim. So that was the way he was going to play it. Betty needed some time to think about this. She examined the box again.

"It really is lovely," she said, trying to smile.

"Consider it a house-warming present. More of a suite-warming present really, but I thought it would do for all your treasures, like the old one. You can put all your papers and photos and stuff in there."

"Thank you, Ephraim. It's a beautiful gift. And so thoughtful. I'll give it pride of place on my desk."

"Does this mean I'm forgiven?" asked Ephraim.

"There's nothing to forgive," she lied glibly. "These things happen."

"Friends?" he asked her.

Betty nodded. "Friends."

Ephraim sighed deeply and took her hand in his. "You don't know how much that means to me," he said.

"Nor me."

Ephraim went away, happy. Betty stared after him. Friends? The man did not know the meaning of the word. Just you wait, Ephraim, just you wait, she muttered. I'll show you friends.

Betty was starting to worry about Mrs King. The woman seemed to be a shadow of her former self these days. Weight was dropping off her and her once-tight suits now hung loosely. Betty thought she looked the better for it but thought it prudent not to say anything. Mrs King's famously static candy-floss hair was now showing signs of grey and stray wisps stuck damply to her face and neck. She was obviously not taking as much care of her appearance as she used to and Betty wondered what was the cause. She mentioned it to Ephraim. He was still a useful source of information, whatever else he'd done.

"It was the Sinclair incident," as it had become known at Friars. "The young Inspector. Remember him? Well, he's talking of suing Mrs King because he's not been able to work since. Got some sort of stress issue, so I hear."

"Stress? All he saw was Sinclair."

Ephraim shrugged his shoulders. "Nightmares. Flashbacks. Can't sleep at night. Every time he shuts his eyes, all he can see is Sinclair's body in the bath." Betty felt awful, momentarily racked with guilt. If she'd known Sinclair's death was going to cause so much distress, she'd have found another, less dramatic, way of disposing of him. "Mrs King's worried she's going to lose the place. Been hitting the bottle rather hard lately." That would explain the faraway look in her eyes.

"This is awful. What can we do about it?" asked Betty, wanting to help. She was where she'd always wanted to be, in the Rose Suite, and if that might now be taken away from her, not to mention her new home, something would have to be done about it. She had no idea what. Did Ephraim?

"I don't know what we can do to help. What's done is done."

Indeed, thought Betty. And cannot be undone. "Let me give it some thought," she said, confident that, like Lady Macbeth, she'd find a way. Now there was a woman who got things done.

Betty would sit for hours by the window looking out over the gardens, spring flowers everywhere. It was a wonderful sight but she was troubled. What could she do to take away some of Mrs King's pain? The woman was suffering, that was clear and Betty felt she might be partly responsible. She'd been well-looked after here from day one, not just by Mrs King but by all the helpers. Everybody had done what they could to help her settle in and to make the most of her time in Friars. And what had she done? Apart from a very few, Betty had been stand-offish and unpleasant with nearly everyone, residents included. There was no real malice in it, it was just the way she was. Ever since Barry had died, she vowed that she was never going to be hurt again, by anyone. So, apart from Mark, she allowed nobody to get close to her. She'd grown a hard shell, to keep people at bay and to protect herself. Sometimes it worked too well; sometimes it didn't work at all. She'd let Ephraim get close and look what had happened. He'd betrayed her, just like Barry. Betty put it to the back of her mind. It could wait. It was more important to concentrate on what she could do to help poor, wretched Mrs King. After all, if Betty was partly to blame for some of the accidents that had happened here at Friars it should be up to her to make amends. But how?

Several weeks after Betty had moved into the Rose Suite, Mrs King knocked on her door.

"Come to see how I'm doing, have you? That's very kind." Betty reeled back from the overpowering smell of stale sherry and sweat.

"Partly. What do you think of the suite?" Mrs King sat in the armchair, leaned back and crossed her legs. When was she last able do that? wondered Betty.

"It's gorgeous," replied Betty. "I can't believe It's finally mine."

"Yes, it took some doing, didn't it?" said Mrs King.

What a strange thing to say, thought Betty. What was she referring to? As Mrs King examined her chipped nails Betty took a good look at her. Poor woman did not look good at all. Her skin was pale and there were huge bags under her eyes.

"If you don't mind me saying, Mrs King, you don't look too well."

"Just a bit tired, that's all. Been a lot going on."

"I don't suppose there's anything I can do to help, is there?"

"Well, actually, Betty. There is."

"You name it and if I can do it, I will."

Mrs King wriggled uncomfortably. "This is not easy, Betty, Mrs Mortimer, but I am thinking of asking you to leave."

"Leave Friars?" Betty was horrified.

"I'm afraid so. Such strange things have happened since you arrived, so many people have died. I'm not suggesting that you had anything to do with any of them. Except Lizzie. And Roberto. And Sinclair. And they were all accidents, I know. But I think it might be best if you found another home."

Another home? Betty could not believe what she was hearing. For the first time she felt finally settled, now that she was in the suite that she had wanted since day one. And now she was being asked to give it up and move out altogether. The woman was out of her mind.

"But why?" she whispered.

"I just think there have been too many coincidences. Five people have died since you moved in, four residents and one member of staff. The Health Care Inspectors are talking about asking the Police to re-open some of the cases."

"Why would they do that? Even that Inspector Corndolly, whatever her name was, she said there'd be no more enquiries. So why would the Health Care people bother?"

"As I say, there are too many coincidences."

"But you know they were all accidents," said Betty. "Every single one of them."

Mrs King shrugged her shoulders. "That's certainly how they appeared."

That's certainly how I made damned sure they appeared, thought Betty. I went to a lot of effort to make them look that way. Honestly, some people were just not appreciative of hard work and imagination.

"Don't I get any say in the matter? Some sort of right of appeal? Don't you have to consult anybody else about this decision?"

Mrs King shook her head. "No. I'm the owner of Friars. It's my decision and mine alone."

"So you haven't discussed this with anyone else?"

"No, I just told you. I don't have to."

"It seems really harsh to me," sniffed Betty. "This is the only home I have."

"I know. And, believe me, it's not been an easy decision." Any feeling of sympathy for Mrs King had gone right out of the window. "We'd help you find somewhere else, of course."

"But I don't want to go anywhere else. I want to stay here."

"I'm afraid I don't think that's a good idea."

"Don't you think you're being a bit heartless?" asked Betty. "I mean, you haven't told me why you want me to go. Other than the fact that some people have died. This is an old folks home. Of course people are going to die."

"It's a Retirement Home," said Mrs King. "There's a difference. Some of the people who choose to live here may be elderly but they are all in good health. At least they were until you came."

"So you're saying I killed them?" Betty folded her arms and stared at her adversary. "What proof do you have?"

"Please don't make this any more difficult than it is," pleaded Mrs King.

"Show me the proof!" demanded Betty, whilst desperately trying to think if there was anything she'd overlooked in all her planning. Could she have left any clues? She'd been so careful every time. But there had to be something that she'd missed otherwise why was Mrs King asking, no, telling, her to go?

"But if you know they were all accidents, Mrs King, I don't see what the problem is. You know I never meant to harm Lizzie. She was my friend. I didn't know she shouldn't drink alcohol with her medication. And Roberto? I didn't plan to drop my jewellery box on his head. Or are you saying I did?"

"I'm not saying that at all," replied Mrs King, "but one accident is understandable. But two? Three? Maybe more?"

"More? What do you mean?"

"Johnny and Sinclair. Quite a coincidence that they were both ahead of you on the list for this suite."

"Are you suggesting that I killed the two of them because I wanted to move into the Rose Suite? That's obscene!" Betty thought Mrs King was delusional. Her killing them had nothing to do with the Rose Suite. It was simply a matter of her not liking either of the brothers. How could the woman not see that? "And anyway, don't you think that Friars is a much nicer place without them?"

"That's neither here nor there. The fact is that they were both ahead of you on the list and then suddenly they're both dead. Awfully convenient, wouldn't you say?" Some people simply refused to see the bigger picture, thought Betty. "And then there was Reggie," Mrs King continued.

Aah, there she may have a point, thought Betty. That one was a bit more difficult to explain.

"You know I can't remember what happened that night. It was as if I'd had some sort of blackout."

"Awfully convenient, wouldn't you say?" Mrs King sounded so cynical. She uncrossed her legs and stood up. Betty had never felt such pure hate for anyone, not since Madame Cutlass. And Barry. "I'll leave you to think it over, Mrs Mortimer."

Betty stood too. "Please," she begged, "I don't want to to go. I like it here." She put her hand on Mrs King's arm. "Please. Don't make me leave."

"I'm sorry, Mrs Mortimer. My mind's made up." She opened the door and stepped out into the corridor. Betty followed her.

"It won't happen again," cried Betty. "There'll be no more accidents, I promise you."

Mrs King stopped and looked at her. "What do you mean, no more accidents? How can you guarantee that unless..."

Before she could say anything more, Betty grabbed both Mrs King's shoulders and propelled her toward the fire exit. With her hip, she pushed against the release bar and the door sprang open and outwards into the pouring rain. At the same time a screeching alarm sounded, announcing that a fire exit had been opened. Betty wouldn't have long before someone came to investigate. With difficultly, she manhandled a writhing and screaming Mrs King out of the door and onto the fire escape. Her stilettos slipped dangerously on the wet metal surface and she let go of Betty with one of her hands to grasp the stair rail to steady herself. With as much strength as she could muster Betty hit Mrs King's hand with her clenched fist and the woman let go, shrieking in pain. At that moment, Betty shoved with all her might and Mrs King fell headlong down the two flights of the fire escape, letting out a terrified scream on the mid-way landing. Betty watched in silence as the woman bounced from step to step, head then feet then head again, until she lay in a crumpled pile at the bottom of the stairs, not moving. Betty screamed and, without further ado, staggered back into the Rose Suite and promptly fainted.

CHAPTER TWENTY - NINE

The Rose Suite
March

Darling Eva,

I moved into The Rose Suite a wee while ago and it's been worth the wait. And Mrs King was so right. It is worthy of the THE! It makes it sound so much more grandiose. It's absolutely gorgeous with so much space and wonderful views over the gardens. I even have a walk-in bath. Such luxury. I try not to think about Sinclair's final moments as I lie there, bubbles aplenty, reminiscing about what a good time I've had at Friars these past six months. Because they have been good times. I may have spoken a tad harshly about some of my fellow residents and one or two of the helpers, but most of them are absolutely delightful. I really do like it here, Eva, I've decided. How different from when I first wrote to you. I was so depressed then, thinking my life was over. Nothing to look forward to. Now look at me! Sometimes I have to pinch myself. What have I done to deserve this? It's never too late to change, that's what I always say. And I feel so positive now. I've got something to look forward to. And I had a letter from Mark yesterday telling me he'll be home at Easter for a few days so I'm really thrilled about that. And guess what? He mentioned that he was bringing someone with him he wants me to meet. Does this finally mean grandchildren, do you think? I know you probably consider that a bit of a leap, but big acorns, little trees, as they say. I do hope he's found someone at long last and not just for my sake. It's all so exciting. He'll hardly recognise his old mum when he sees me, Eva. I feel like a completely different person these days and it shows. I look years younger and that black cloud that always seemed to hang over me has quite gone.

You'll laugh, though. I had to work my way up the waiting list for this suite, as you know, but now there's nobody else wanting to move in here, after I've gone. There's a rumour going round that the Rose Suite is cursed. They're calling it an unlucky room because everybody who's been on the list recently has died. Can you imagine? Stuff and nonsense, of course. But it does mean I can sleep peacefully at night and I don't have to keep looking over my shoulder in case someone is trying to bump me off! What an irony that would be!

And now that I'm finally settled and where I want to be, I've decided several things. First and foremost, no more accidents. I don't need to do any more. My days of tidying up problems are over. Almost. I'm not going to bother sorting Ruby out. She's harmless. One tomato short of a salad, if you ask me, and I know I've got nothing to worry about there. Her talk of revenge? Storm in a tea-cup. Although I'm still undecided about Ephraim after what he did to me. So everyone here at Friars, staff and residents alike, can rest easy in the knowledge that my killing days are over. Except that they don't realise it, of course, because they don't know what I've been up to. I have been so clever hiding my tracks. And secondly, Eva, I'm going to make a full confession. Tell you everything that's happened so you can make your own mind up what sort of sister you have. I don't think you'll love me any the less. I hope not. It's like a new beginning for me, moving into the Rose Suite, so I want to make a clean breast of it. And I know I'll be a lot happier when I've told you the whole story.

Before I start I should mention Mrs King. It's sad she died but she would insist on wearing those frighteningly high stilettos. I said she'd break her neck one day and I was right. Fell down the fire escape, head over high heels. She'd popped into my suite to see how I was settling in and for some unexplained reason as she left my room, instead of turning left to go down the corridor she opened the fire exit door and went out onto the fire escape. I followed her, of course, wanting to see what she was up to. Do you know what my first thought was, Eva? She wanted to commit suicide by throwing herself down the stairs. And she'd chosen a good day to do it, if you want my opinion. It had been raining and everything was slippery out there. Wet metal stairs and six inch heels don't mix. But she'd have known that, of course. I thought about trying to grab her before she launched herself down the stairs – I could see it playing in slow motion before my very eyes – but I knew it was not my place to intervene. Poor Mrs King had the weight of the world on her shoulders and if she chose to end it this way, who was I to intercede? So she fell. All the way to the bottom. And don't forget Eva, we were on the first floor and it was a long way down. Broken neck, sadly. It'll be viewed as another accident of course, (who would believe anyone would take their own life this way?) but I would like to take a bit of credit for ending her pain, because I did not stop her on her chosen path. She was going through hell, poor woman. About to be sued, about to lose Friars – we're being taken over, I didn't tell you. Her son, Frank, I think his name is, stands to inherit the business but doesn't want to be involved in running a retirement home. So he's selling out to the highest bidder and I can't say I blame him. Mrs King's ex-husband (I never gave much thought about her personal life) was apparently going to contest the will but Ephraim, fount of all knowledge as usual, said he hadn't got a leg to stand on; Tabatha King left everything to her son. There's a lot of interest in the place – retirement homes, care homes, call them what you will. It's a growing market and there's no shortage of prospective buyers coming to look at us. Favourite is a youngish couple from Middlehampton, who've already got two care homes. They've promised that nothing will change if they buy the place. Nobody will be made jobless or homeless and everyone will stay exactly where they are. Of course they can change their minds when they take over the place but I've taken that to mean that I'll stay in the Rose Suite, so I'm happy. Frank King likes it too, apparently, the fact that somebody is going to continue his mother's work in the way she would have wanted. He's minding the shop at the moment so to speak, until the sale goes through. He's got no experience of this sort of thing – he's something to do with designing sets for television shows. Sounds very glamorous but he assures me it's not. Pleasant young man. Shame he's not staying. He's taken time off from his job to make sure that the place continues to operate smoothly. Not that we need him here. Even when his mother was off on one of her sunny jaunts, there was nobody left in charge; the place ran itself. Which, I think, speaks volumes about what a tight ship Mrs King ran.

Do you know, Eva, I miss that woman. I do wish she hadn't died and that things had remained the same but she was in so much pain, I just couldn't bear it. I had to do something for her and now her suffering is over. I'd like to think she would have thanked me for my kindness, if she could. And it's been the same with all of the others, pretty much.

All I've been doing is trying to be kind. Helping solve their problems once and for all. Except maybe for Johnny. He just plain annoyed me. No question, he deserved what he got. And Roberto. And Reggie. I never liked him. And Sinclair. Oh, and Madame Cutlass too. Absolutely. And Barry. They all got what was coming to them. I don't consider any of them victims. Do you know, when I think about it, Eva, that's the first time I've used that word. Because it's not relevant. It doesn't apply to any of them. And because they're not victims, then you can't blame me for a single one of their deaths. Whoa! I hear you say. Barry? Did you think I was trying to slip him in without you noticing? You always were a sharp one. Yes, Barry. He was one of those on my list of those who got their just deserts. I know what I've done could be counted as murder and that I shouldn't have done it, but something tells me I've not really done any harm. I've simply removed people, people who needed eliminating either for their own benefit or for the benefit of others. So I have mixed feelings about my actions. Guilt? Yes, to a small extent. But also a quiet satisfaction. For the most part, I think I've done them, me and the whole world a favour by causing the departure, if premature, of those who, because of their behaviour, really had relinquished their right to be here. Go on, Betty, I can hear you shouting, stop getting side-tracked! Tell me about your husband!

Barry. I really did love him, you know. And it broke my heart when he died. Our marriage wasn't perfect – whose is? But we muddled along. There was no indication that anything was amiss, at least not in the early days. But then he began to spend more and more time at work. The demands of running your own business, he told me. But there was more to it than that. I wasn't stupid, Eva. I knew there was somebody else, right from the moment it started. I didn't find out that it was Madame Cutlass until later but it didn't matter who it was. He could have been having an affair with a one-legged walrus and it wouldn't have mattered; betrayal is betrayal. There was nothing obvious but when you know someone, and I knew Barry, you can tell when things change. A slight shift in your centre of gravity. A feeling. At first I ignored it, pretending it wasn't happening. But then when I knew, when I really knew, my world collapsed. I couldn't say anything of course. Why not? I hear you asking. Why not confront him with it? Because that would have made it real, Eva. Can you understand that? It's hard to explain. I knew, but I didn't, if you get my meaning. Until he admitted it I could go on pretending it wasn't happening. But I didn't want him to admit it. So I sorted it out. My way.

When the Police came round to tell me about his heart attack, I acted as if I knew nothing. What a performance, Eva. Oscar-winning! I was so convincing, you would have been proud of me. Remember those little plays we used to act out in the back garden after school? I was so much better at them than you. Yes, I played it for all it was worth. Shock. Tears. The works! I knew it was going to happen but even I couldn't have planned the timing better. With Madame Cutlass, in flagrante dolce de latte or whatever. Yes, the papers had a field day and I hid myself away. But only because I didn't dare be seen with a smile on my face. And I had Mark to look after. And how did I know it was going to happen? Because I planned it. Simple.

Barry had recently been diagnosed with diabetes. Should have been picked up years ago, but typical man, refused to go to the doctor. And when he finally did he was told that he'd have to be careful; his high sugar levels over the years had damaged his heart. He still looked pretty good and there were few obvious signs he had any medical problems. Anyway, I remember it so well. It was a Saturday and he said he had some paperwork to clear in the office. I knew that was a lie, of course, and that he was really going off to see his paramour (such a romantic word – French I think it is – but at the same time, so tawdry). I'll cool your ardour a bit, I thought to myself, so I injected some extra insulin into his Weety Wot-Nots. Maybe it was a lot, I can't exactly remember. He looked flushed as he left the house, sweating slightly. Gave me the usual peck on the cheek and that was the last time I saw him alive. I next saw him at the hospital, as you know, dressed in all his finery, his lipstick smudged. I continued playing the grieving widow, naturally, and nobody, not even Madame Cutlass herself, suspected it was anything other than a heart attack. Any suggestion that his insulin levels were high was put down to his poor management of his condition and this was reinforced by my written statement to the Coroner. I didn't go to the inquest if you remember – I knew I couldn't hide that smirk! - but I wrote in detail explaining how Barry often struggled with his diabetes and the correct dosage required to keep it in check. And bingo! No questions asked. Done and dusted.

Don't you feel any remorse for what you did? I hear you asking. For any of them? For Barry? I'm afraid the answer is no. Barry let me down and there was a price to pay for doing so. The only accident I genuinely regret was Lizzie. I really did not mean to kill her. I can't say it often enough. Of course I knew about not mixing alcohol with medication. Everybody knows you shouldn't. But I like to think she thought, what the hell! I'm going to do it anyway. Why not live a little dangerously at the age of 96? So I suppose I aided and abetted, as they say on that Police show. Did I tell you I was now watching old re-runs of Z Cars? I bet that takes you back a bit!

Anyway, I'm off to dinner now. I've ordered a couple of bottles of champagne for our table tonight. If anyone asks me, I'll tell them it's because I'm excited about Mark and the thought that, finally, I may become a grandmother. A bit premature, I hear you say, but really I need an excuse to celebrate the fact that with Mrs King gone, all my worries are over. It doesn't look as though she told anyone she was going to ask me to leave Friars and I don't think the Police have opened their investigations into any of the accidents here, so I can sleep easy in my bed tonight with a clear conscience. It's a wonderful feeling.

I'll write soon,

Your loving sister,

Betty.

CHAPTER THIRTY

"To what do we owe this unexpected treat?" asked Melanie, raising her champagne flute. "I know it's not your birthday."

"I just feel like celebrating," Betty replied. "Mark's coming to visit me next month, all the way from America. And he's bringing someone for me to meet. I'm hoping he may have found someone to settle down with at long last. I'm so happy for him."

This news was greeted by a loud burp from across the table. "Always does that to me," explained Ruby.

Tonight of all nights, Betty was not going to let that awful woman spoil her quiet celebration. She could burp as much as she wanted.

"Does that mean the person he's bringing is an American?" asked Melanie.

Betty put down her glass. She'd never thought of that. Oh well, she'd cross that bridge when she came to it.

"What's this, ladies and gents? Champagne?" It was Frank, doing a tour of the Dining Room, stopping at each occupied table. "Celebrating?"

Betty smiled at him. "My son's coming to visit me next month. That's always a cause for celebrating. Would you like a glass?"

"Do you know, I would love one. May I?" He took what used to be Reggie's seat, still vacant, and sat down next to Ashley. Melanie poured him a glass of champagne. "Cheers. Bottoms up."

"Bottoms," muttered Ruby.

"I may be able to give you another reason to celebrate. I've decided not to sell Friars after all. I'm staying."

"What?" shrieked Betty, alarmed. Would this change things? Just when she thought everything was settled and she had nothing more to worry about. Her heart sunk.

"You sound as surprised as I am," said Frank. "I've just been letting everybody here know tonight but I will be sending individual letters out to everyone."

"I thought the place was sold. Going to that couple who'd already got retirement homes," said Melanie.

"It was under offer but, the more I thought about it, I decided not to sell. You probably all know that I took leave from my job to look after the place after my Mum died until a buyer could be found."

"God rest 'er soul," said Ruby mournfully. "Lovely woman. Angel, she was."

Frank looked sad. "I know how much you all thought of her. Well, over the past few weeks I've come to realise what a wonderful place she's made here. She'd put her heart and soul into it over the years and you can tell. I know nothing about the retirement home business or how to run a place like this but, from what I've seen, there's so much happiness here. The residents, all of you, you're lovely, and all the people who work here are an absolute delight. The couple who were going to buy it are very disappointed that I've changed my mind but I think it's the right thing to do."

Betty felt smug. Thanks in no small part to me, she thought. I've got rid of the deadwood and the unwanted. Not forgetting, Mr Frank King, that you owe me a debt of gratitude too. If it wasn't for me disposing of your mother, you would not now be embracing a change in career.

"It's so very different from where I work. It's dog eat dog in the television business and, do you know, I'm not missing it at all." He took another sip of champagne. "So I've handed in my notice and I'm going to have a stab at this."

Stab, thought Betty. Now there was something she'd never tried. And she still had to teach Ephraim a lesson. How difficult would that be? She could get a knife from the kitchen. They'd be super sharp. And all she had to do was walk up behind him, then trip. She'd have to make sure she wasn't wearing something that would spoil; you could never get blood out of clothing, no matter how long you soaked it. Yes, that might work. She'd have to explain why she was carrying a knife but it wasn't beyond the realms of possibility to make it look like an accident. Betty smiled and shelved the idea for later. Work in progress, as they said on Starsky and Hutch.

"So cheers, everybody," said Frank. They all raised their glasses.

"Does that still mean that nothing will change?" asked Melanie. "We were told that the couple who were taking over had said they wouldn't change anything, but anything could have happened once they were in."

Frank shook his head. "If it ain't broke, don't fix it. If it worked well for my Mum, it can work well for me. Everything will be just the same, I promise you that."

"So we all stay where we are, same rooms? Everything?" Betty asked, on tenterhooks. So much depended on his answer.

"Yes. No reason for anyone to move."

"And no-one loses their job?" She was thinking about Ephraim in particular. She wanted him around so he could get his just desserts.

Frank smiled. "No, no redundancies." Things just got better and better. "I'm taking the whole place on, kit and caboodle."

Ruby looked up from her soup, spoon mid-air. "Caboodle? Is that my main course, Ashley?"

"No," he replied. "You're having the beef."

Betty smiled across the table at the pair of them. Despite what she had promised Eva, maybe there was still a bit of room for some fine tuning with Ruby after all. Frank emptied his glass and got up to leave.

"Does that meet with your approval?"

"Absolutely," Betty was grinning from ear to ear. "And I think this calls for another bottle of champagne."

By the end of the meal everyone was in high spirits. Betty in particular was feeling happier than she could ever remember. Her future at Friars was guaranteed and she had nothing to worry about. The Rose Suite was hers, she'd heard it from the horse's mouth. Mark was coming to visit her next month. Things were looking good.

"Do you know, I'm going to have a nightcap," she declared. "Anyone care to join me? My treat."

"I'll give it a miss, thanks," said Melanie. "Had far too much as it is."

No-one else on the table showed any sign of interest, except for Ruby.

"I'll 'ave one."

Oh well, thought Betty, more fool me for offering.

"What about you, Ashley?" Ruby offered generously. "You not 'avin' one?"

Ashley removed his finger from his ear, examined the contents closely, and grunted.

Janice was setting the table next to theirs ready for breakfast. Betty caught her eye.

"Could we have some drinks in the lounge please? A small Tia Maria for me. Ruby?"

"Same. Large."

"Go on, Ashley? Betty's payin'," Ruby offered generously.

"Whisky. Double."

Not quite the company she'd been hoping for, so Betty decided she'd make it a quick one then head up to bed.

The three of them sat in the lounge, not speaking, waiting for their drinks. I've never seen either of these two smile, mused Betty. They could make a fortune as professional mourners.

Unusually it was Ephraim who brought their drinks to them. Betty smiled her thanks. Trying to ingratiate yourself with me? she wondered. Well, you may find it a wee bit late for that. She downed her drink in two gulps then stood up, wobbling a little. "Oops," she said, "Definitely time for bed. Goodnight."

"Night," muttered Ashley, watching as Betty wove her way unsteadily between the tables and out of the Dining Room.

"'Ad a lot to drink, that one," commented Ruby. "Be out for the count in no time at all. Another?"

"Don't mind if I do, then I'm off to my bed. Put it on her bill, shall we? Ephraim! Same again."

Betty took the lift up to the first floor and walked carefully along the corridor towards the Rose Suite, holding on to the wall for balance. Undressing for bed, she sang quietly to herself. If this place is to be my home for the future, I could do a lot worse, she thought. Mark was right. It had got so much going for it and, since she felt well and truly settled, perhaps now was the time to really start making the most of what it had to offer. The world was her oyster. Betty decided that first thing tomorrow she would check the Activity Notice Board and sign up for something she'd never done before. Maybe it would be useful to know how to fold serviettes. Or how to make hedgehog pin cushions out of old tennis balls and curlers. She might even become the Friars Rest champion of indoor bowls. She smiled to herself as she got into bed. You can teach an old dog new tricks and tomorrow she was going to prove it.

There was a quiet knock at the door of The Rose Suite but there was no response. Betty was sound asleep, snoring softly. The door opened and in crept Ruby and Ephraim.

"Betty, oh Betty," whispered Ruby, shining her torch into her face.

"Sshh!" Ephraim hissed. "And turn that bloody thing off. We don't want to wake her."

"Nothing'll wake that old trout, the amount she's 'ad to drink. Anyway, we need the torch so we can see what we're doin'." Ruby tiptoed over to the bed. "Piece o' cake."

"You reckon?"

"Take that cushion off the chair."

Ephraim did as he was told. "Now are you sure about this? It is murder, isn't it?"

Ruby shook her head. "No, it's self defence. You've seen 'ow everyone's started dyin' since she got 'ere. If we don't do this, there'll be none of us left. An' 'ave you seen how she looks at me? Pure 'atred. I know I'm next on 'er list so it's 'er or me. And don't forget about my poor Reggie. I always reckon it was 'er who tossed 'im into the river."

"But you don't know for sure, do you? Not really."

"I can feel it in me waters."

Bit like Reggie, thought Ephraim.

"An' don't forget, I saw 'er comin' out of Sinclair's room just after 'e got electrified. You saw 'er too. Now we all know what that was about. An' if we 'adn't been 'avin' a little 'ow's yer father in the Quiet Lounge, we'd be none the wiser. Now, 'old it over 'er face."

Ephraim placed the cushion over Betty's face and pressed down gently. There was a slight whimper. "I can't do this," he told her, dropping the cushion on the bed. "I can't commit murder."

"It's not murder, I tell you," said Ruby, picking up the cushion and placing it squarely over Betty's face. She pushed down hard. Betty's started to writhe and moan as her air supply was cut off and Ruby gasped as she struggled to keep the cushion in place. The whimpering grew louder and Betty began to thrash, her legs pedalling under the duvet and her arms flailing wildly.

"Stronger than I thought," panted Ruby. "Bitch!"

Slowly the violent thrashing was replaced by a quiet spasm or two until, finally, there was no movement at all from the bed.

"I think that's it," said Ruby, taking the cushion away from Betty's face.

"She's not moving at all," noted Ephraim.

"Still as a lamb chop," replied Ruby.

"Is she dead then?"

They both peered at the lifeless body. Ruby lifted one of Betty's eyelids and nodded.

"Gone." She handed the cushion back to Ephraim who returned it to the chair.

"God, I need a stiff drink," he said, not taking his eyes off Betty.

"'Ow about a little nightcap? You got some of that rum?"

Ephraim nodded.

"Sorted!"

"Come on! Let's get out of here."

Ruby tucked Betty's arms under the duvet, gave the room a quick once-over, then closed the door quietly behind them. Now this was a cause for celebration, she thought.

It was Mercy who'd discovered Betty's body. When she hadn't turned up for breakfast, and had missed lunch too, she'd been sent up to see if Betty was alright. Clearly she wasn't. She appeared to be fast asleep but when Mercy shook her and called her name she realised Betty was never going to wake up. She stared down at the inert body, deeply saddened, but happy too. Betty looked so peaceful, lying there, already swept up into the welcoming arms of sweet Jesus. She straightened the duvet and fluffed up the pillow. Spitting on her hands, Mercy did her best to flatten Betty's mussed hair. There, that was better. Kissing her gently on the forehead, Mercy went downstairs to break the news to Frank.

Poor Frank. His mother had had to deal with so many deaths in the Home. Now it was his turn.

EPILOGUE

The next day, after the ambulance had collected Betty's body, Frank was in the Rose Suite boxing up Betty's few possessions. He opened the painted wooden box which Ephraim had given to her and sat at the writing desk examining its contents. What were all these letters written in old-fashioned hand-writing? They appeared to be in chronological order – Betty was nothing if not organised – but why had they not been posted? Frank had no intention of reading the letters but he was so intrigued by the beautiful but almost illegible calligraphy that he couldn't stop himself. He slowly read the first letter. Poor Betty Mortimer. How unhappy she'd been. He picked out another at random. It was the contents of this second letter that made his skin crawl. He put all the letters back in the box, took them downstairs to what was once his mother's, and was now his, office, poured himself a strong cup of coffee, and spent the next several hours reading each letter from start to finish. When he'd done he sat back in his chair and poured himself a large glass of his mother's sweet sherry. What to do? If these letters ever became public, Friars was doomed, surely? The Retirement Home had been harbouring a serial killer. It was all carefully documented by the murderer herself. Frank counted up the deaths. Eight, he made it, including his own mother. Tabatha King hadn't committed suicide; this woman, this monster, had killed her. Betty Mortimer had killed twice before she'd even arrived at Friars, her husband and the woman he'd paid to spank him. And then she'd added an assortment of residents and one of the helpers to her tally. If this got out Friars would have to close. The Press would have a ball. Frank could see the headline now; Mayhem, Madness and Murder! Serial Killer at Large in Care Home!

Frank took Betty Mortimer's personal file out of a grey steel cabinet to find details of her next of kin. He flicked through the meagre contents. Nothing out of the ordinary at all. No health or dietary issues. And pretty mundane hobbies and interests – she'd made no mention of being a serial killer when she filled in the form. No, there was no indication whatsoever that there was another darker side to this apparently innocuous, ageing widow. She was a serial killer when she moved in to Friars; she was an even bigger one now. Frank took a deep breath and rang the number on the Admission Record.

"Hello? Is that Mark Mortimer? Betty Mortimer's son?"
"Yes, who is this?"
"You don't know me but I'm Frank King. Mrs King's son."
"Who?"
"Mrs King. The owner of Friars Rest."
"Oh, yes. Hello. What can I do for you?"

"I'm afraid I've got some very sad news for you. I'm afraid your mother died last night."

There was silence on the phone. "Did you hear me?"

"Yes. Sorry. My Mum died? But there was nothing wrong with her. What happened?"

"We don't know but it looks as if she died in her sleep. I'm very sorry."

"Frank, did you say your name was? I don't understand."

"Sometimes it just happens. It's a very peaceful way to go." Unlike most of Betty's victims, he thought, some of whom had died in unbearable agony which she'd described at some length in her letters. "She had a few bits and pieces. What do you want me to do with them?"

"What sort of things? I know she didn't take much into Friars when she moved in."

Frank looked at the letters in his hand. If he gave these to Mark then his plans to run the Home were ruined. But by rights they belonged to him. Maybe he could just give him some of them? Ones that made no mention of his mother's 'accidents'? After all, wouldn't it be kinder if Mark never knew that his mother was a serial killer?

"There's a pair of baby bootees," Frank could hear a sob in Mark's throat, "and some letters."

"Letters?"

"About a dozen or so. Handwritten but never posted. Written by your mother."

"Who are they to?"

"Someone called Eva."

"I don't know anyone called Eva."

"They're all addressed to her," said Frank. "In Canada."

"Oh, hang on a minute, I remember now. My Mum had a twin sister. Emigrated to Canada just after she got married. I can remember Mum mentioning her once or twice. That's the only Eva I can think of."

"I wonder why she never posted them," said Frank. "We post letters for residents all the time. It was one of the many extra services my mother was pleased to offer."

"Eva died in a car crash. In Canada. Along with her husband and two children. She was only 25 at the time."

"But..." There was a long pause. "But if she was your mother's twin, and your mum was, what, 76, that means Eva died..."

"...over 50 years ago." Mark finished the sentence for him. "So why was she writing to her?"

Neither said anything.

"What do you want me to do with the letters, then?" Frank asked, "and her other things? Send them out to you in the US or keep them till you get back?"

Mark thought about it for only a moment. "Give her bits and pieces away to charity, if you will, please. And as for the letters, I think you may as well burn them."

"Are you sure?" Frank tried not to sound too eager.

"Yes. It's not as if they're of any interest to anyone. My Mum writing to a dead sister. How weird is that? No, I can't see anybody being interested."

Mark couldn't see Frank smiling. "No, me neither. You sure now?"

"Yea. Chuck 'em."

"Will do."

There was another pause. "Mark, what do you want us to do about the funeral? Would you like me to make all the arrangements?"

"That's very kind. Thank you, Frank."

"Are you planning on coming home?"

"I don't see the point, do you? The funeral's only a ceremony, after all. It makes no difference whether I'm there or not. Mum's gone and that's that. No, go ahead and do what you need to do and send me the bill."

"Will do," Frank repeated.

"And Frank? Thanks for sorting my Mum's things out. Can't have been the most exciting thing to do."

You have no idea, thought Frank. None at all.

ACKNOWLEDGEMENTS

An enormous THANK YOU to the NYPT (that's the North Yorkshire Production Team and not the New York Police), for their truly invaluable assistance in getting this book into print. Thanks to my proof-readers, Glyn, Christine, Lynn and Angela; and thanks to my tech team, Jason and Piers. Without them I would be lost.

And a very big THANK YOU to you for buying this book and I really hoped you enjoyed it. If you could please write a review on Amazon for me, that would be great – I read every review and they all help shape my future work. Similarly, if you have any comments about this or any of my other books, please feel free to share them with me at maggiewhitley5@gmail.com.

Maggie Whitley

Printed in Great Britain
by Amazon